STINKY CECIL
in MUDSLIDE MAYHEM!

STINKY CECIL
in MUDSLIDE MAYHEM!

PAIGE BRADDOCK

Andrews McMeel
PUBLISHING®

TO MY BROTHER, GUETH,
THE FORESTER.

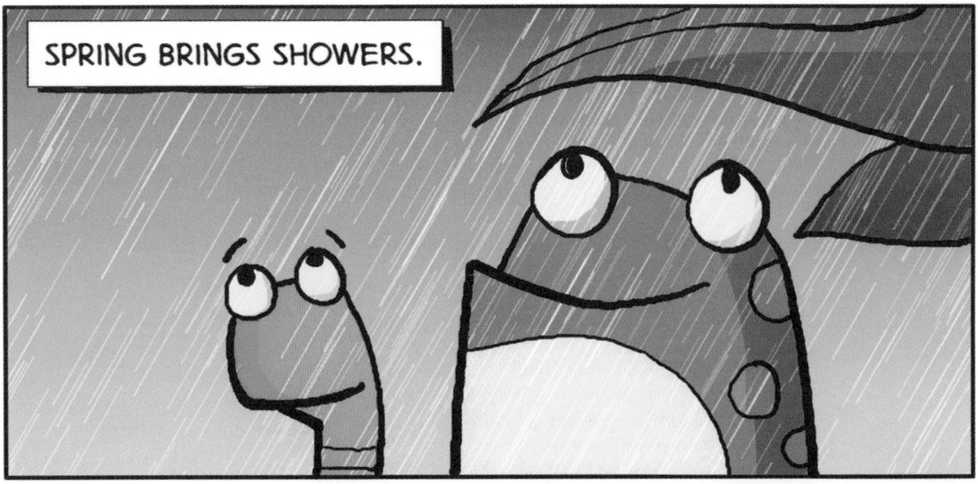
SPRING BRINGS SHOWERS.

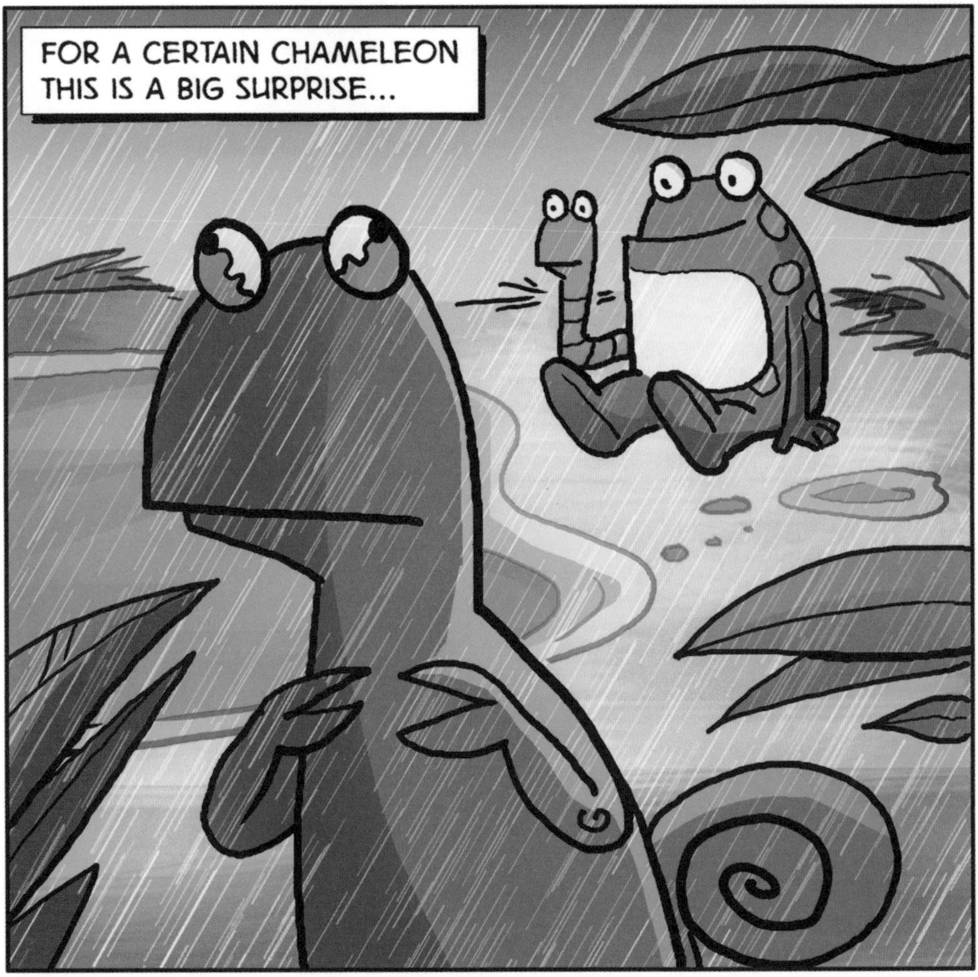
FOR A CERTAIN CHAMELEON THIS IS A BIG SURPRISE...

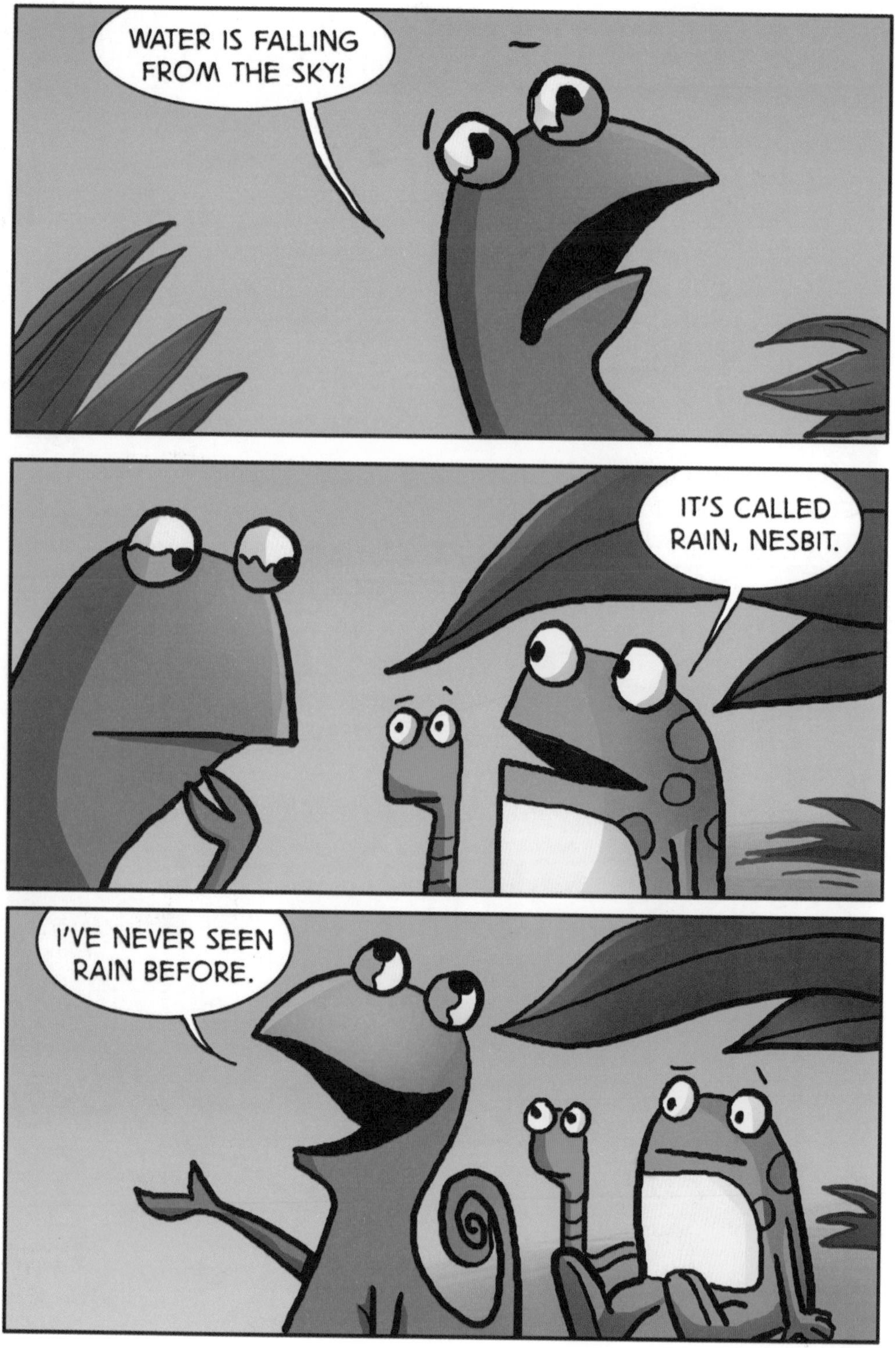
WATER IS FALLING FROM THE SKY!
IT'S CALLED RAIN, NESBIT.
I'VE NEVER SEEN RAIN BEFORE.

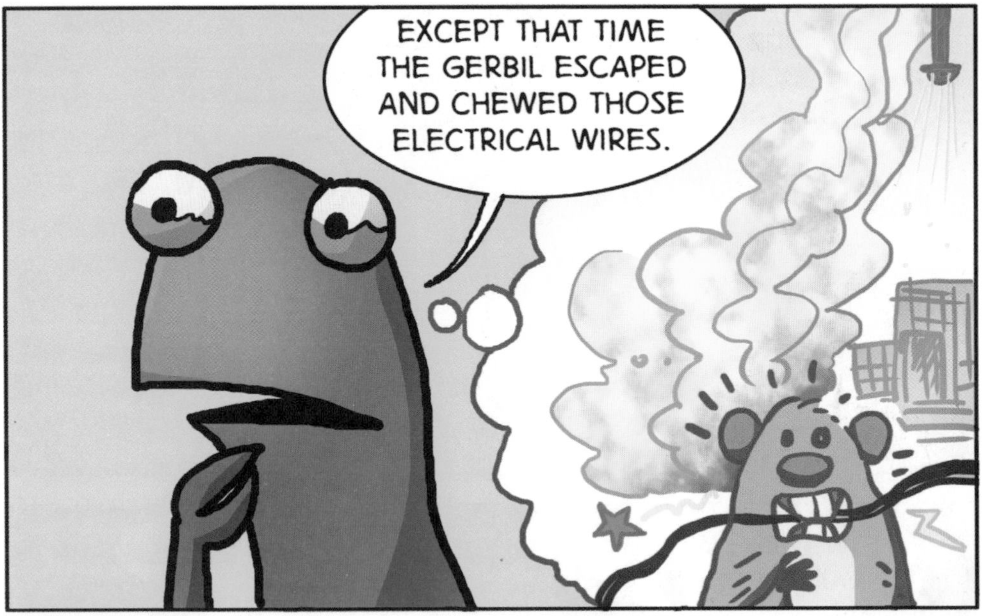
EXCEPT THAT TIME THE GERBIL ESCAPED AND CHEWED THOSE ELECTRICAL WIRES.

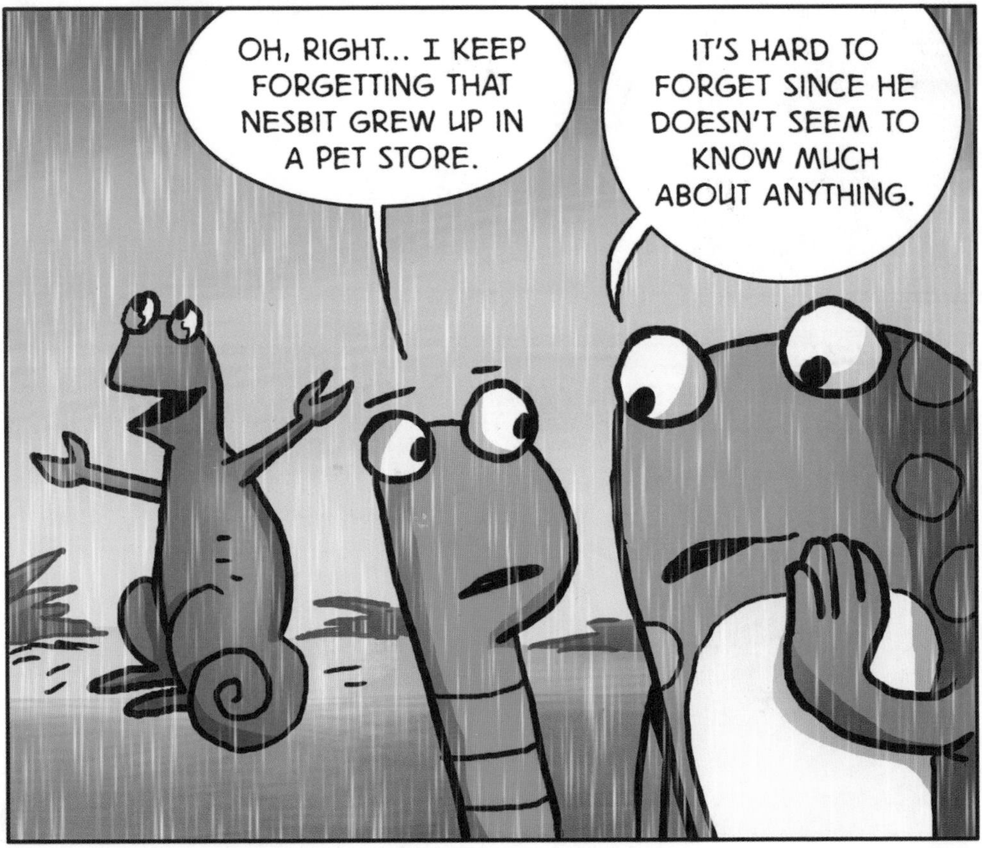
OH, RIGHT... I KEEP FORGETTING THAT NESBIT GREW UP IN A PET STORE.
IT'S HARD TO FORGET SINCE HE DOESN'T SEEM TO KNOW MUCH ABOUT ANYTHING.

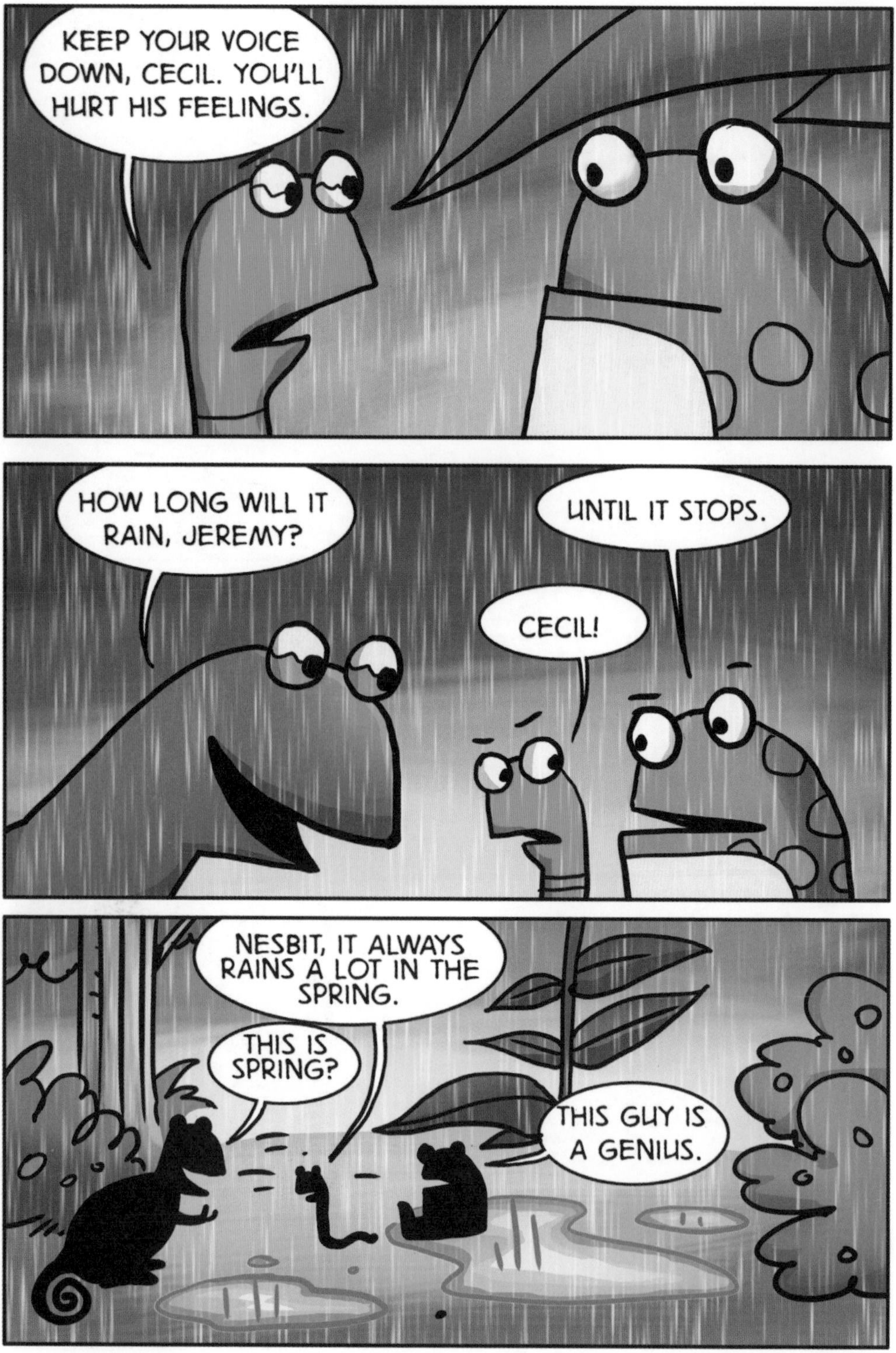
KEEP YOUR VOICE DOWN, CECIL. YOU'LL HURT HIS FEELINGS.
HOW LONG WILL IT RAIN, JEREMY?
UNTIL IT STOPS.
CECIL!
NESBIT, IT ALWAYS RAINS A LOT IN THE SPRING.
THIS IS SPRING?
THIS GUY IS A GENIUS.

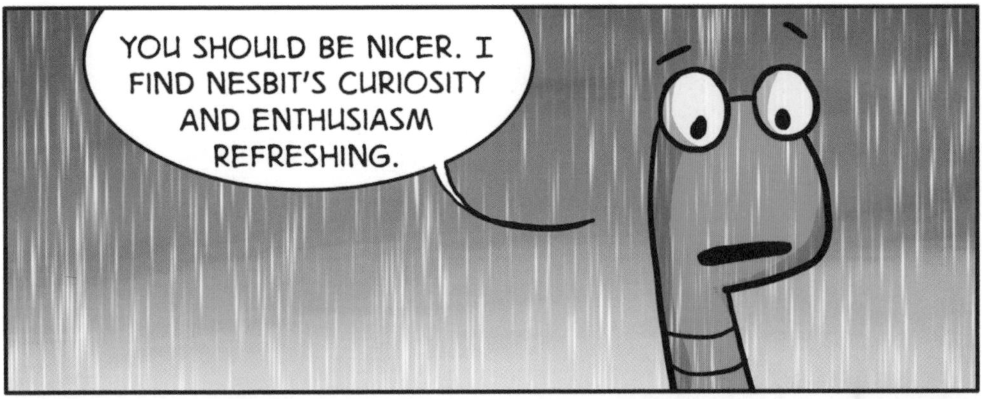
YOU SHOULD BE NICER. I FIND NESBIT'S CURIOSITY AND ENTHUSIASM REFRESHING.

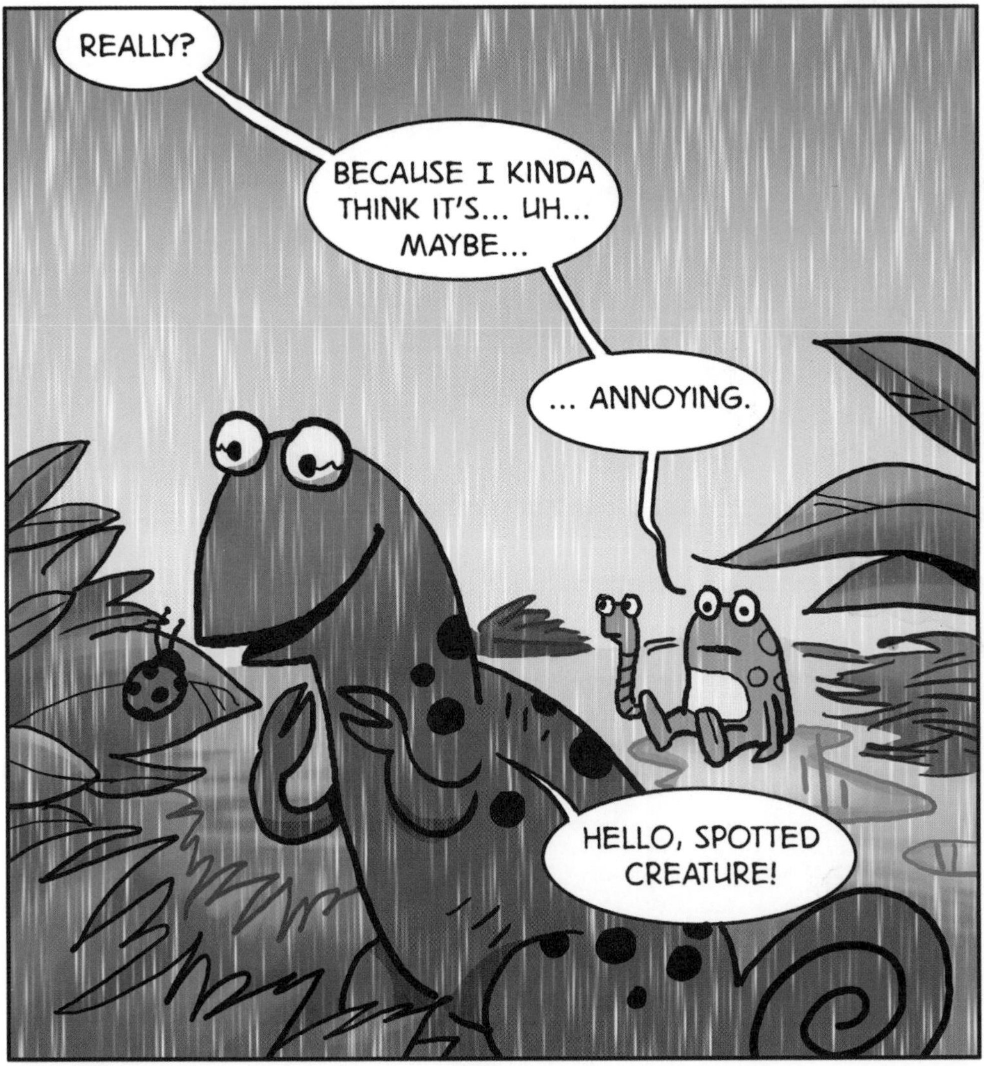
REALLY?
BECAUSE I KINDA THINK IT'S... UH... MAYBE...
... ANNOYING.
HELLO, SPOTTED CREATURE!

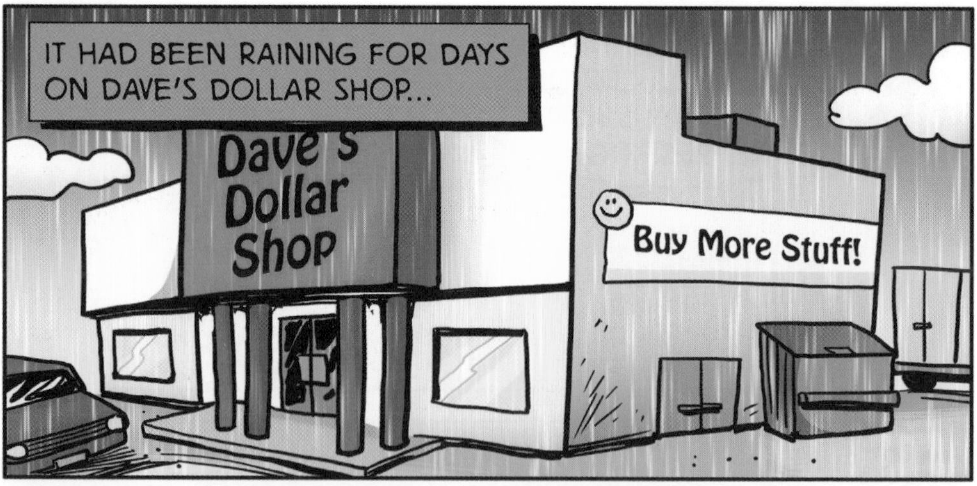
IT HAD BEEN RAINING FOR DAYS ON DAVE'S DOLLAR SHOP...
Dave's Dollar Shop
Buy More Stuff!

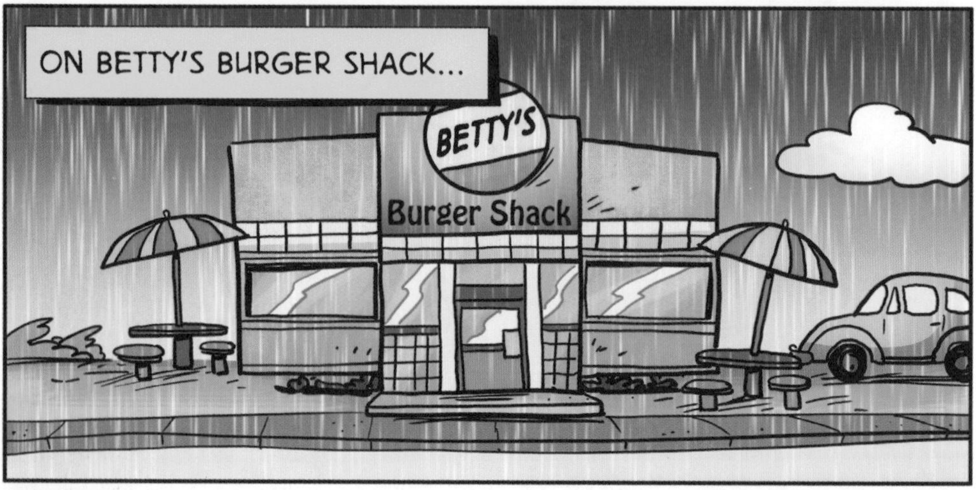
ON BETTY'S BURGER SHACK...
BETTY'S
Burger Shack

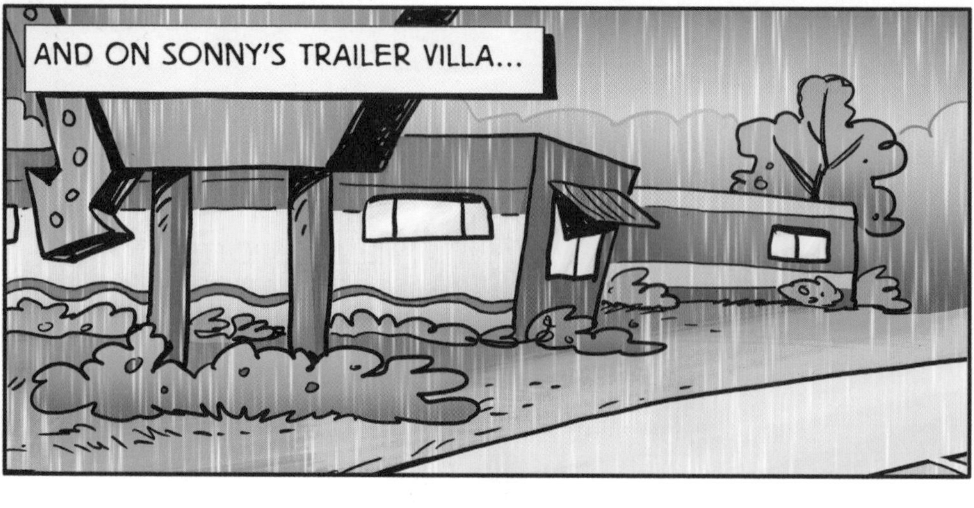
AND ON SONNY'S TRAILER VILLA...

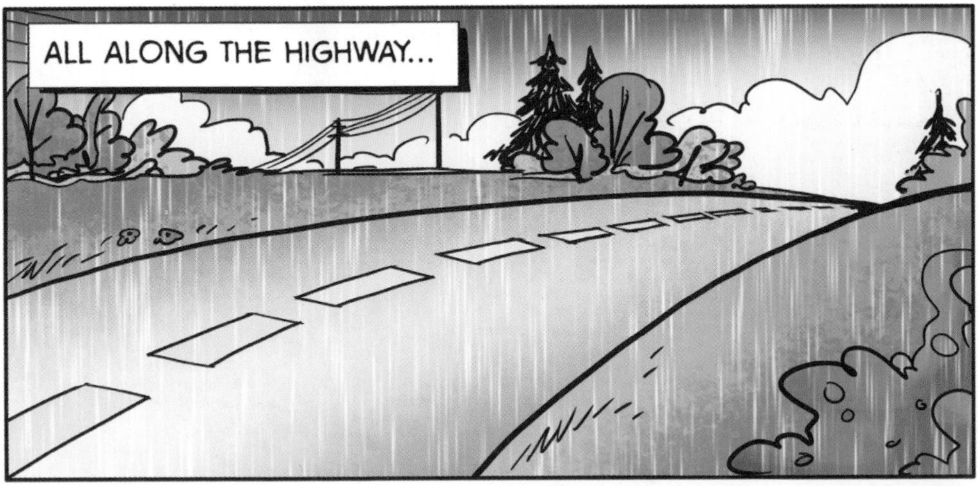
ALL ALONG THE HIGHWAY...

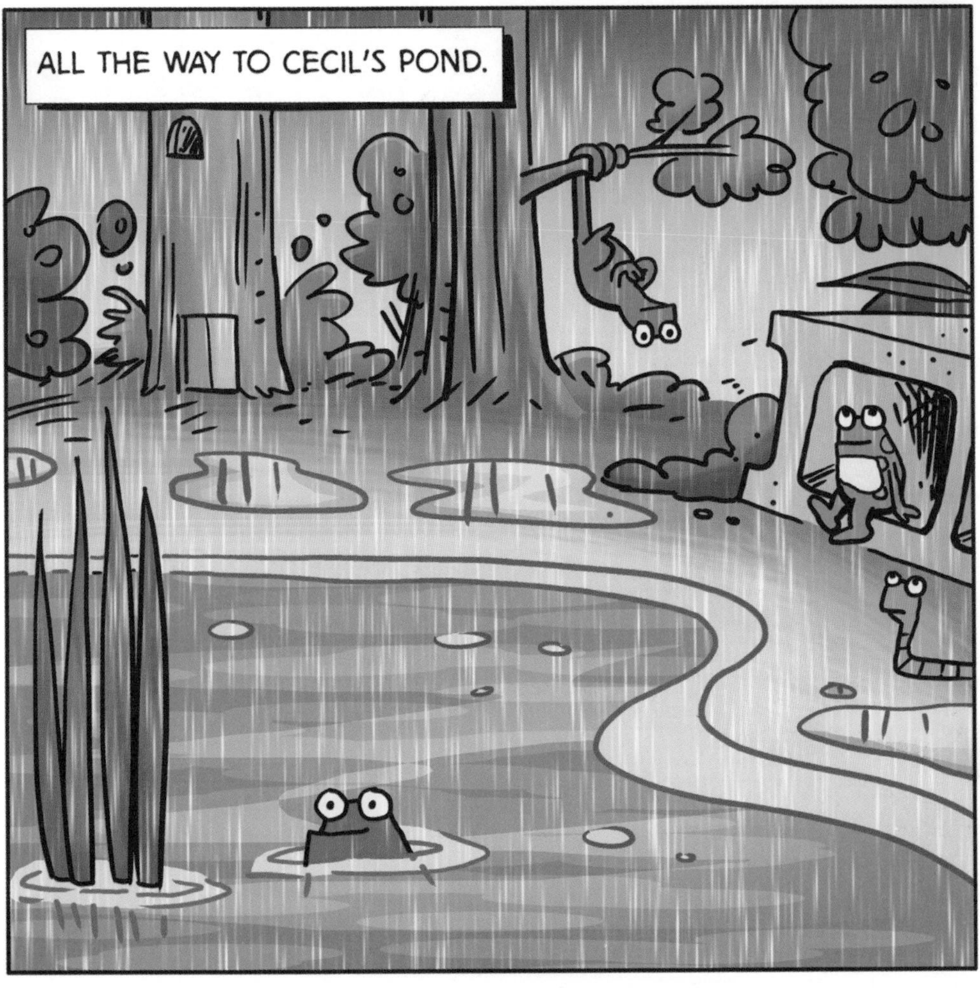
ALL THE WAY TO CECIL'S POND.

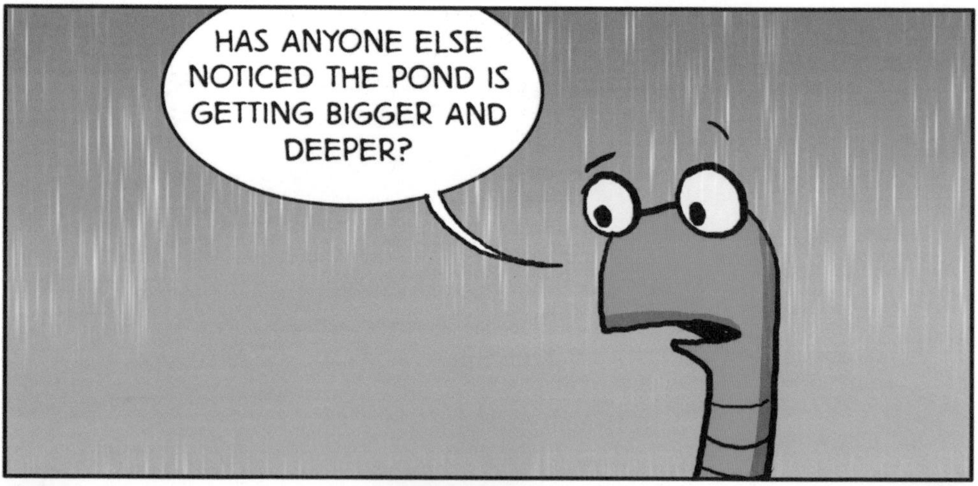
HAS ANYONE ELSE NOTICED THE POND IS GETTING BIGGER AND DEEPER?

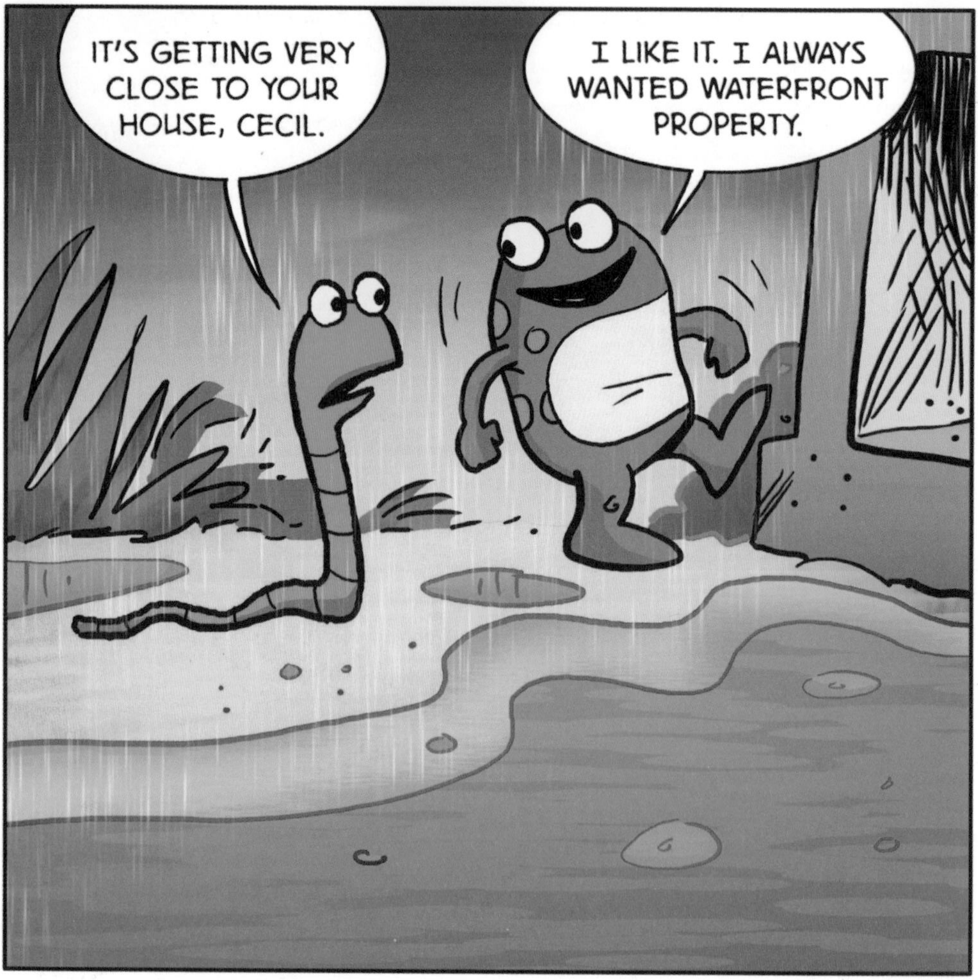
IT'S GETTING VERY CLOSE TO YOUR HOUSE, CECIL.
I LIKE IT. I ALWAYS WANTED WATERFRONT PROPERTY.

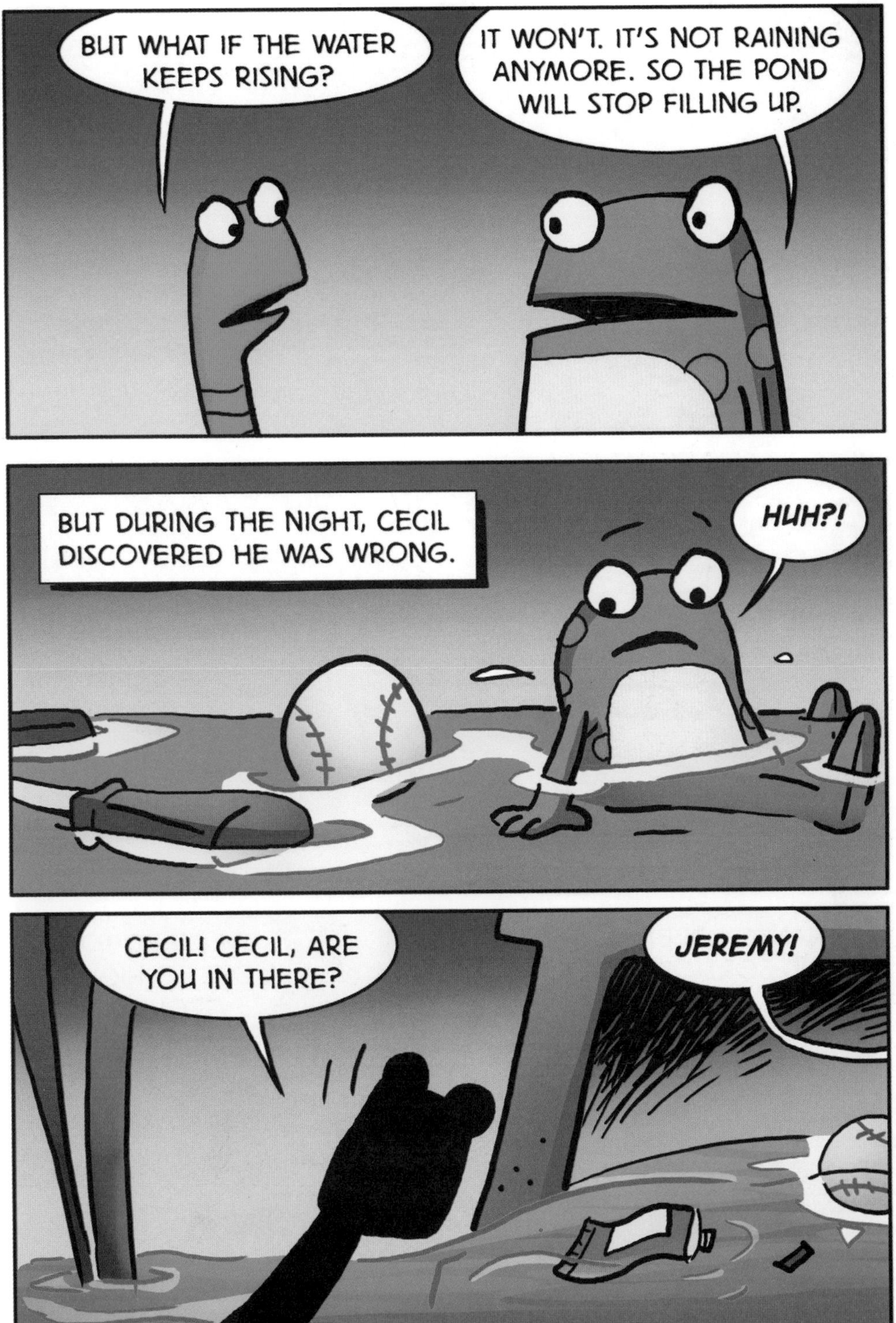

BUT WHAT IF THE WATER KEEPS RISING?
IT WON'T. IT'S NOT RAINING ANYMORE. SO THE POND WILL STOP FILLING UP.
BUT DURING THE NIGHT, CECIL DISCOVERED HE WAS WRONG.
HUH?!
CECIL! CECIL, ARE YOU IN THERE?
JEREMY!

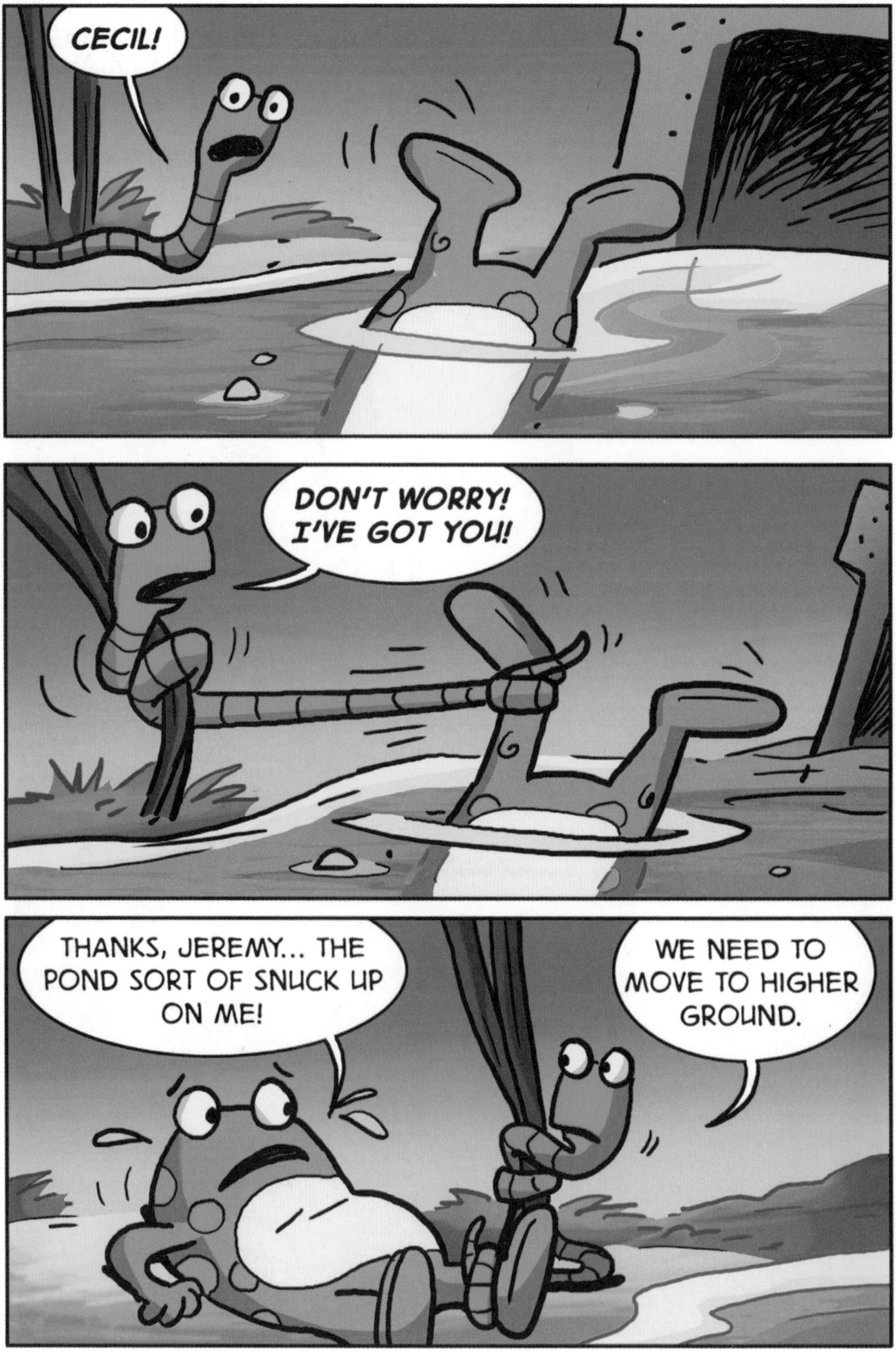
CECIL!
DON'T WORRY! I'VE GOT YOU!
THANKS, JEREMY... THE POND SORT OF SNUCK UP ON ME!
WE NEED TO MOVE TO HIGHER GROUND.

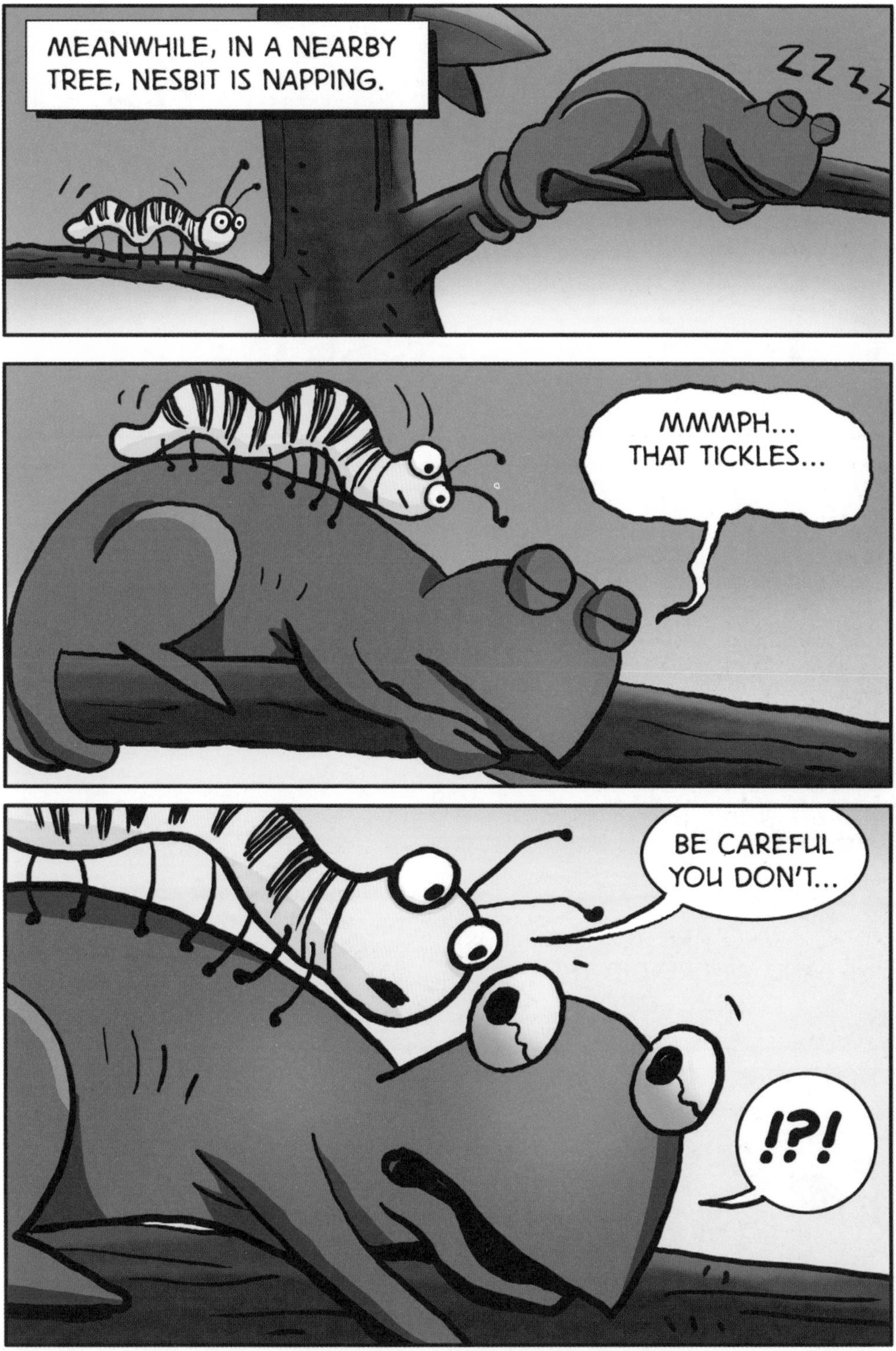
MEANWHILE, IN A NEARBY TREE, NESBIT IS NAPPING.
ZZZZ
MMMPH... THAT TICKLES...
BE CAREFUL YOU DON'T...
!?!

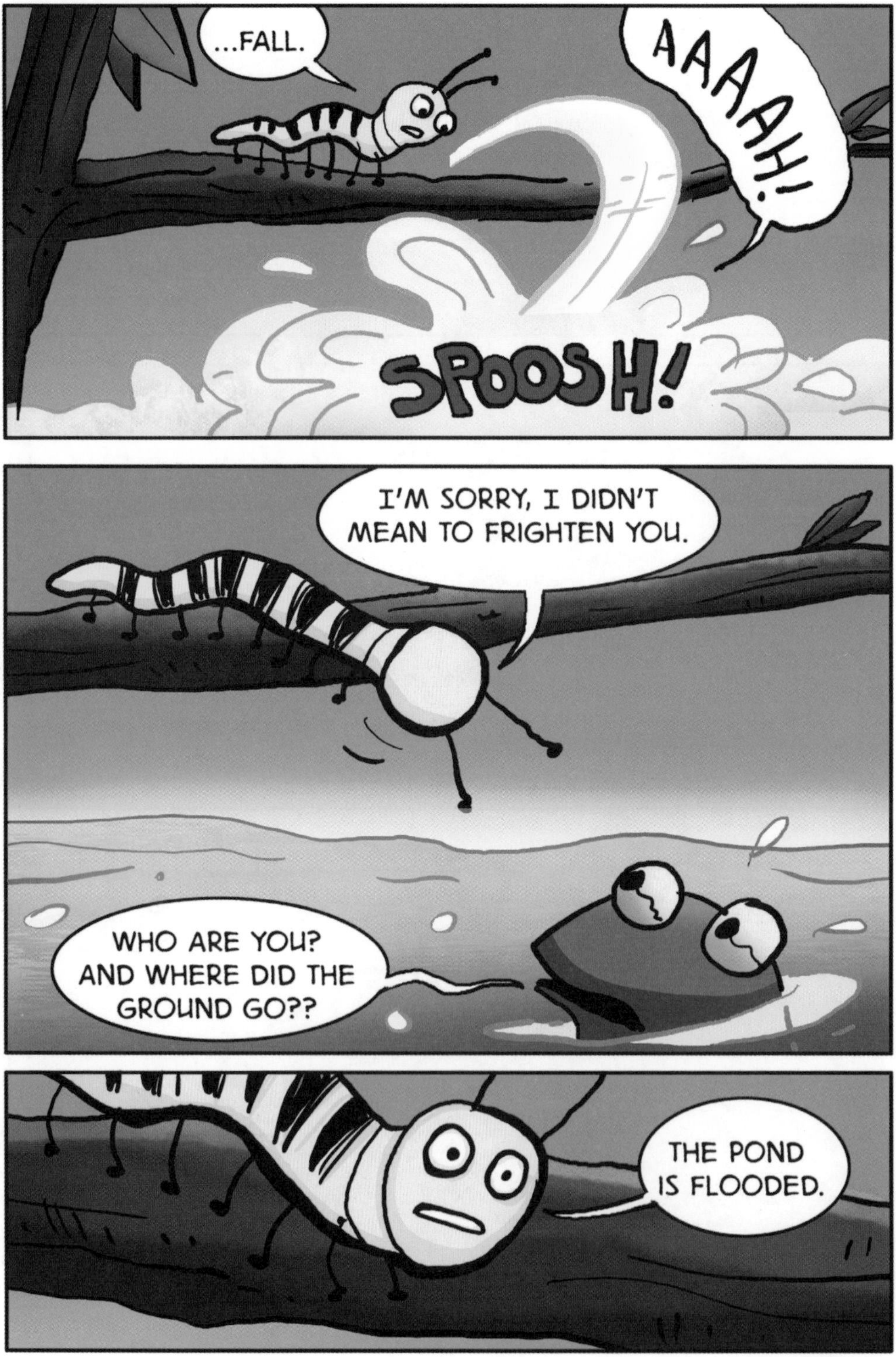
...FALL.
AAAAAH!
SPOOSH!
I'M SORRY, I DIDN'T MEAN TO FRIGHTEN YOU.
WHO ARE YOU? AND WHERE DID THE GROUND GO??
THE POND IS FLOODED.

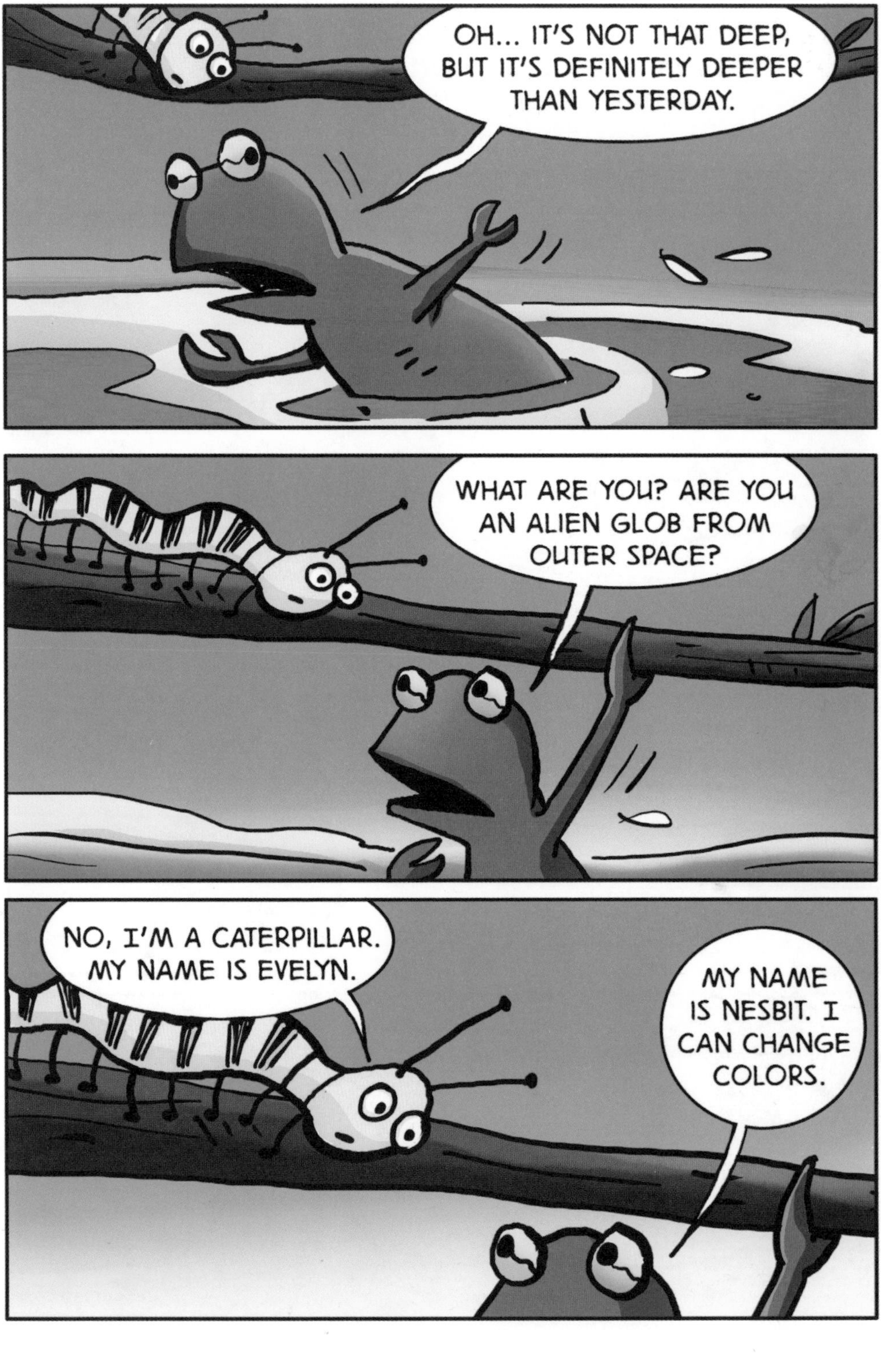
OH... IT'S NOT THAT DEEP, BUT IT'S DEFINITELY DEEPER THAN YESTERDAY.
WHAT ARE YOU? ARE YOU AN ALIEN GLOB FROM OUTER SPACE?
NO, I'M A CATERPILLAR. MY NAME IS EVELYN.
MY NAME IS NESBIT. I CAN CHANGE COLORS.

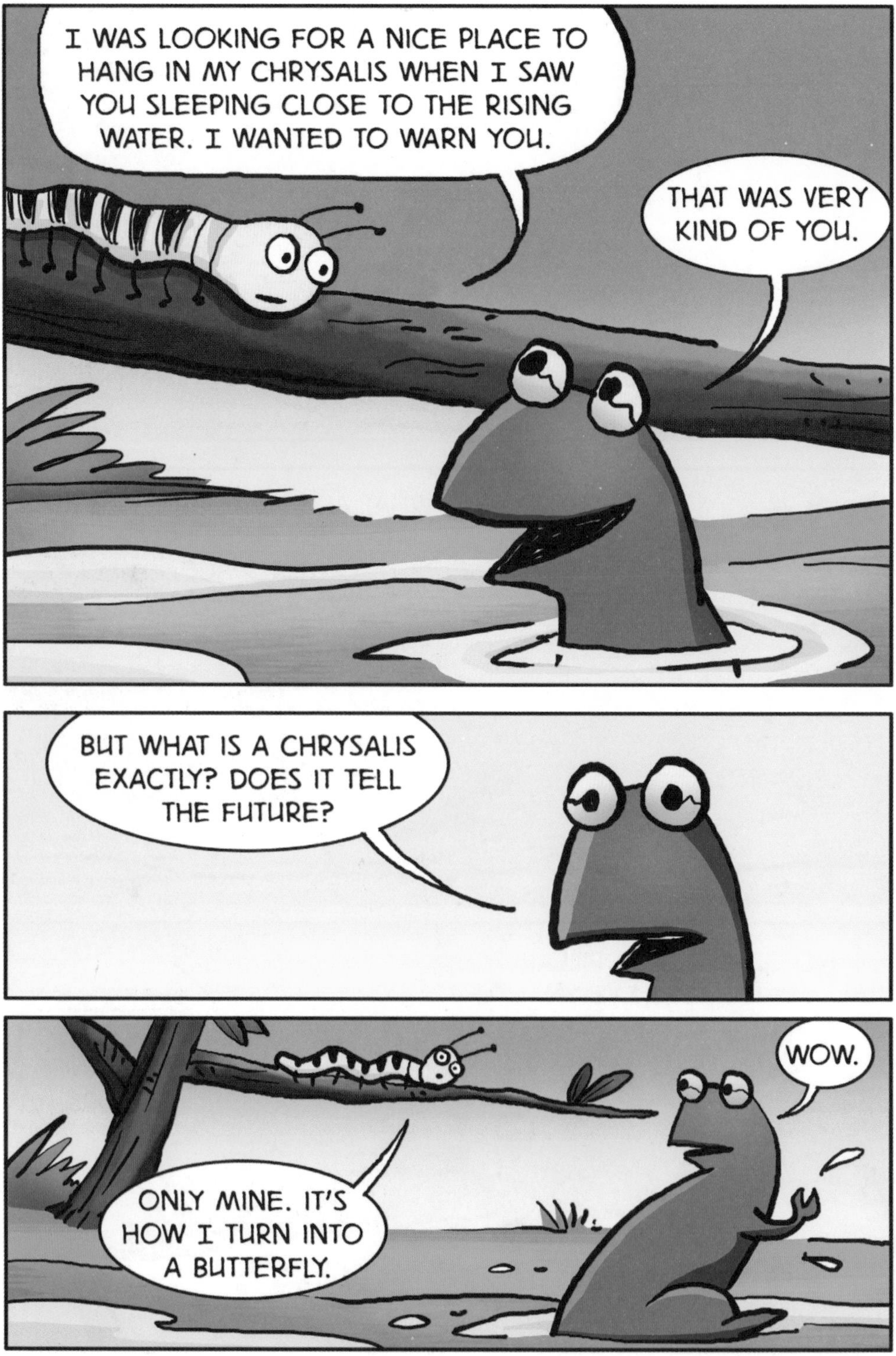
I WAS LOOKING FOR A NICE PLACE TO HANG IN MY CHRYSALIS WHEN I SAW YOU SLEEPING CLOSE TO THE RISING WATER. I WANTED TO WARN YOU.
THAT WAS VERY KIND OF YOU.
BUT WHAT IS A CHRYSALIS EXACTLY? DOES IT TELL THE FUTURE?
ONLY MINE. IT'S HOW I TURN INTO A BUTTERFLY.
WOW.

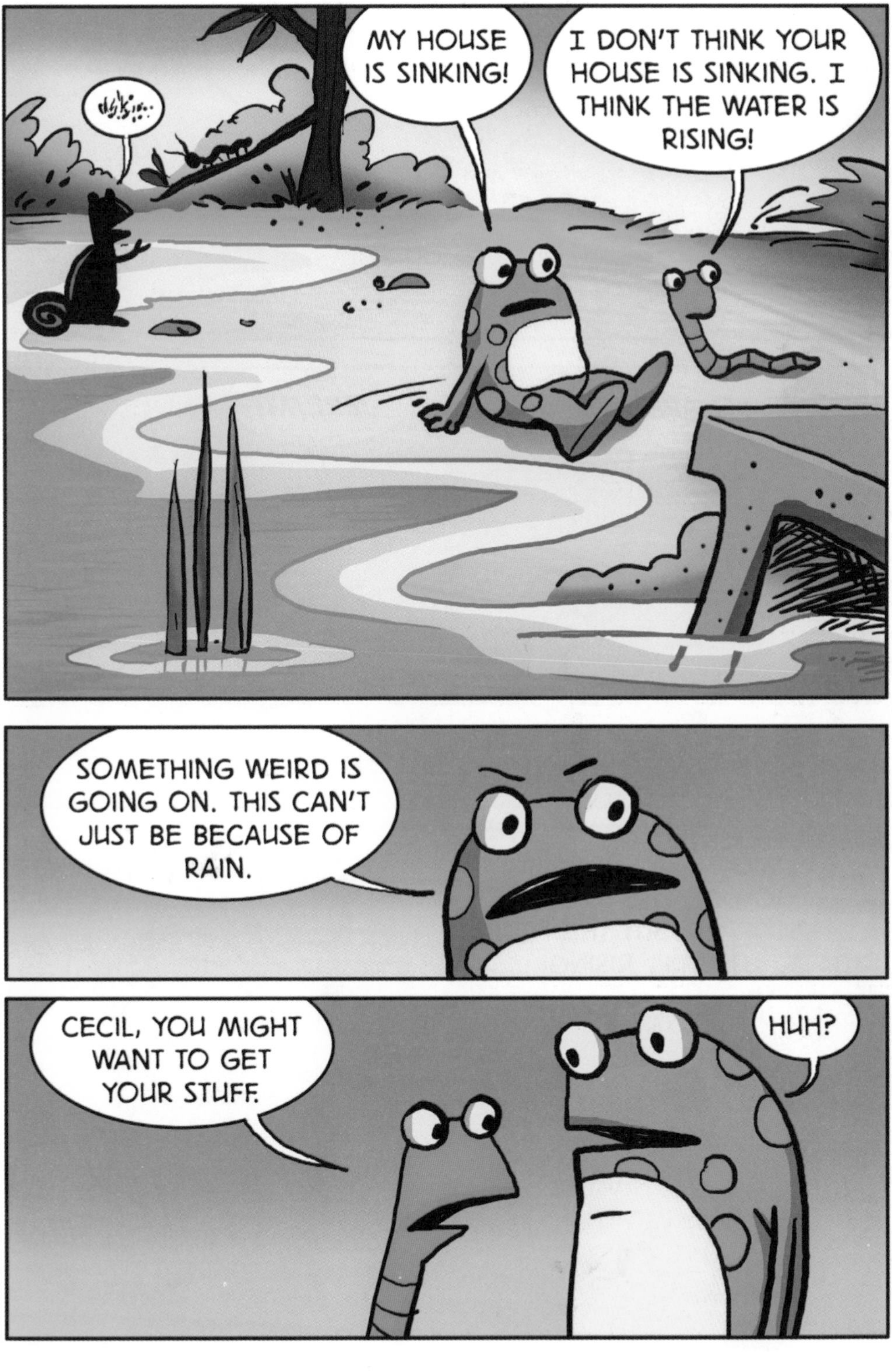
MY HOUSE IS SINKING!
I DON'T THINK YOUR HOUSE IS SINKING. I THINK THE WATER IS RISING!
SOMETHING WEIRD IS GOING ON. THIS CAN'T JUST BE BECAUSE OF RAIN.
CECIL, YOU MIGHT WANT TO GET YOUR STUFF.
HUH?

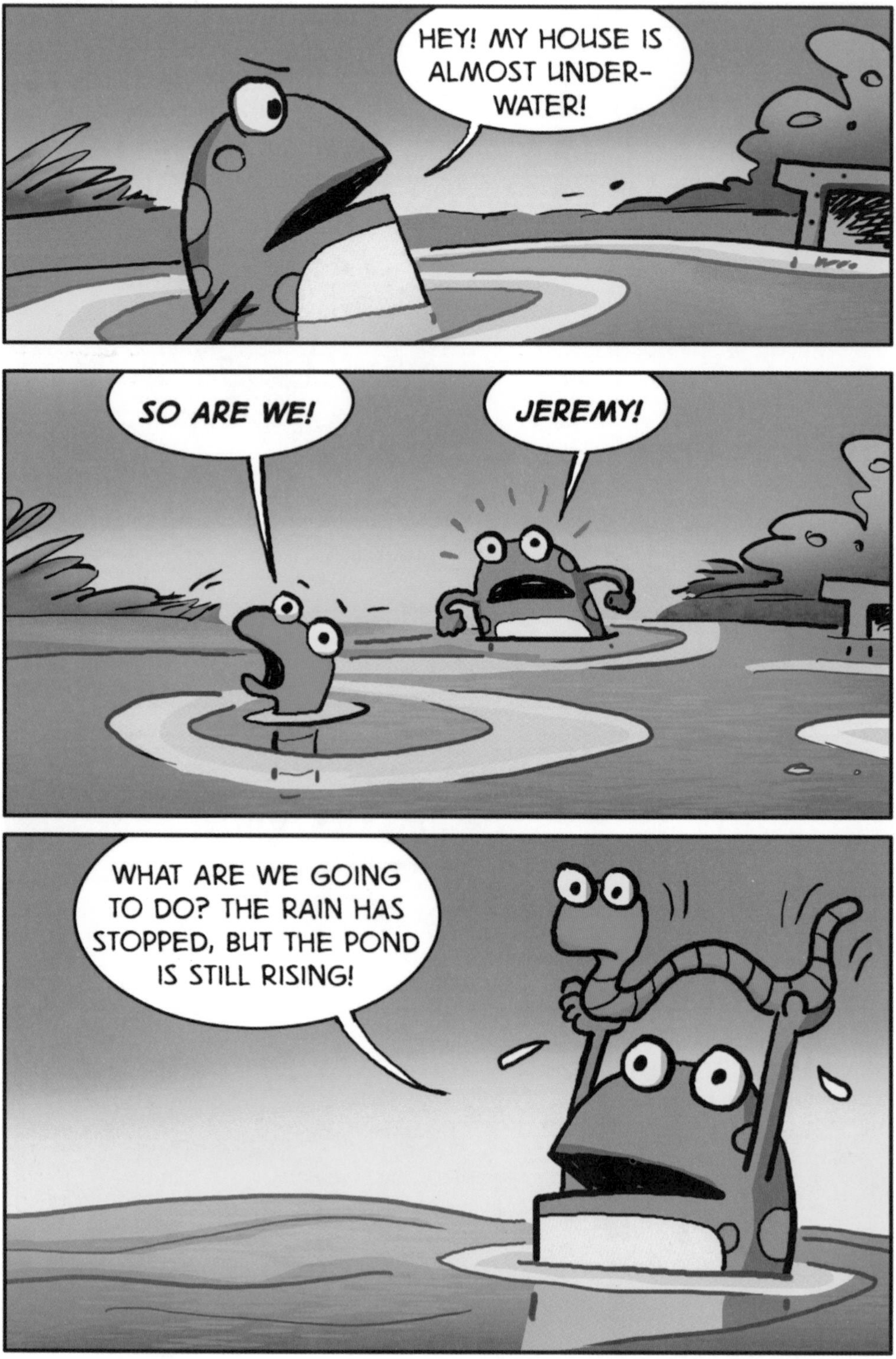

HEY! MY HOUSE IS ALMOST UNDER-WATER!
SO ARE WE!
JEREMY!
WHAT ARE WE GOING TO DO? THE RAIN HAS STOPPED, BUT THE POND IS STILL RISING!

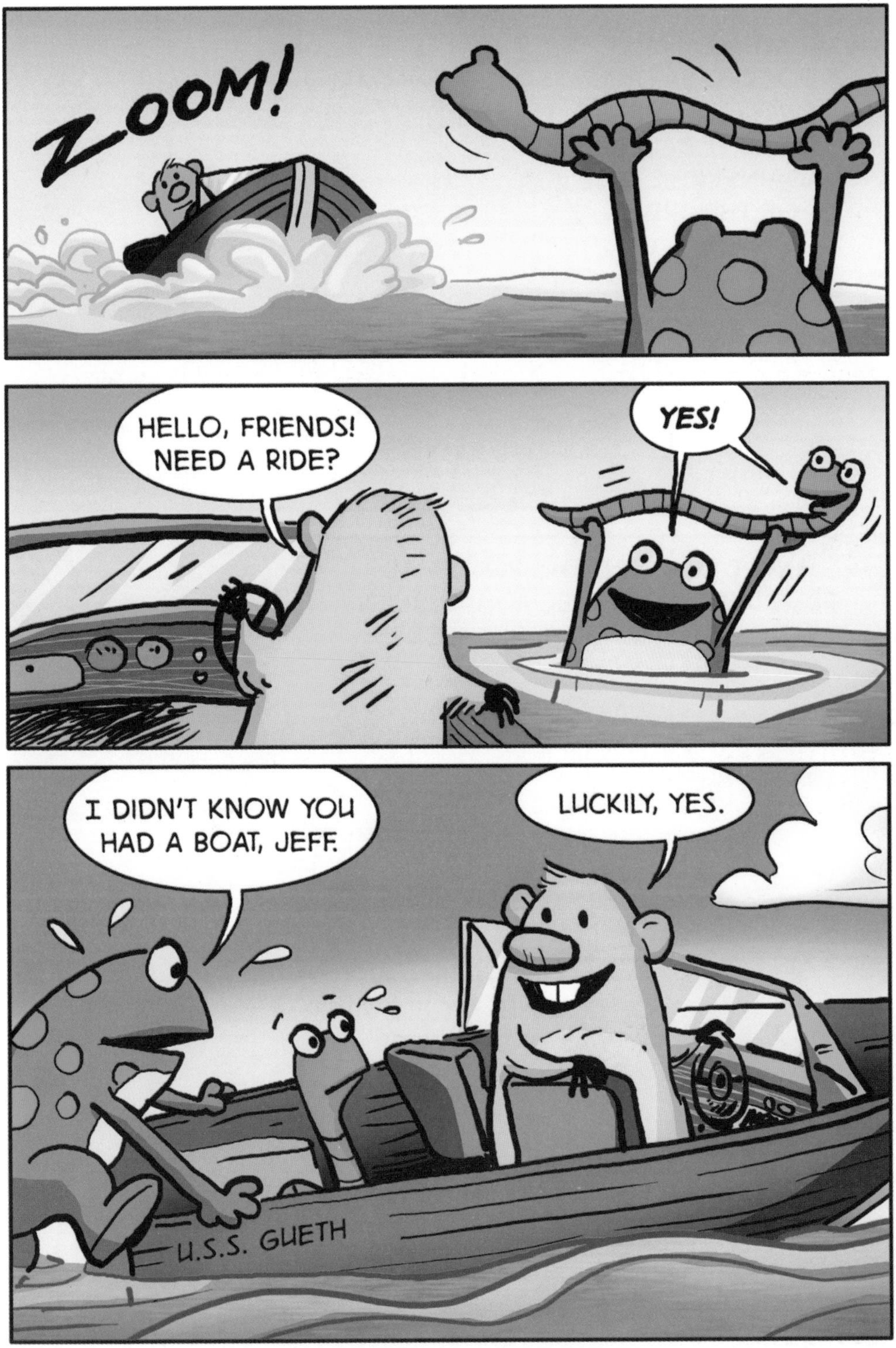
ZOOM!
HELLO, FRIENDS! NEED A RIDE?
YES!
I DIDN'T KNOW YOU HAD A BOAT, JEFF.
LUCKILY, YES.
U.S.S. GUETH

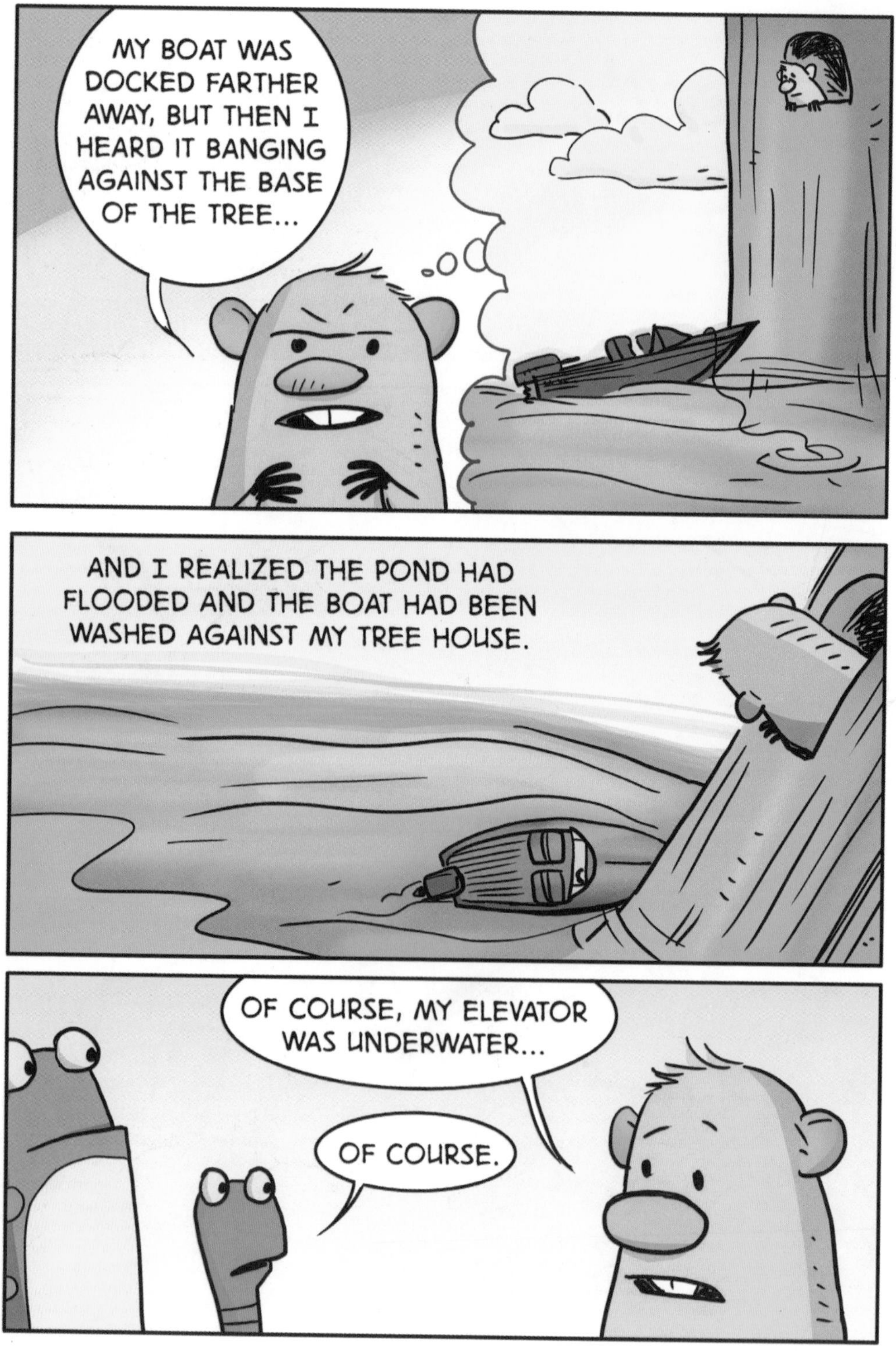
MY BOAT WAS DOCKED FARTHER AWAY, BUT THEN I HEARD IT BANGING AGAINST THE BASE OF THE TREE...
AND I REALIZED THE POND HAD FLOODED AND THE BOAT HAD BEEN WASHED AGAINST MY TREE HOUSE.
OF COURSE, MY ELEVATOR WAS UNDERWATER...
OF COURSE.

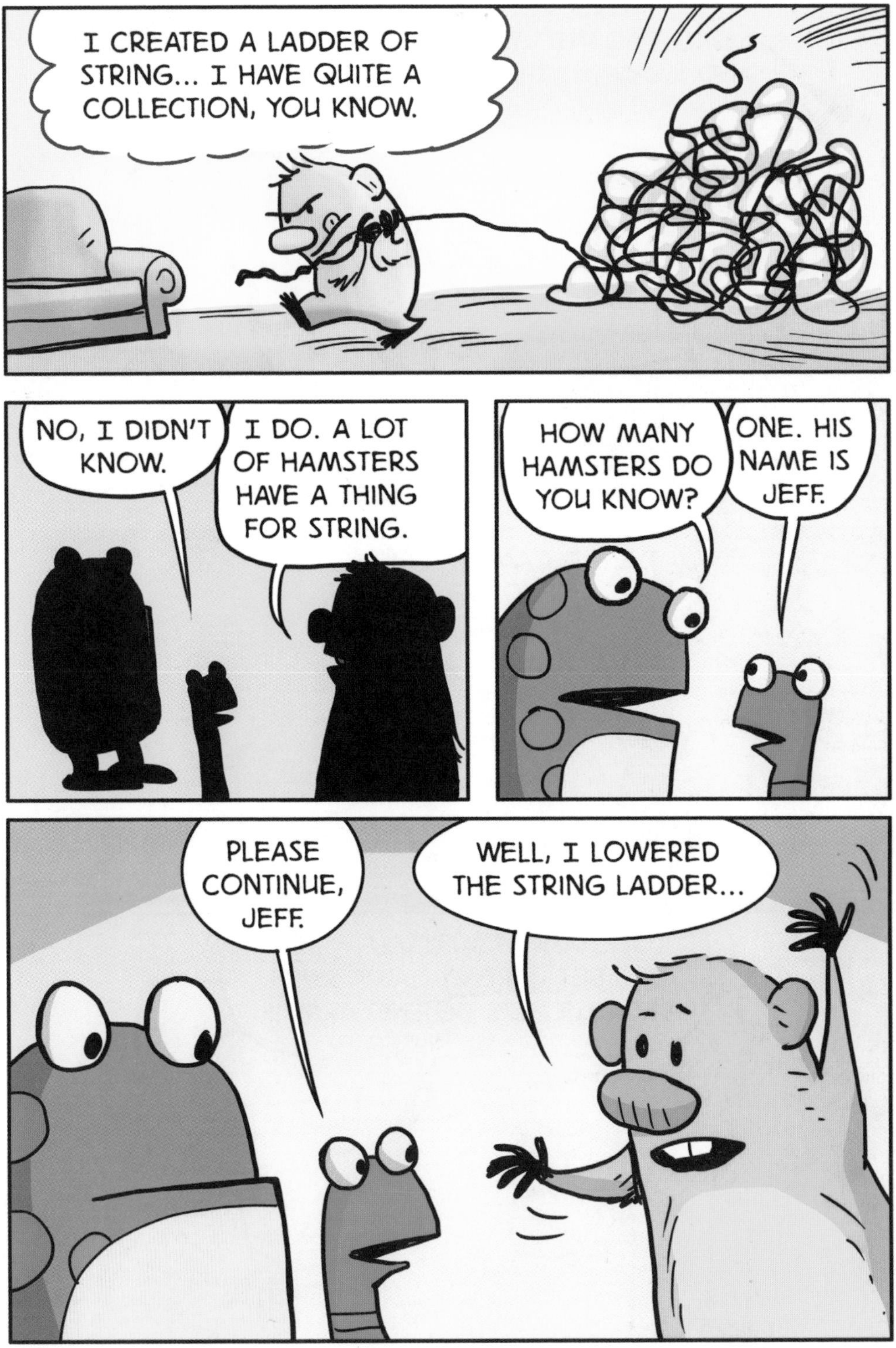
I CREATED A LADDER OF STRING... I HAVE QUITE A COLLECTION, YOU KNOW.
NO, I DIDN'T KNOW.
I DO. A LOT OF HAMSTERS HAVE A THING FOR STRING.
HOW MANY HAMSTERS DO YOU KNOW?
ONE. HIS NAME IS JEFF.
PLEASE CONTINUE, JEFF.
WELL, I LOWERED THE STRING LADDER...

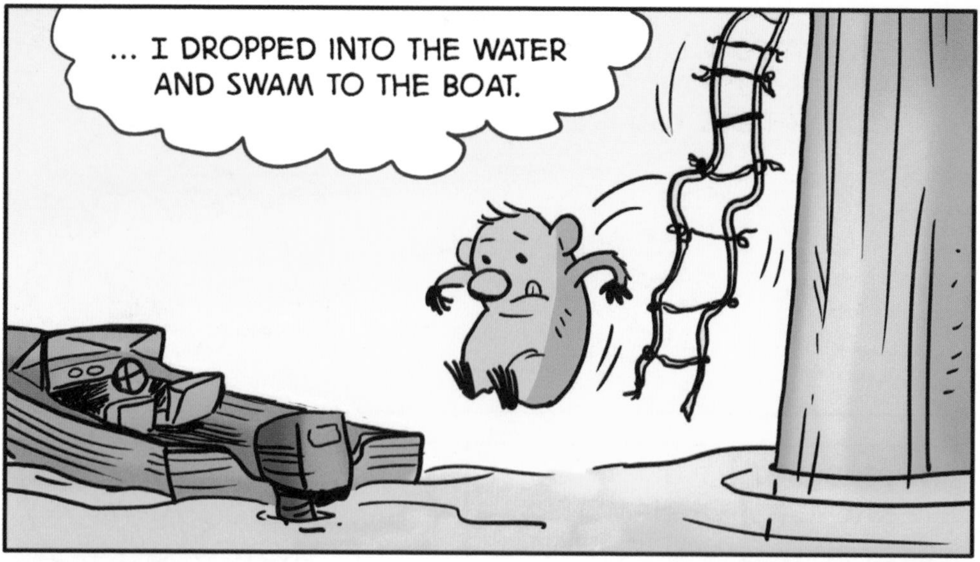
... I DROPPED INTO THE WATER AND SWAM TO THE BOAT.

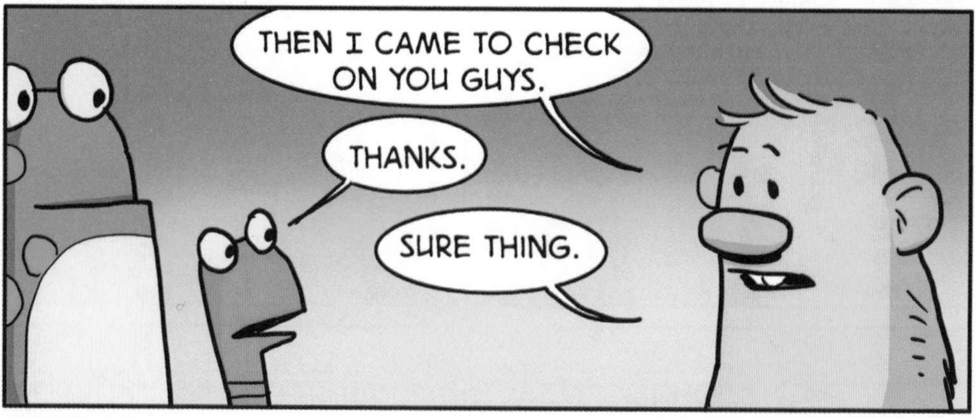
THEN I CAME TO CHECK ON YOU GUYS.
THANKS.
SURE THING.

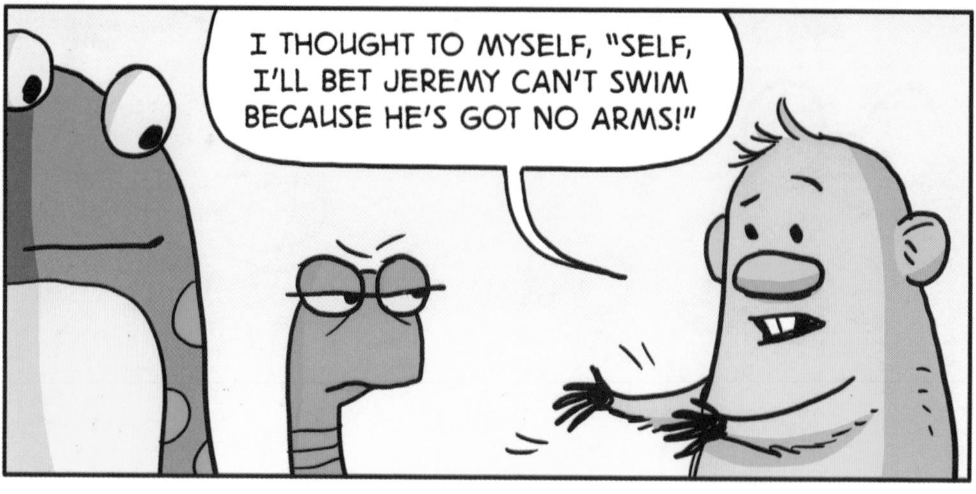
I THOUGHT TO MYSELF, "SELF, I'LL BET JEREMY CAN'T SWIM BECAUSE HE'S GOT NO ARMS!"

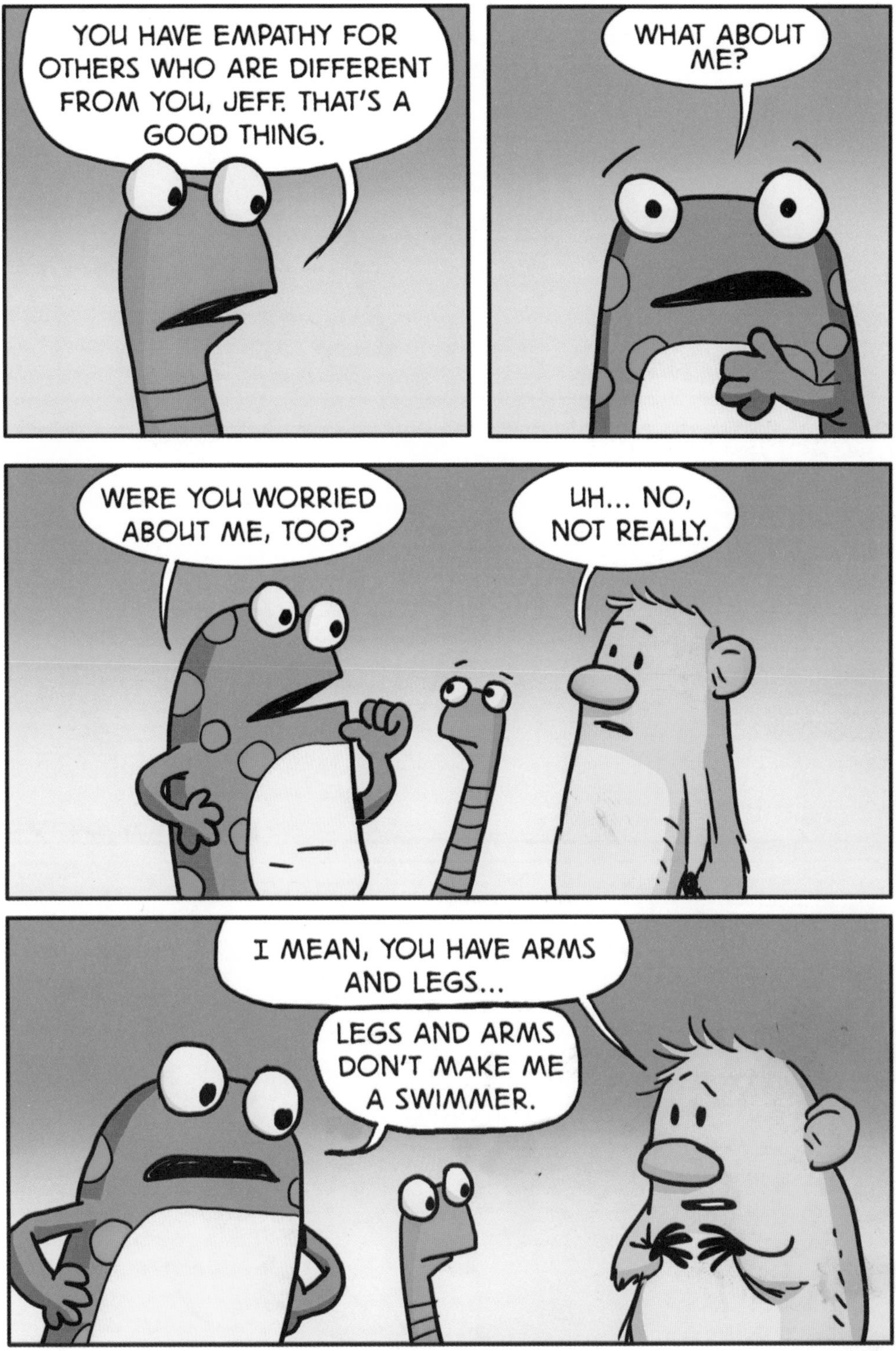
YOU HAVE EMPATHY FOR OTHERS WHO ARE DIFFERENT FROM YOU, JEFF. THAT'S A GOOD THING.
WHAT ABOUT ME?
WERE YOU WORRIED ABOUT ME, TOO?
UH... NO, NOT REALLY.
I MEAN, YOU HAVE ARMS AND LEGS...
LEGS AND ARMS DON'T MAKE ME A SWIMMER.

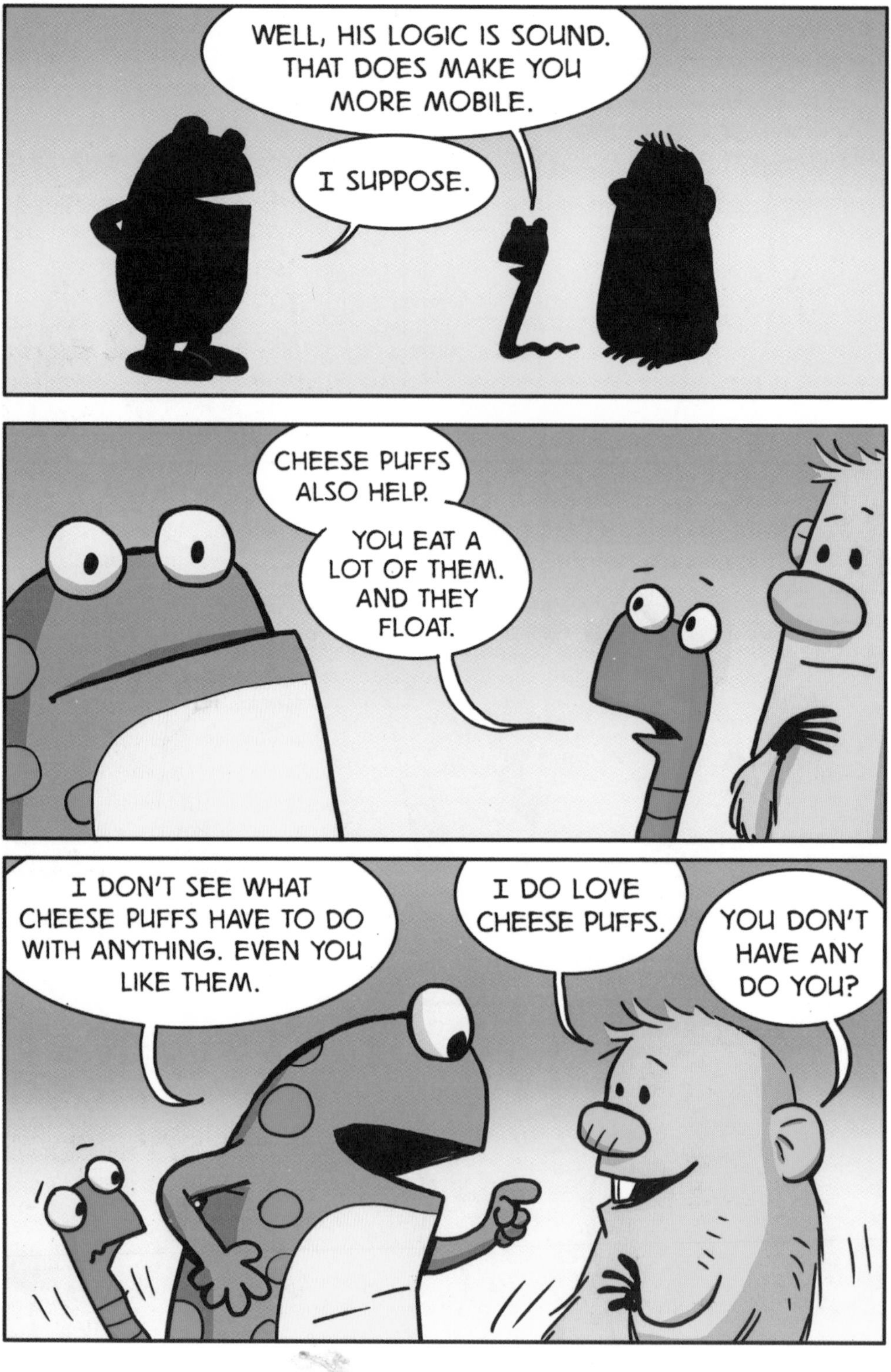
WELL, HIS LOGIC IS SOUND. THAT DOES MAKE YOU MORE MOBILE.
I SUPPOSE.
CHEESE PUFFS ALSO HELP.
YOU EAT A LOT OF THEM. AND THEY FLOAT.
I DON'T SEE WHAT CHEESE PUFFS HAVE TO DO WITH ANYTHING. EVEN YOU LIKE THEM.
I DO LOVE CHEESE PUFFS.
YOU DON'T HAVE ANY DO YOU?

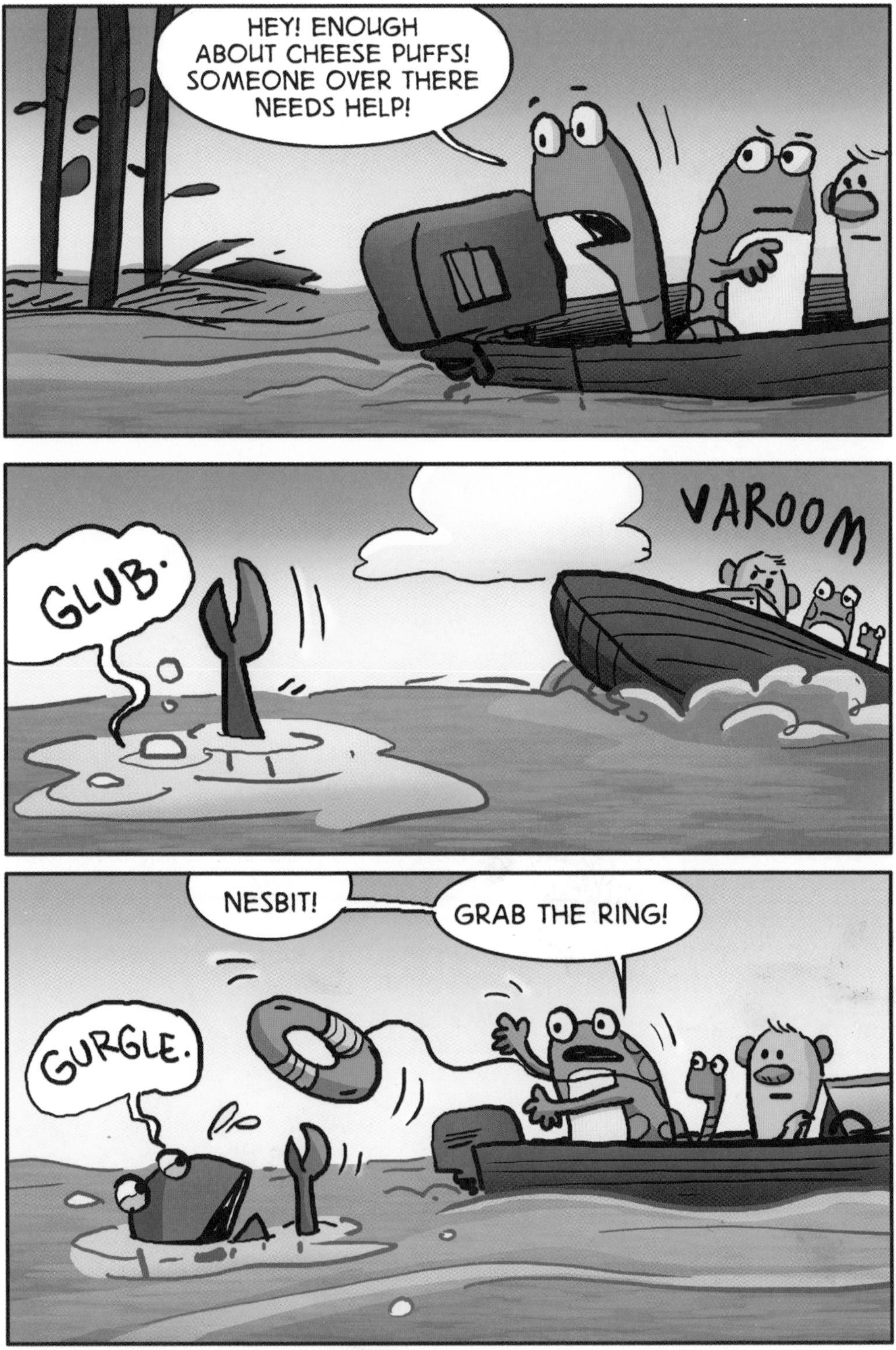
HEY! ENOUGH ABOUT CHEESE PUFFS! SOMEONE OVER THERE NEEDS HELP!
GLUB.
VAROOM
NESBIT!
GRAB THE RING!
GURGLE.

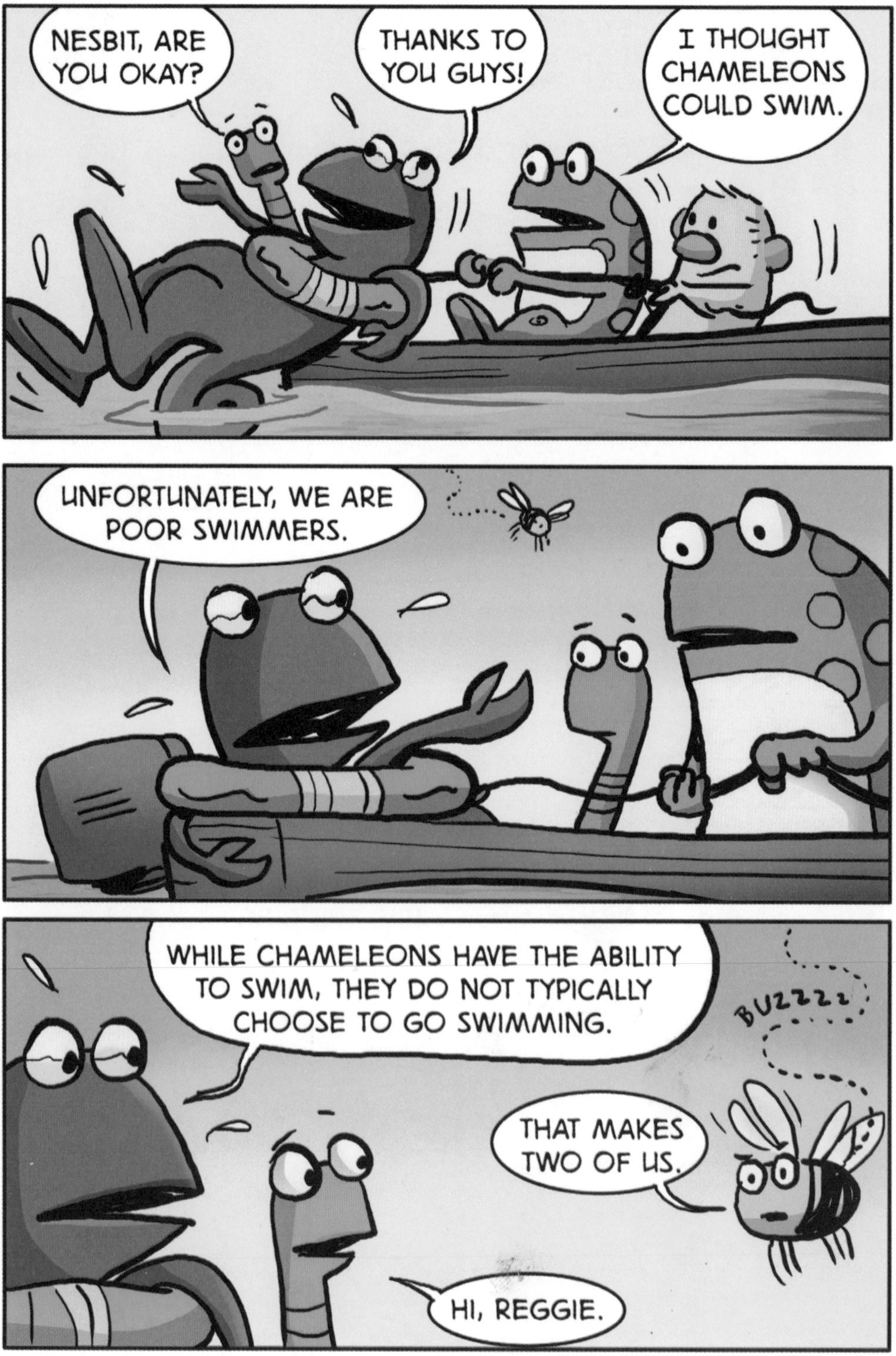
NESBIT, ARE YOU OKAY?
THANKS TO YOU GUYS!
I THOUGHT CHAMELEONS COULD SWIM.
UNFORTUNATELY, WE ARE POOR SWIMMERS.
WHILE CHAMELEONS HAVE THE ABILITY TO SWIM, THEY DO NOT TYPICALLY CHOOSE TO GO SWIMMING.
BUZZZz
THAT MAKES TWO OF US.
HI, REGGIE.

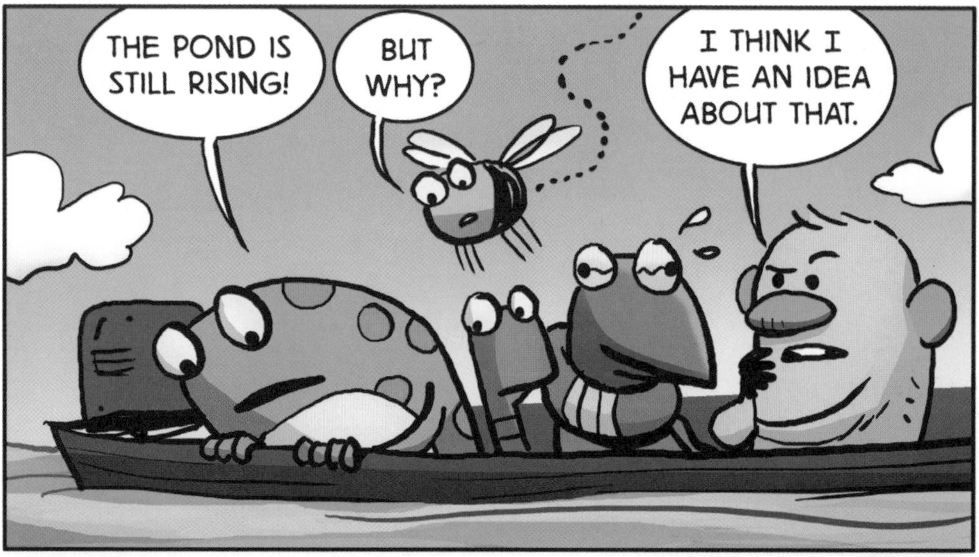
THE POND IS STILL RISING!
BUT WHY?
I THINK I HAVE AN IDEA ABOUT THAT.

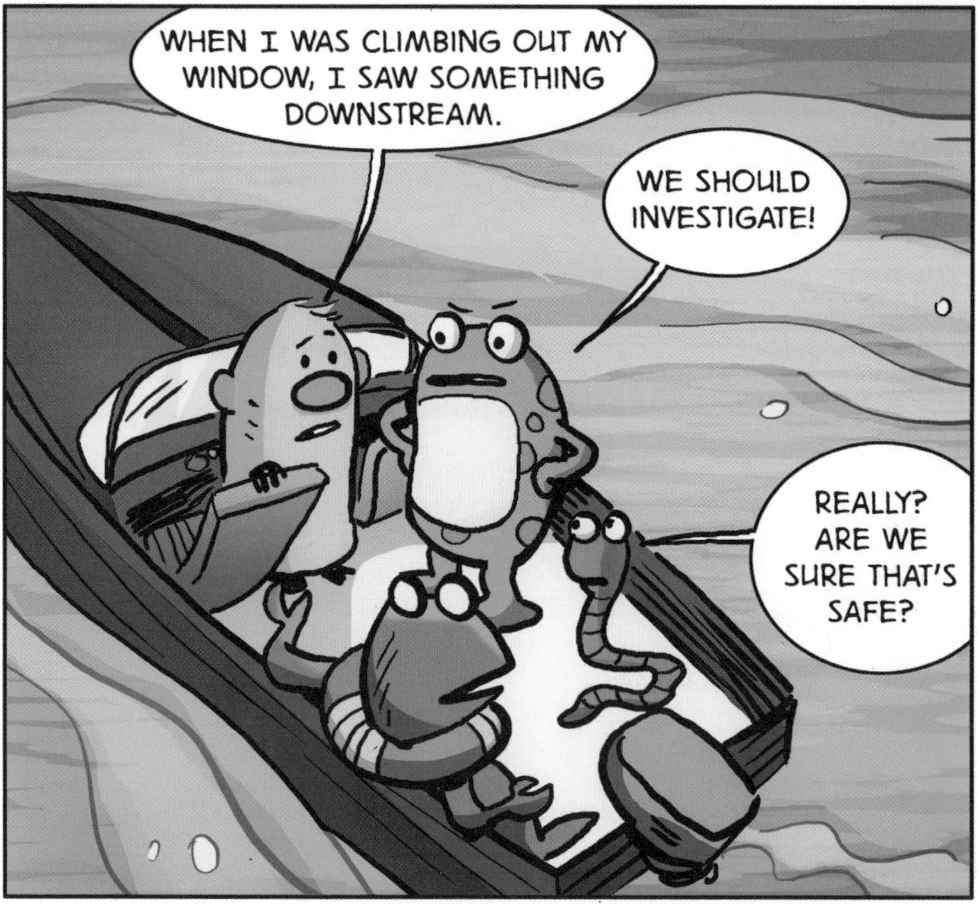
WHEN I WAS CLIMBING OUT MY WINDOW, I SAW SOMETHING DOWNSTREAM.
WE SHOULD INVESTIGATE!
REALLY? ARE WE SURE THAT'S SAFE?

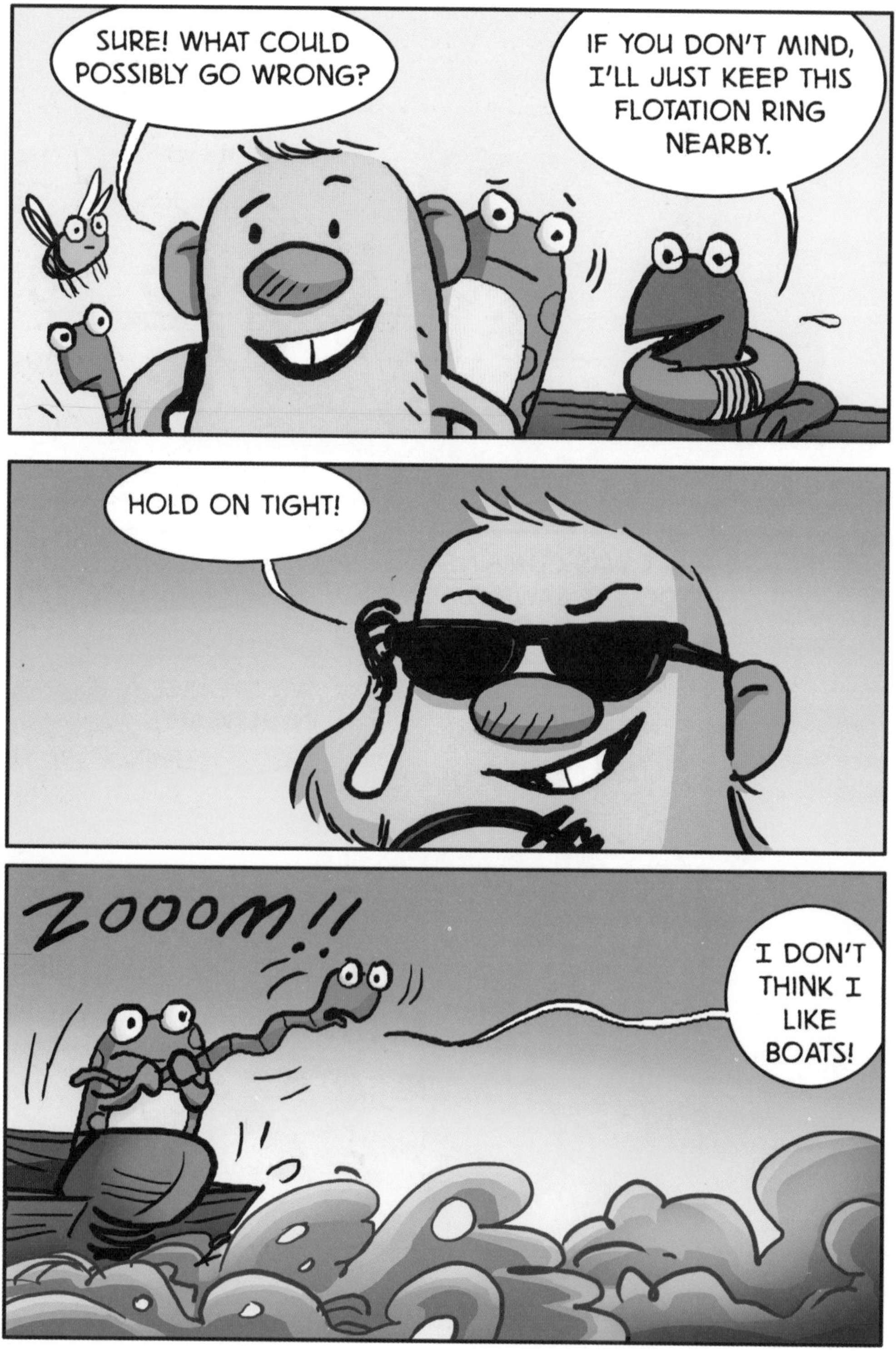
SURE! WHAT COULD POSSIBLY GO WRONG?
IF YOU DON'T MIND, I'LL JUST KEEP THIS FLOTATION RING NEARBY.
HOLD ON TIGHT!
ZOOOM!!
I DON'T THINK I LIKE BOATS!

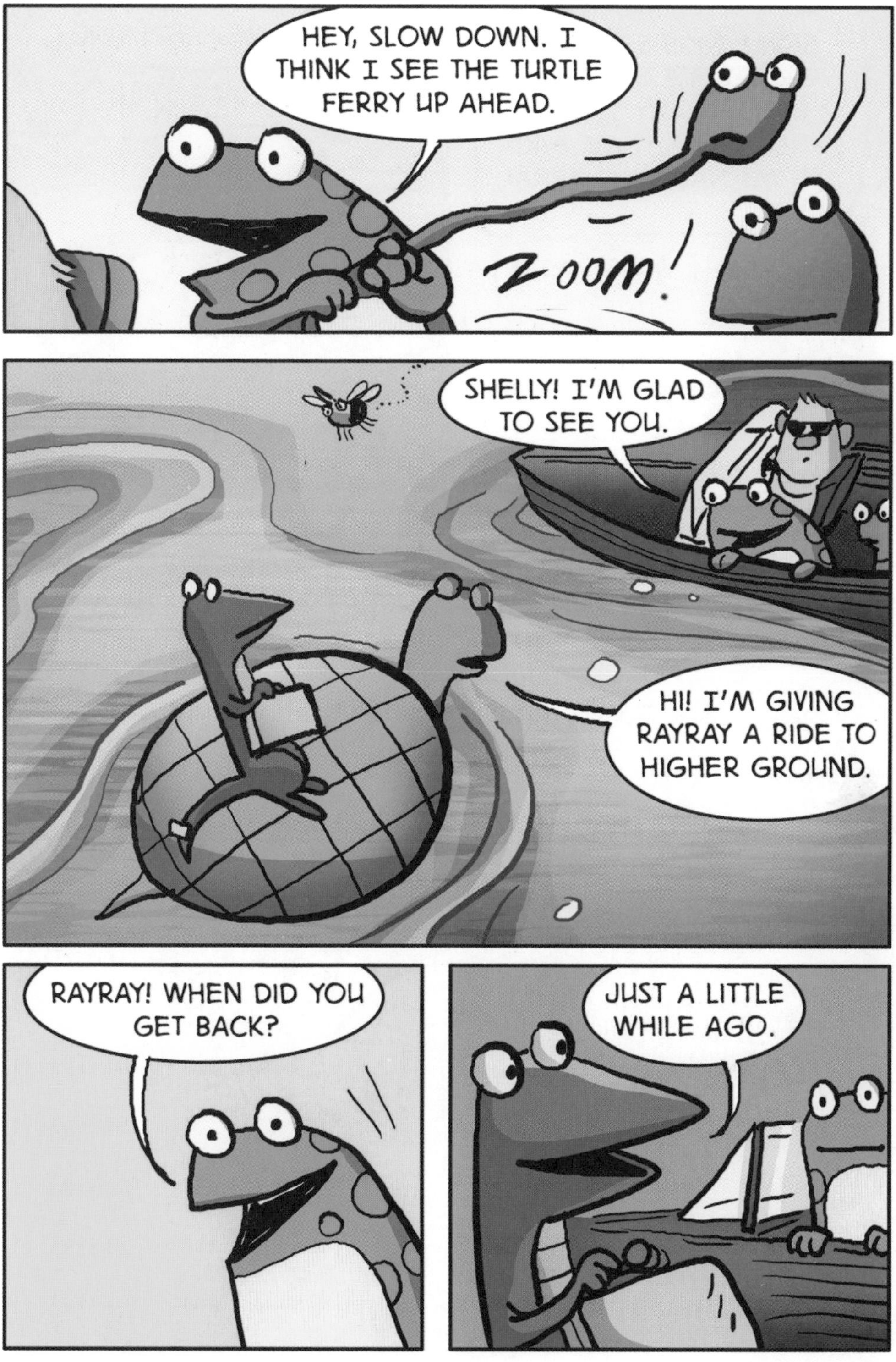
HEY, SLOW DOWN. I THINK I SEE THE TURTLE FERRY UP AHEAD.
ZOOM!
SHELLY! I'M GLAD TO SEE YOU.
HI! I'M GIVING RAYRAY A RIDE TO HIGHER GROUND.
RAYRAY! WHEN DID YOU GET BACK?
JUST A LITTLE WHILE AGO.

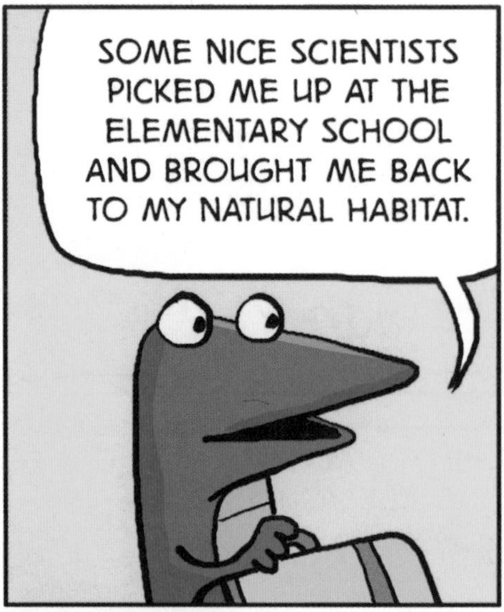
SOME NICE SCIENTISTS PICKED ME UP AT THE ELEMENTARY SCHOOL AND BROUGHT ME BACK TO MY NATURAL HABITAT.

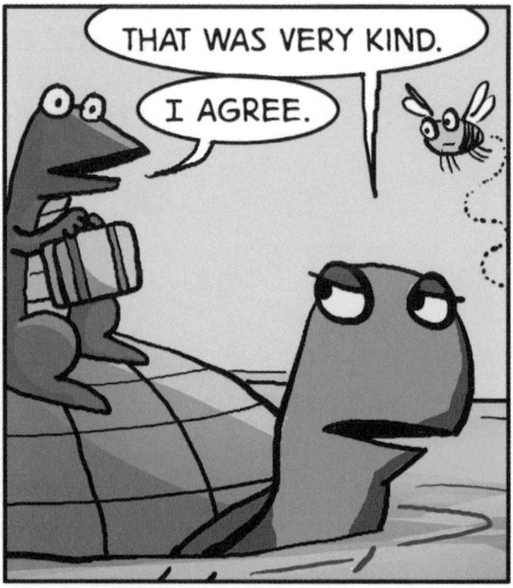
THAT WAS VERY KIND.
I AGREE.

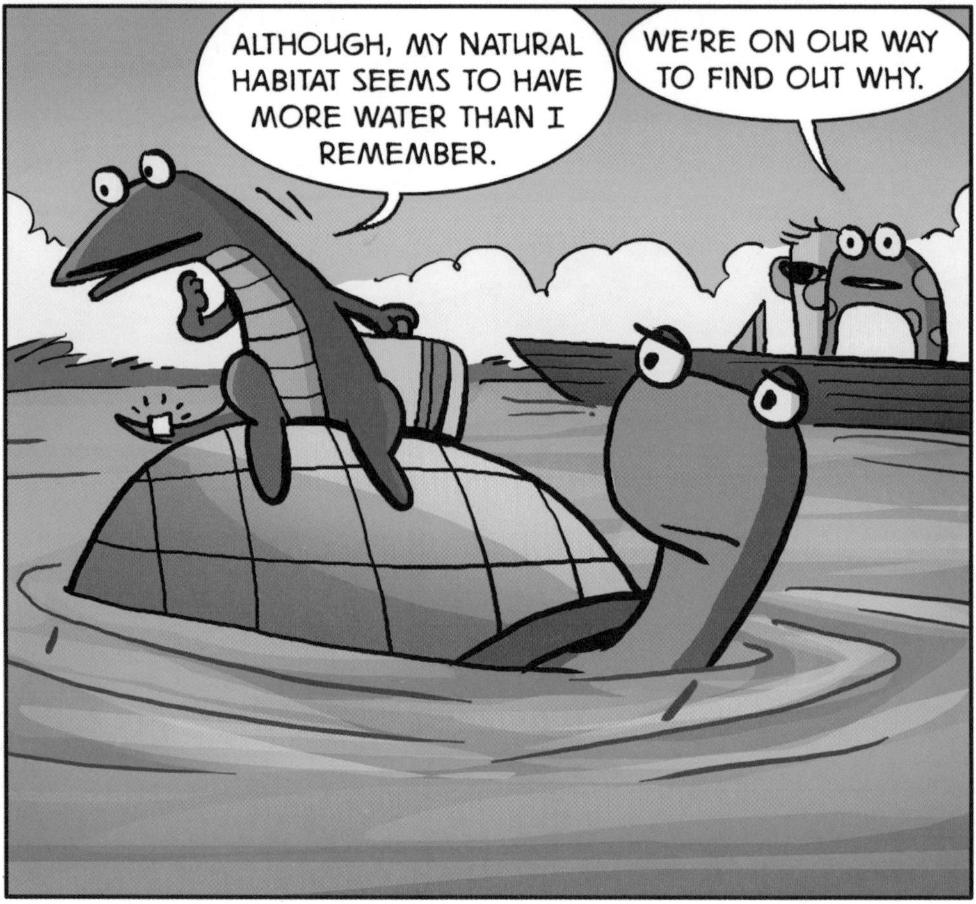
ALTHOUGH, MY NATURAL HABITAT SEEMS TO HAVE MORE WATER THAN I REMEMBER.
WE'RE ON OUR WAY TO FIND OUT WHY.

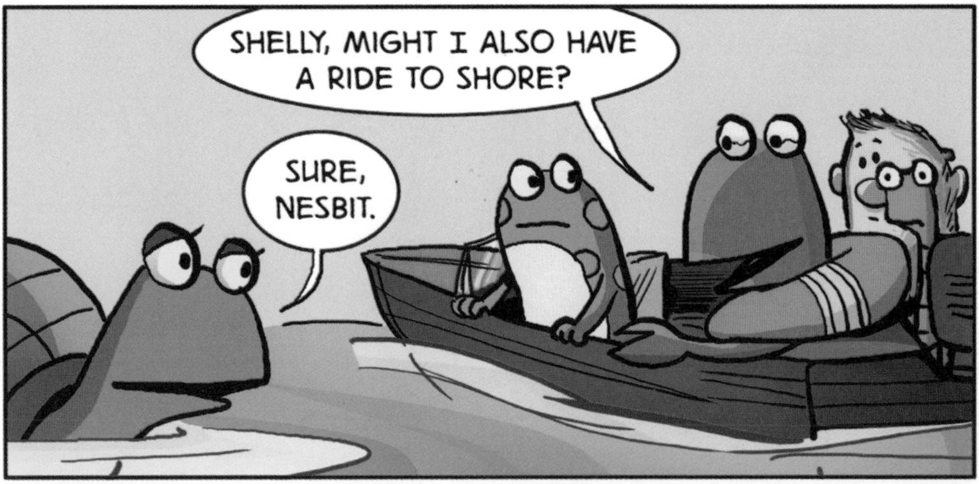
SHELLY, MIGHT I ALSO HAVE A RIDE TO SHORE?
SURE, NESBIT.

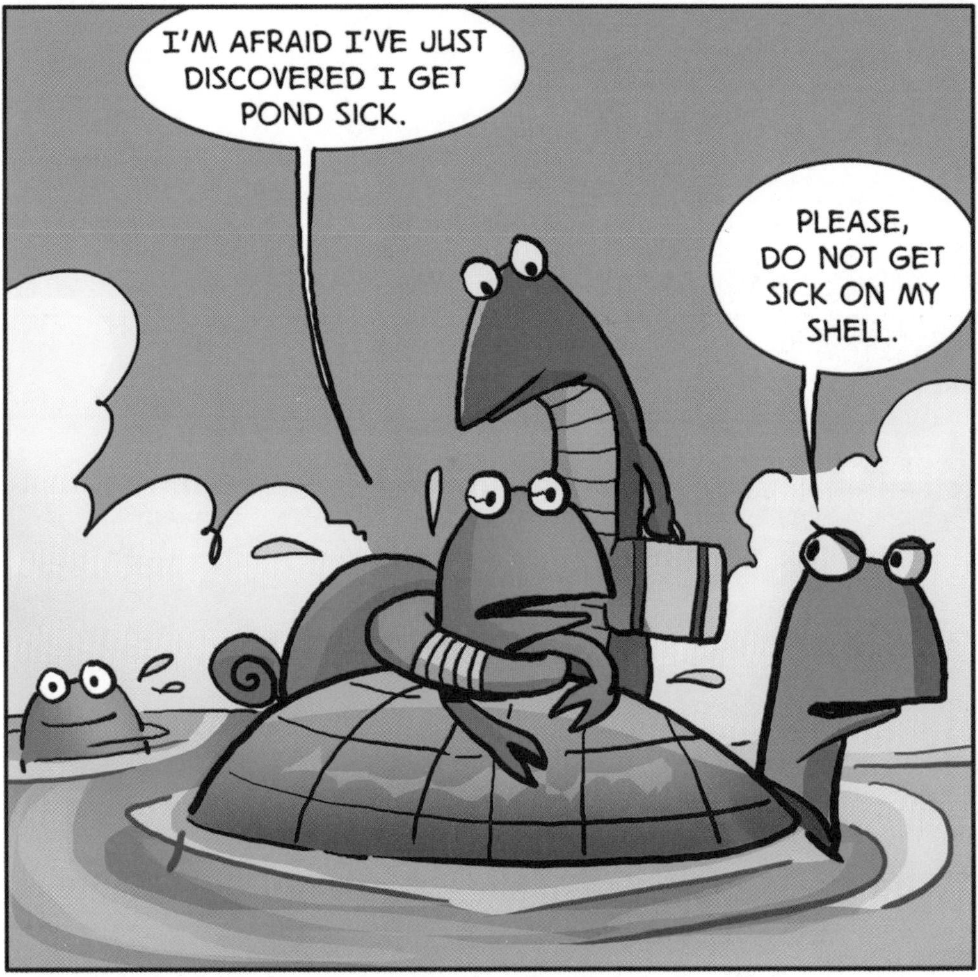
I'M AFRAID I'VE JUST DISCOVERED I GET POND SICK.
PLEASE, DO NOT GET SICK ON MY SHELL.

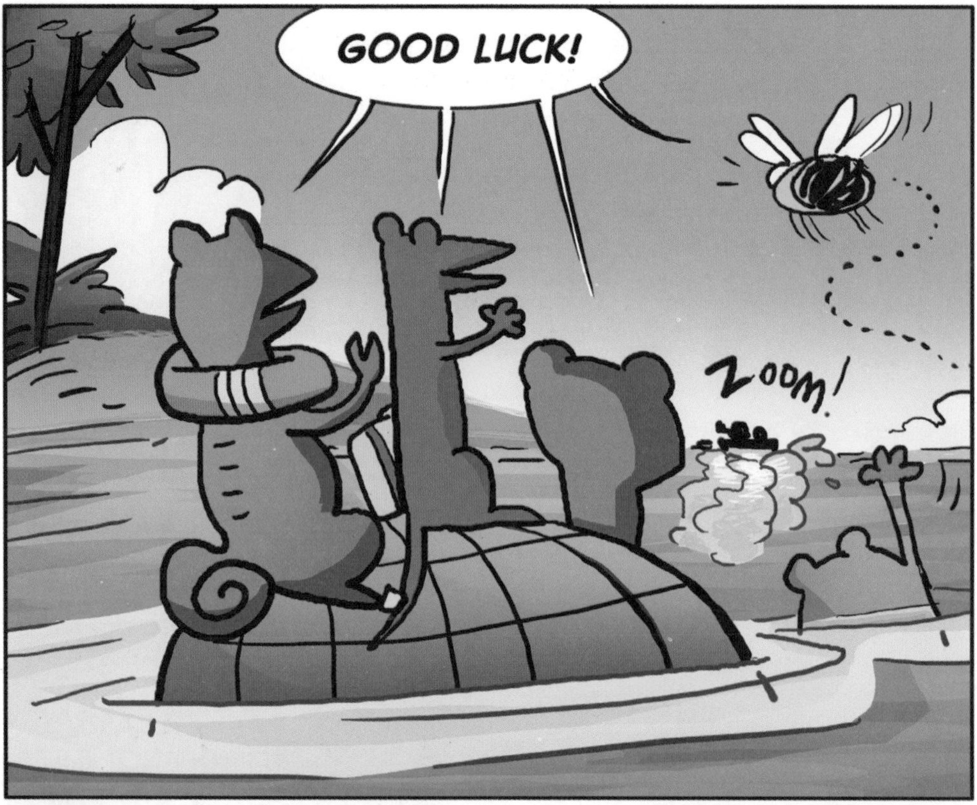
GOOD LUCK!
ZOOM!

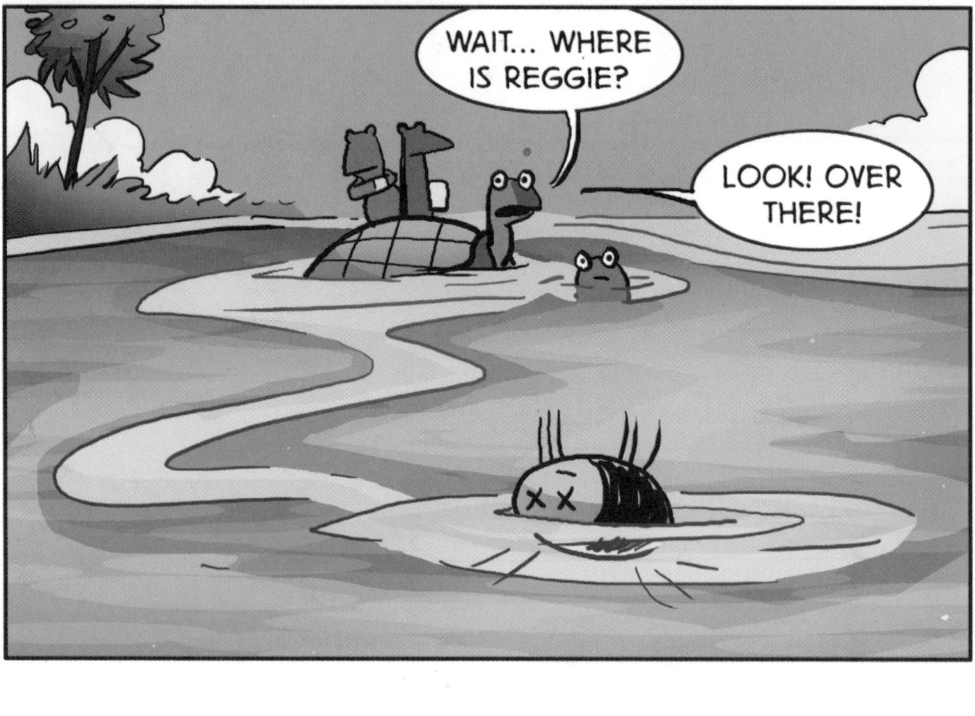
WAIT... WHERE IS REGGIE?
LOOK! OVER THERE!

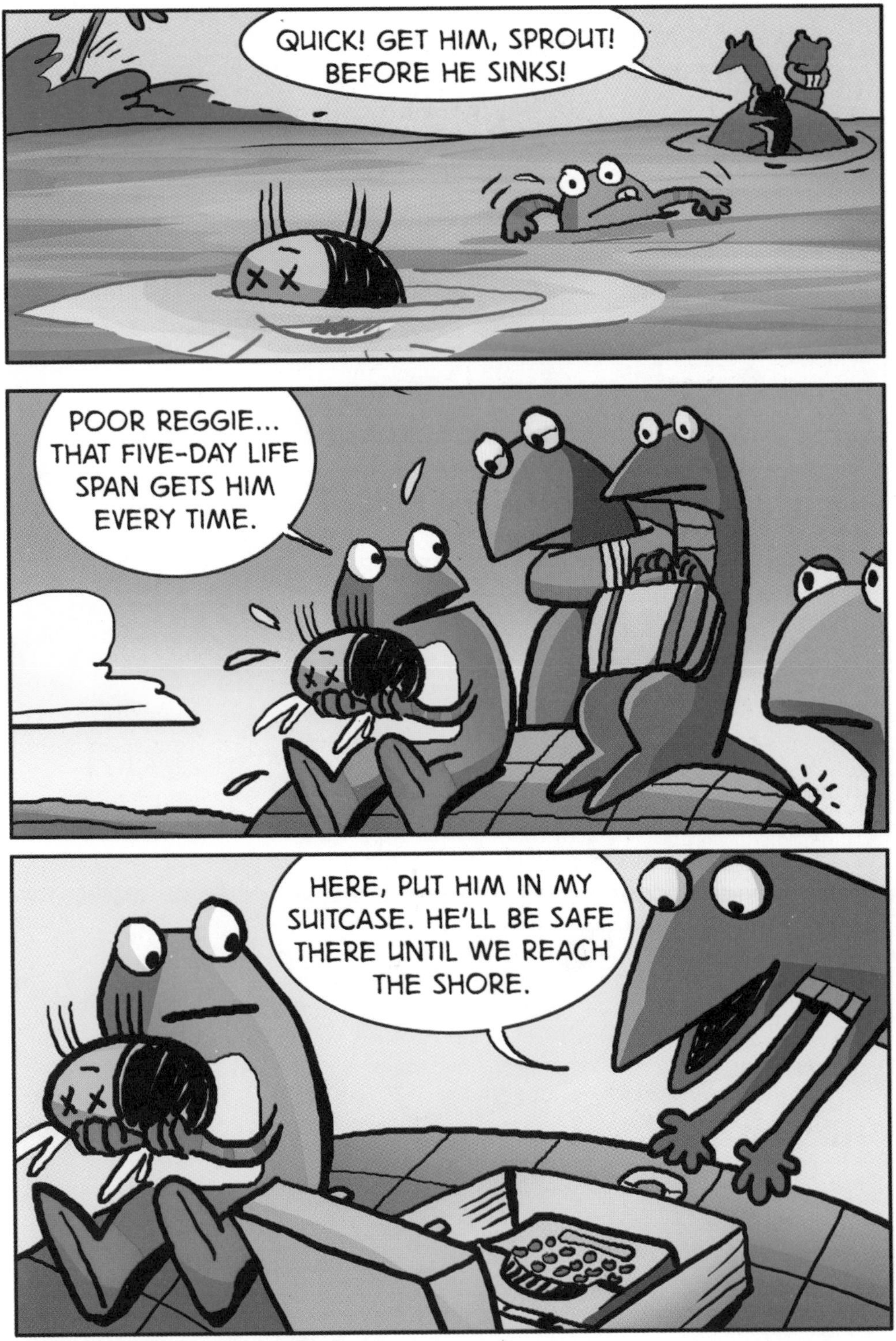
QUICK! GET HIM, SPROUT! BEFORE HE SINKS!
POOR REGGIE... THAT FIVE-DAY LIFE SPAN GETS HIM EVERY TIME.
HERE, PUT HIM IN MY SUITCASE. HE'LL BE SAFE THERE UNTIL WE REACH THE SHORE.

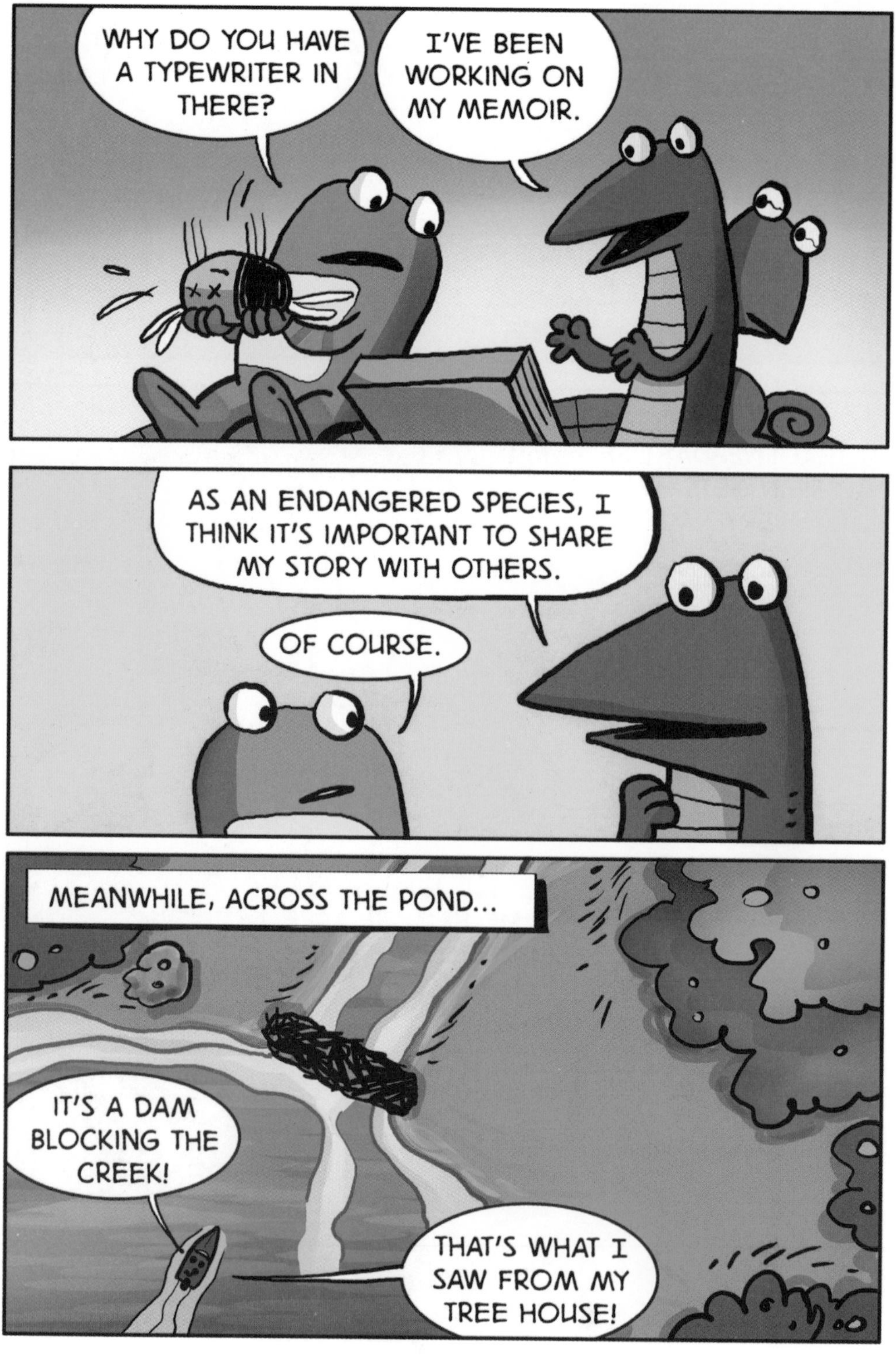
WHY DO YOU HAVE A TYPEWRITER IN THERE?
I'VE BEEN WORKING ON MY MEMOIR.
AS AN ENDANGERED SPECIES, I THINK IT'S IMPORTANT TO SHARE MY STORY WITH OTHERS.
OF COURSE.
MEANWHILE, ACROSS THE POND...
IT'S A DAM BLOCKING THE CREEK!
THAT'S WHAT I SAW FROM MY TREE HOUSE!

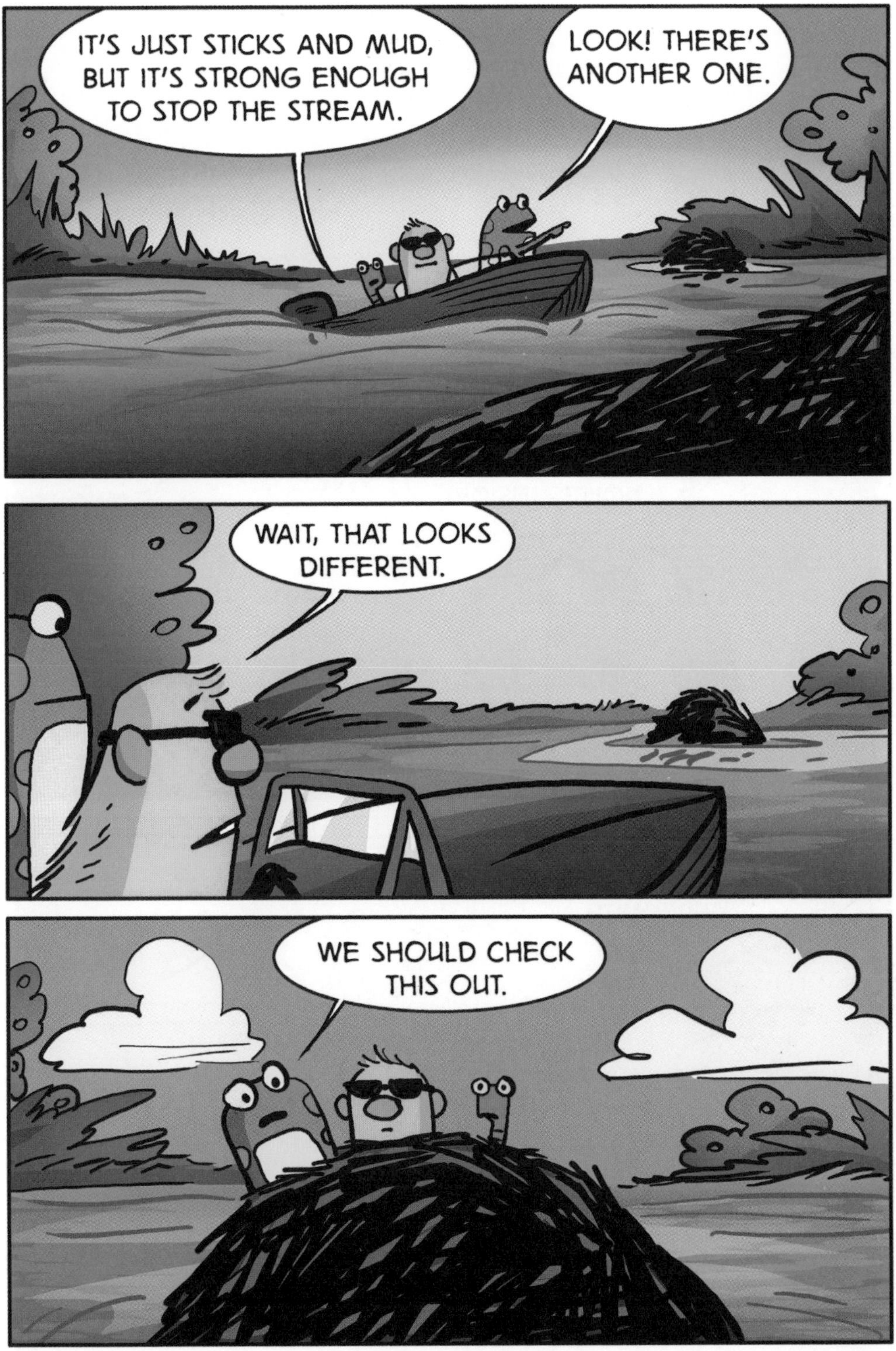
IT'S JUST STICKS AND MUD, BUT IT'S STRONG ENOUGH TO STOP THE STREAM.
LOOK! THERE'S ANOTHER ONE.
WAIT, THAT LOOKS DIFFERENT.
WE SHOULD CHECK THIS OUT.

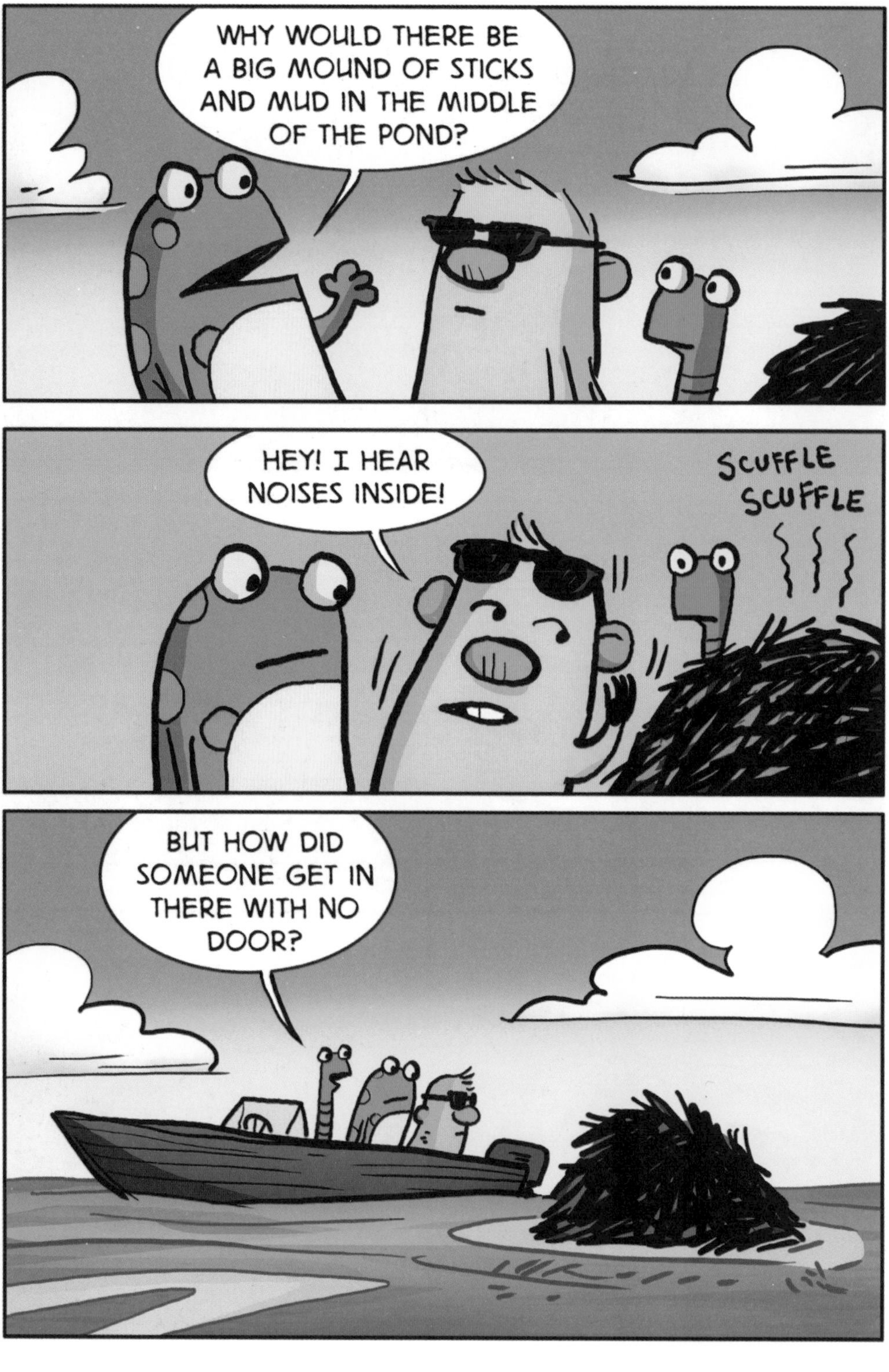
WHY WOULD THERE BE A BIG MOUND OF STICKS AND MUD IN THE MIDDLE OF THE POND?
HEY! I HEAR NOISES INSIDE!
SCUFFLE SCUFFLE
BUT HOW DID SOMEONE GET IN THERE WITH NO DOOR?

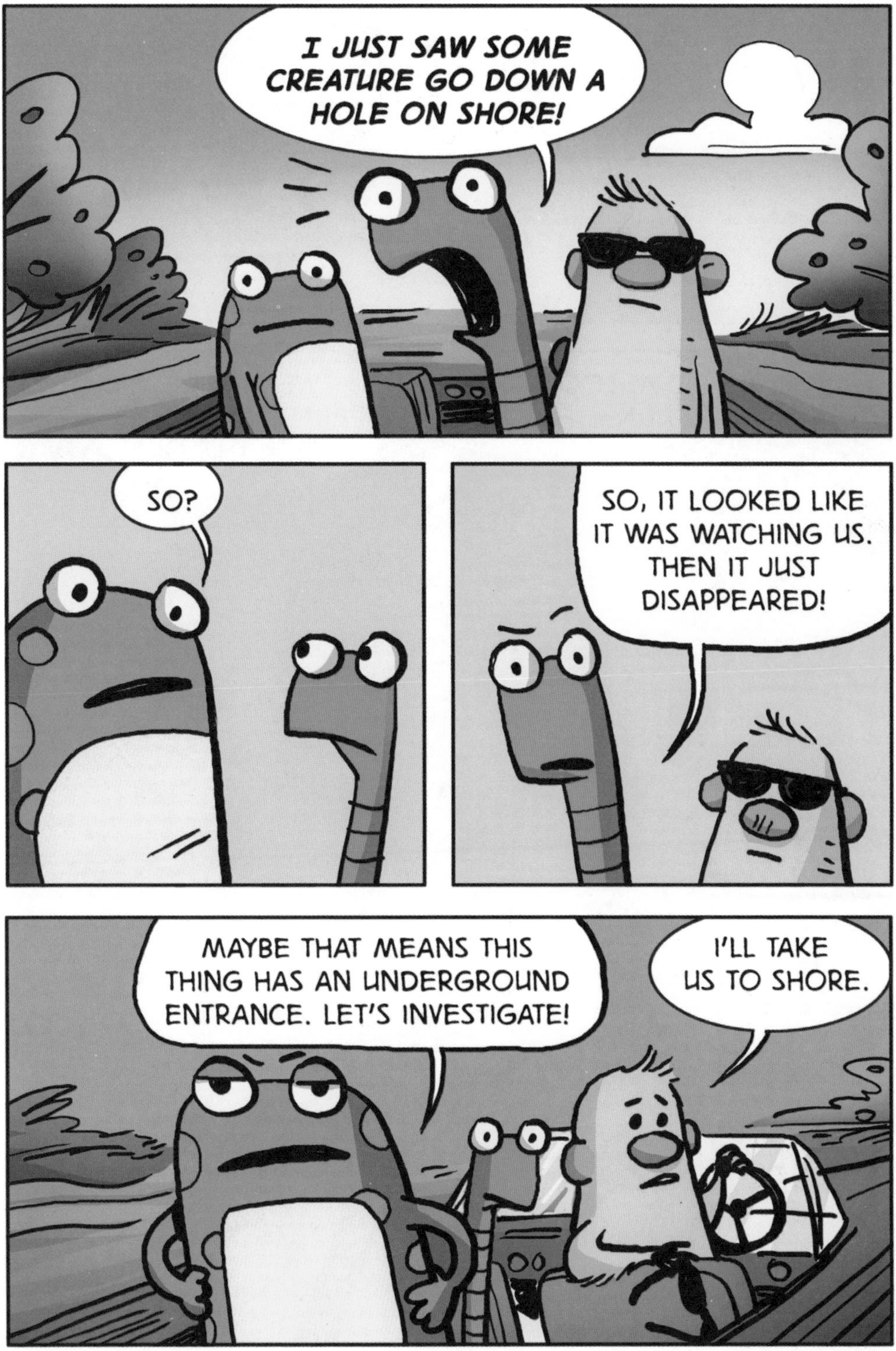
I JUST SAW SOME CREATURE GO DOWN A HOLE ON SHORE!
SO?
SO, IT LOOKED LIKE IT WAS WATCHING US. THEN IT JUST DISAPPEARED!
MAYBE THAT MEANS THIS THING HAS AN UNDERGROUND ENTRANCE. LET'S INVESTIGATE!
I'LL TAKE US TO SHORE.

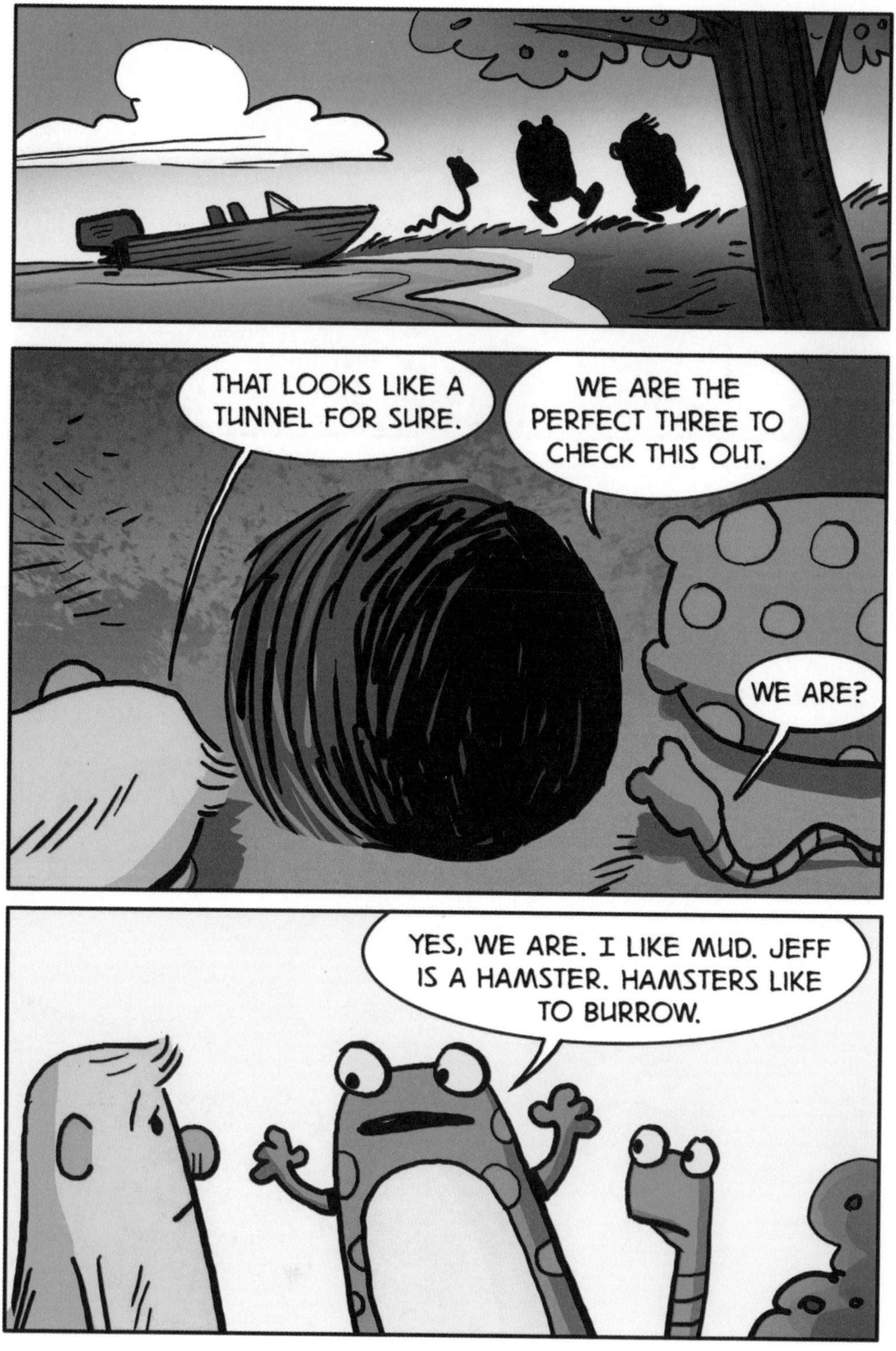
THAT LOOKS LIKE A TUNNEL FOR SURE.
WE ARE THE PERFECT THREE TO CHECK THIS OUT.
WE ARE?
YES, WE ARE. I LIKE MUD. JEFF IS A HAMSTER. HAMSTERS LIKE TO BURROW.

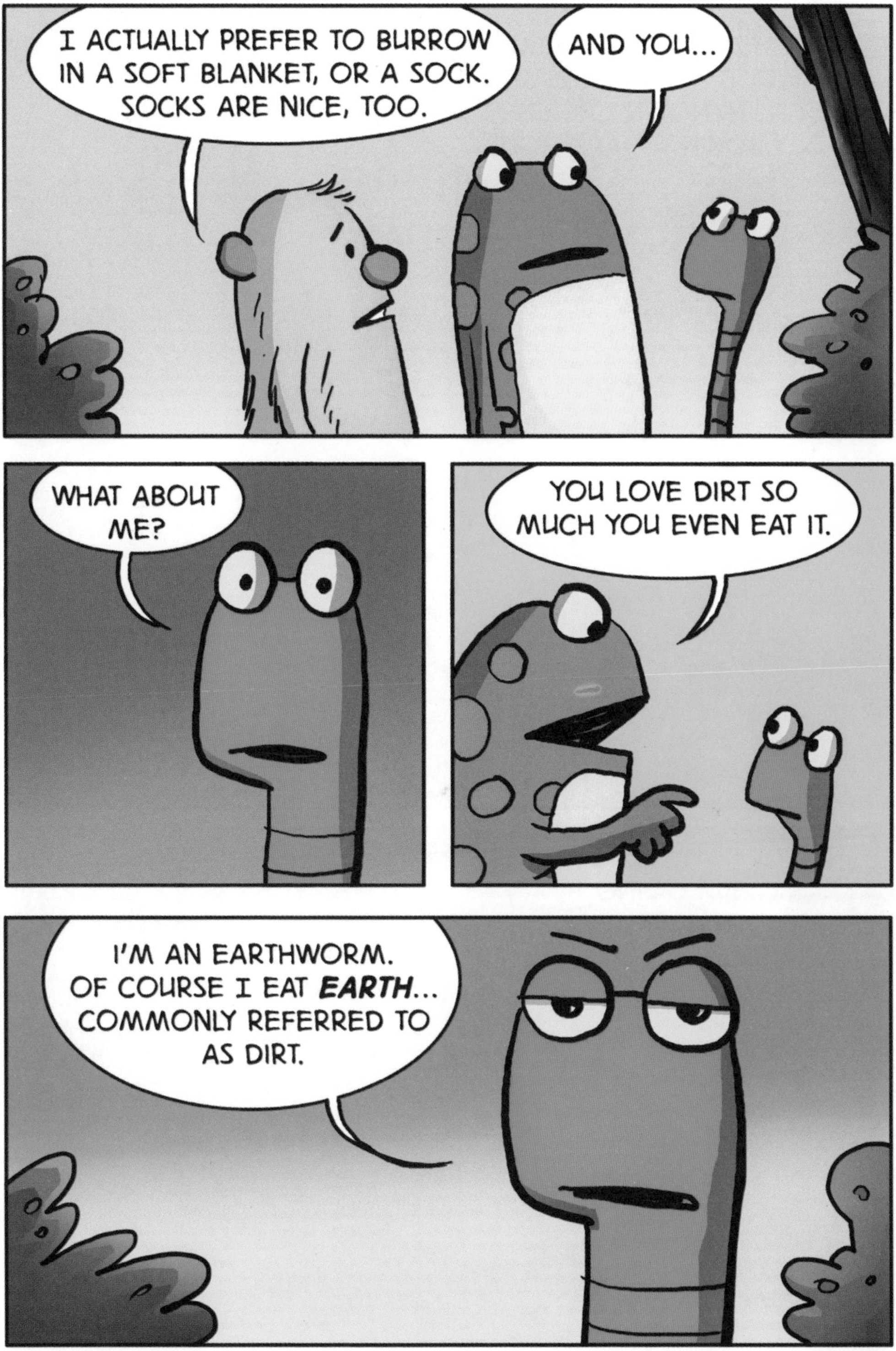
I ACTUALLY PREFER TO BURROW IN A SOFT BLANKET, OR A SOCK. SOCKS ARE NICE, TOO.
AND YOU...
WHAT ABOUT ME?
YOU LOVE DIRT SO MUCH YOU EVEN EAT IT.
I'M AN EARTHWORM. OF COURSE I EAT ***EARTH***... COMMONLY REFERRED TO AS DIRT.

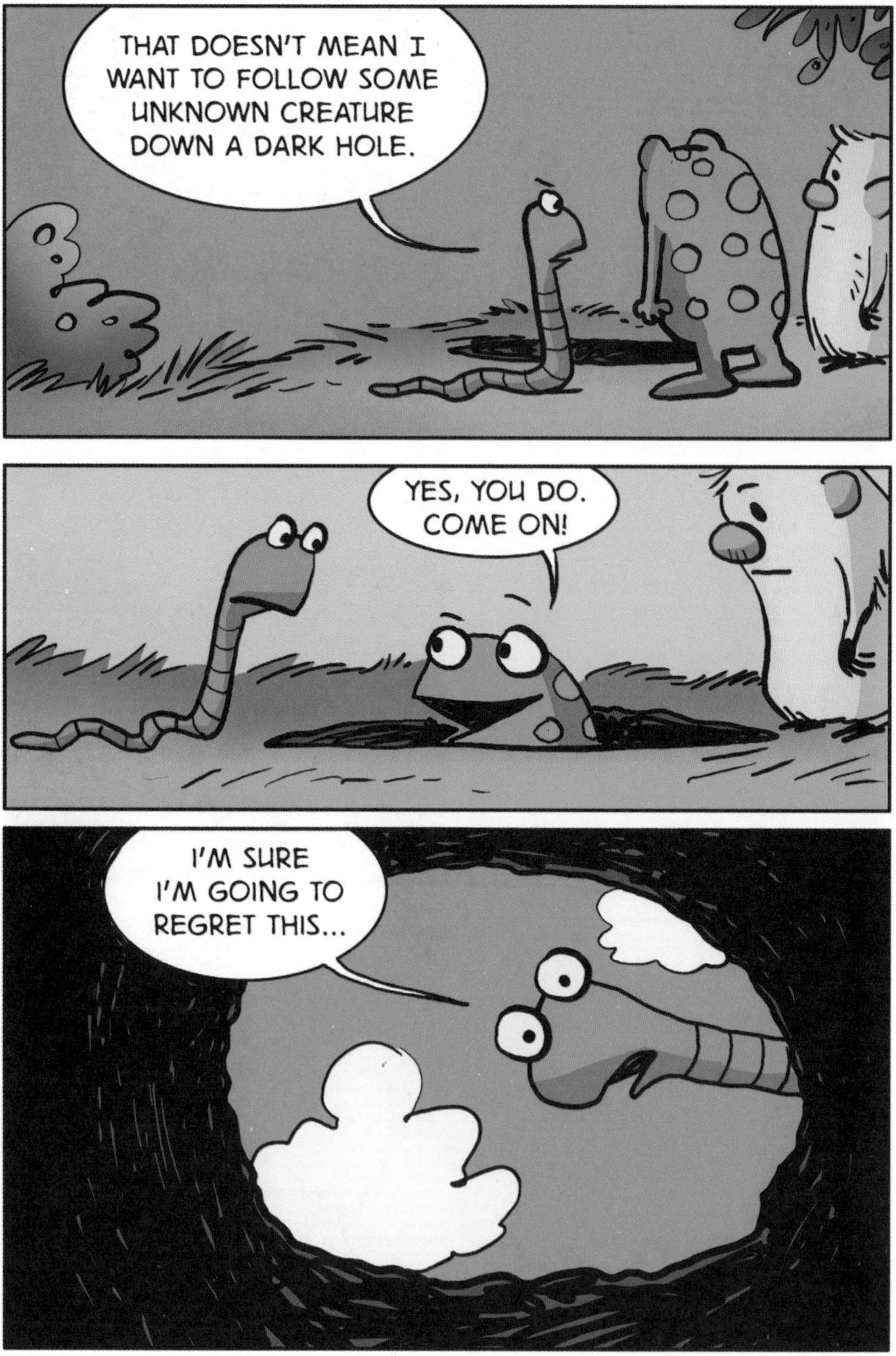
THAT DOESN'T MEAN I WANT TO FOLLOW SOME UNKNOWN CREATURE DOWN A DARK HOLE.
YES, YOU DO. COME ON!
I'M SURE I'M GOING TO REGRET THIS...

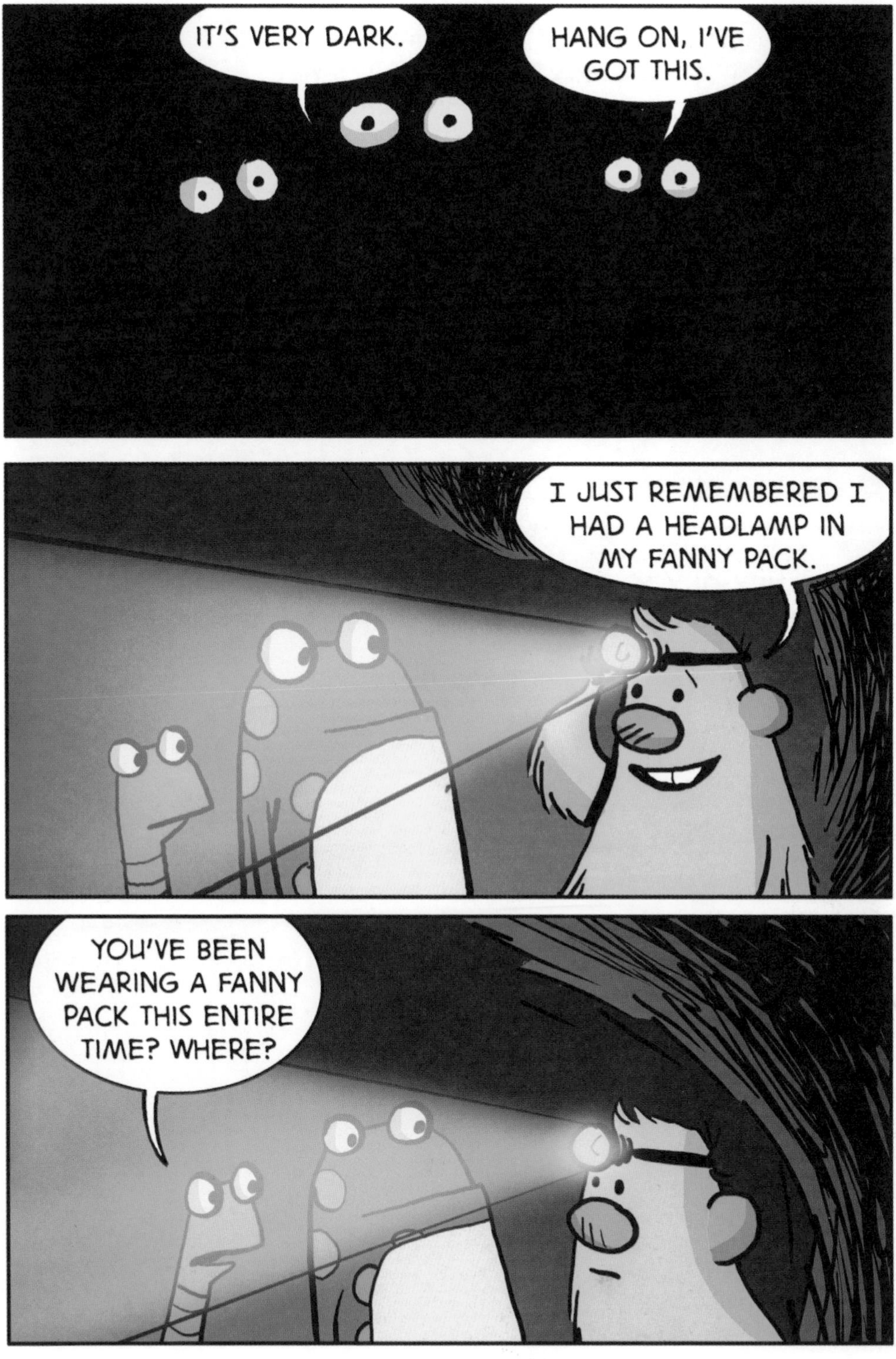
IT'S VERY DARK.
HANG ON, I'VE GOT THIS.
I JUST REMEMBERED I HAD A HEADLAMP IN MY FANNY PACK.
YOU'VE BEEN WEARING A FANNY PACK THIS ENTIRE TIME? WHERE?

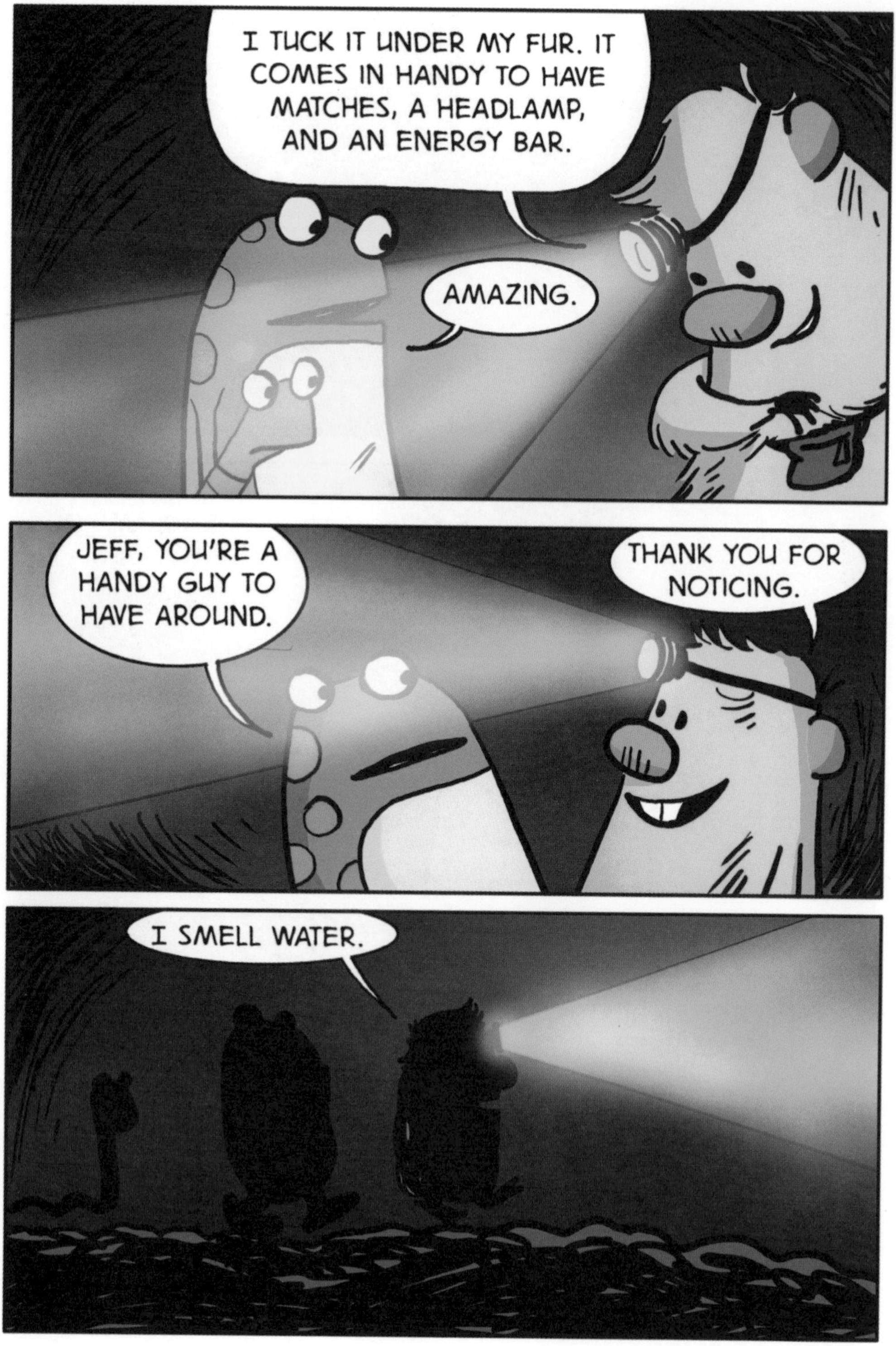
I TUCK IT UNDER MY FUR. IT COMES IN HANDY TO HAVE MATCHES, A HEADLAMP, AND AN ENERGY BAR.
AMAZING.
JEFF, YOU'RE A HANDY GUY TO HAVE AROUND.
THANK YOU FOR NOTICING.
I SMELL WATER.

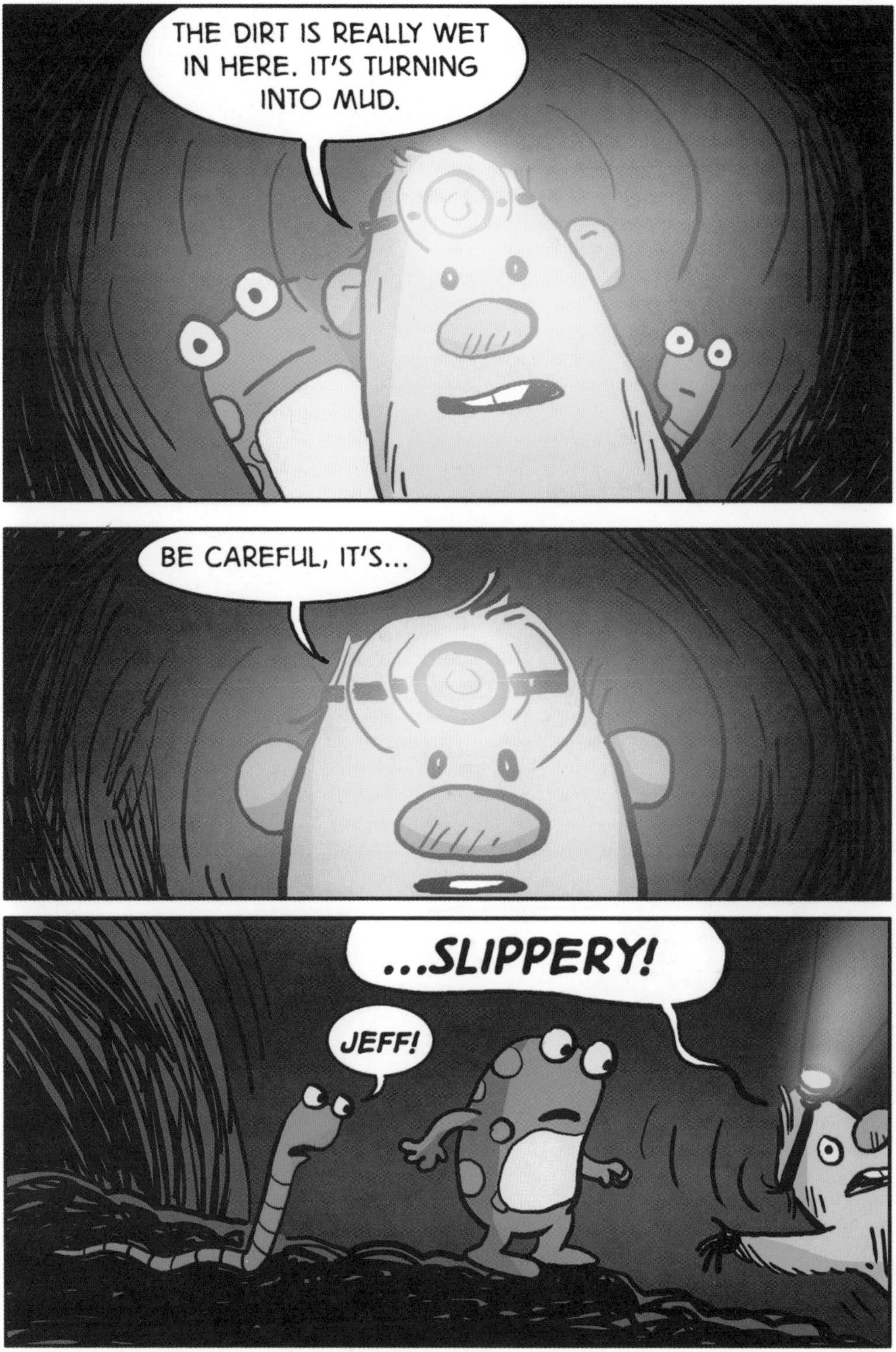
THE DIRT IS REALLY WET IN HERE. IT'S TURNING INTO MUD.
BE CAREFUL, IT'S...
...SLIPPERY!
JEFF!

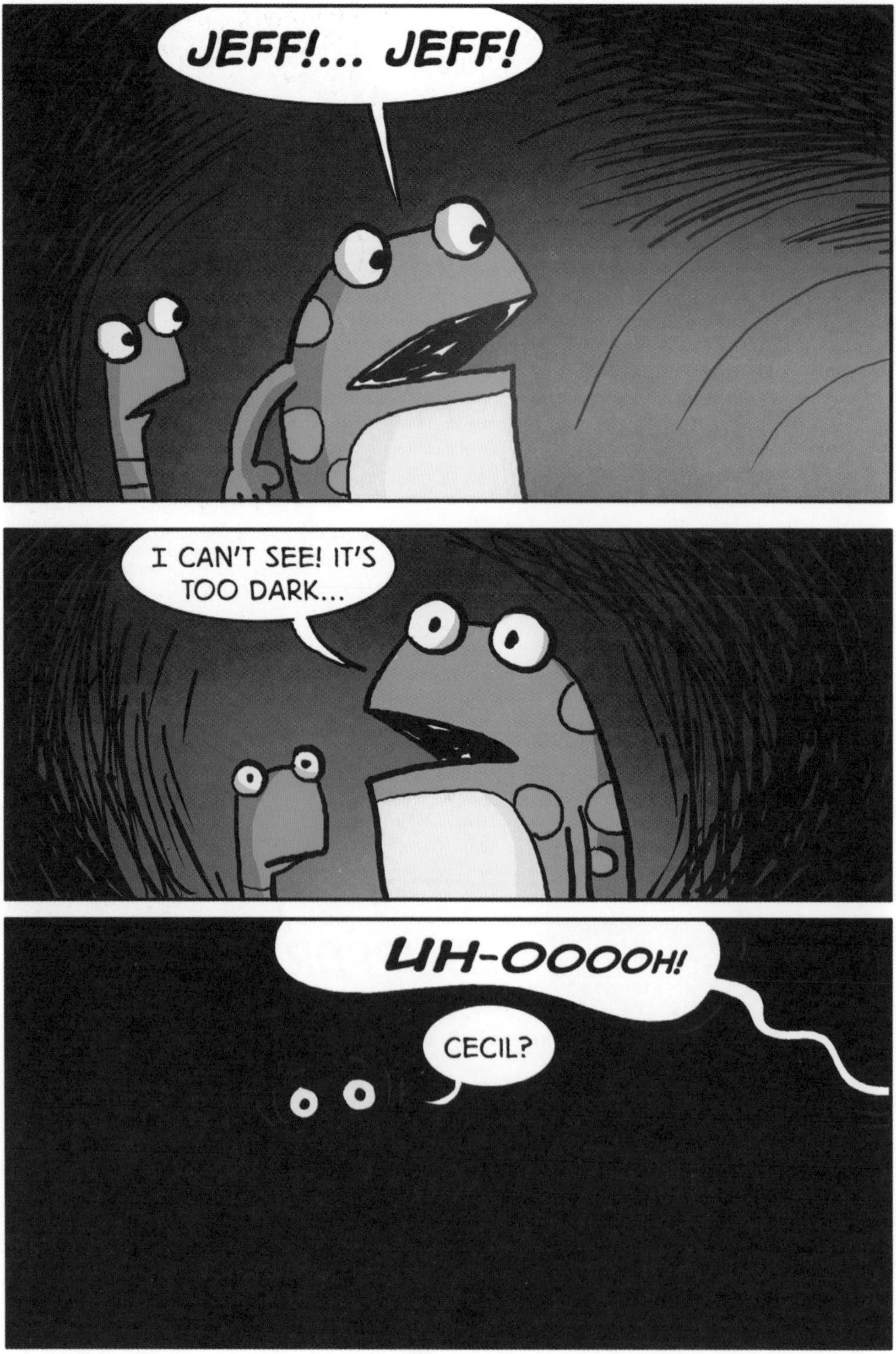
JEFF!... JEFF!
I CAN'T SEE! IT'S TOO DARK...
UH-OOOOH!
CECIL?

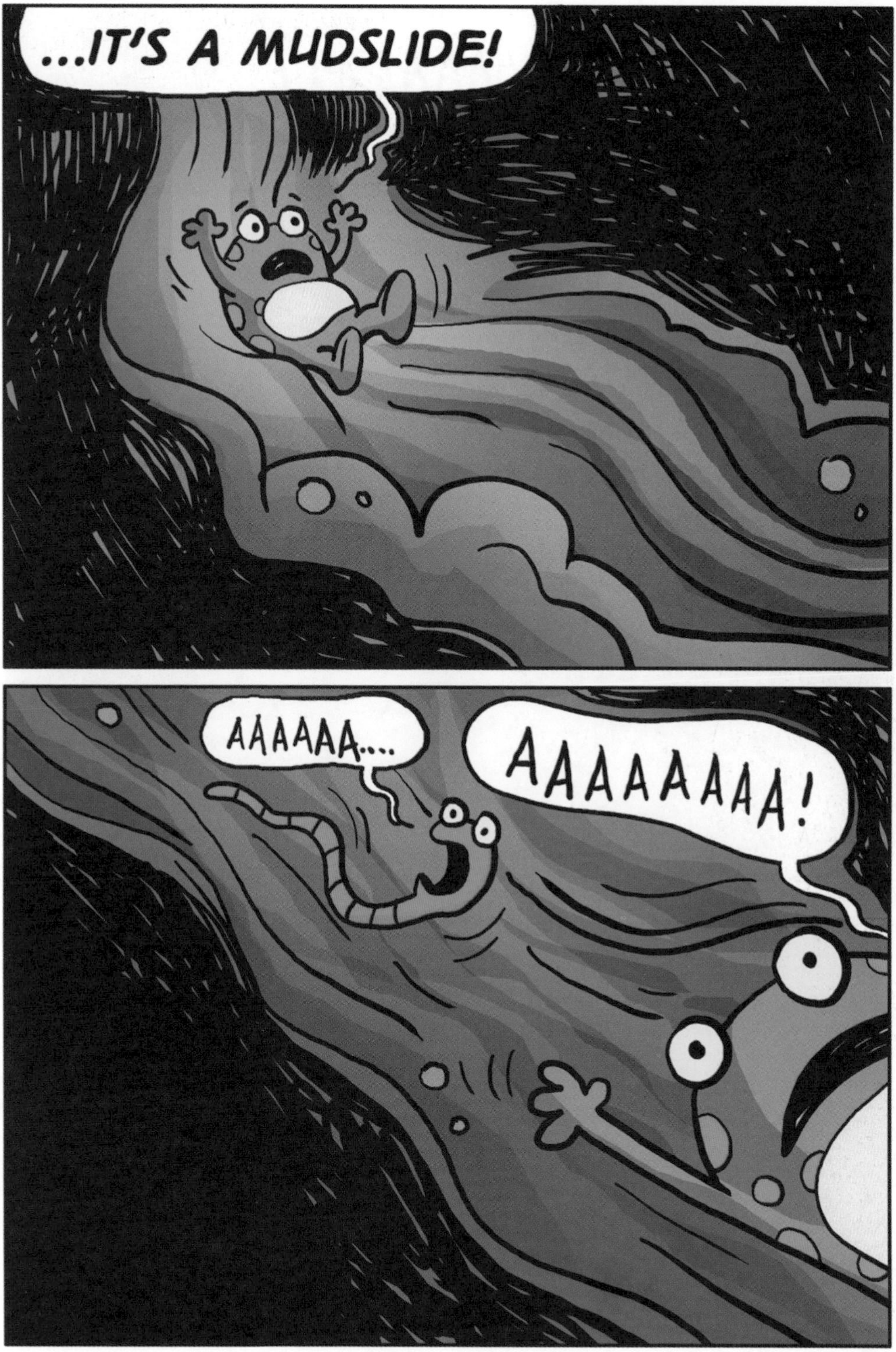
...IT'S A MUDSLIDE!
AAAAAA....
AAAAAAAAA!

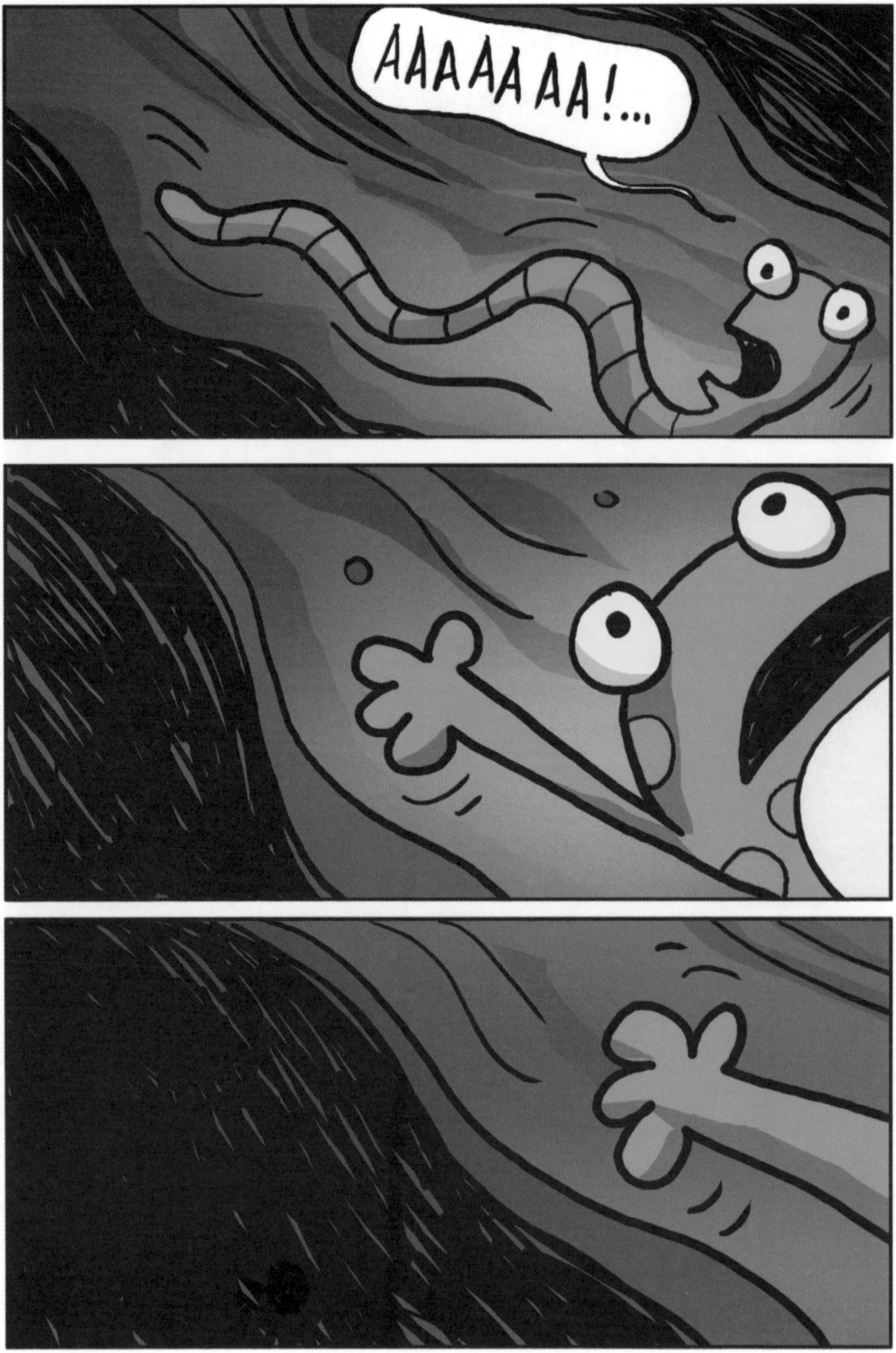
AAAAAAA!...

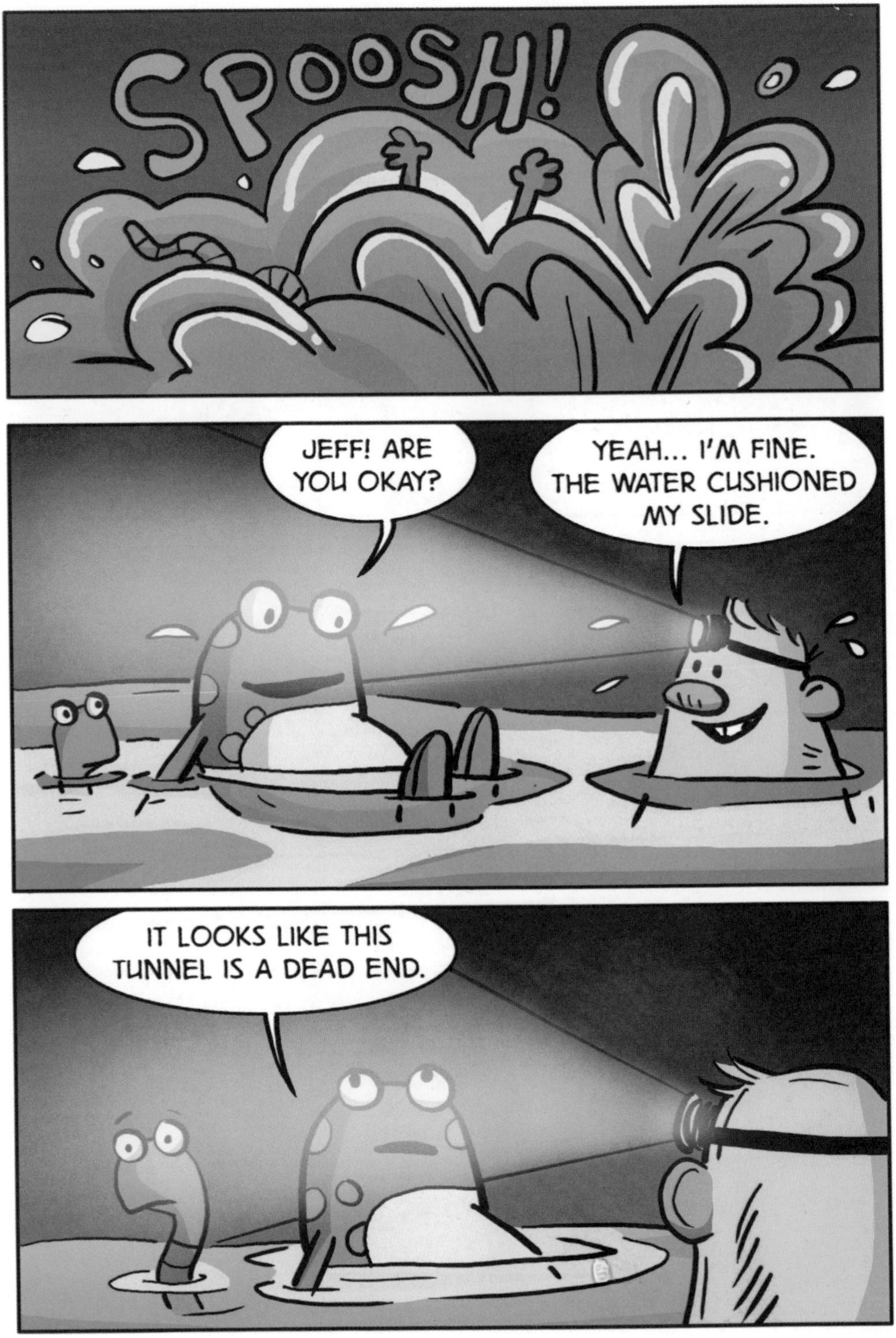
SPOOSH!
JEFF! ARE YOU OKAY?
YEAH... I'M FINE. THE WATER CUSHIONED MY SLIDE.
IT LOOKS LIKE THIS TUNNEL IS A DEAD END.

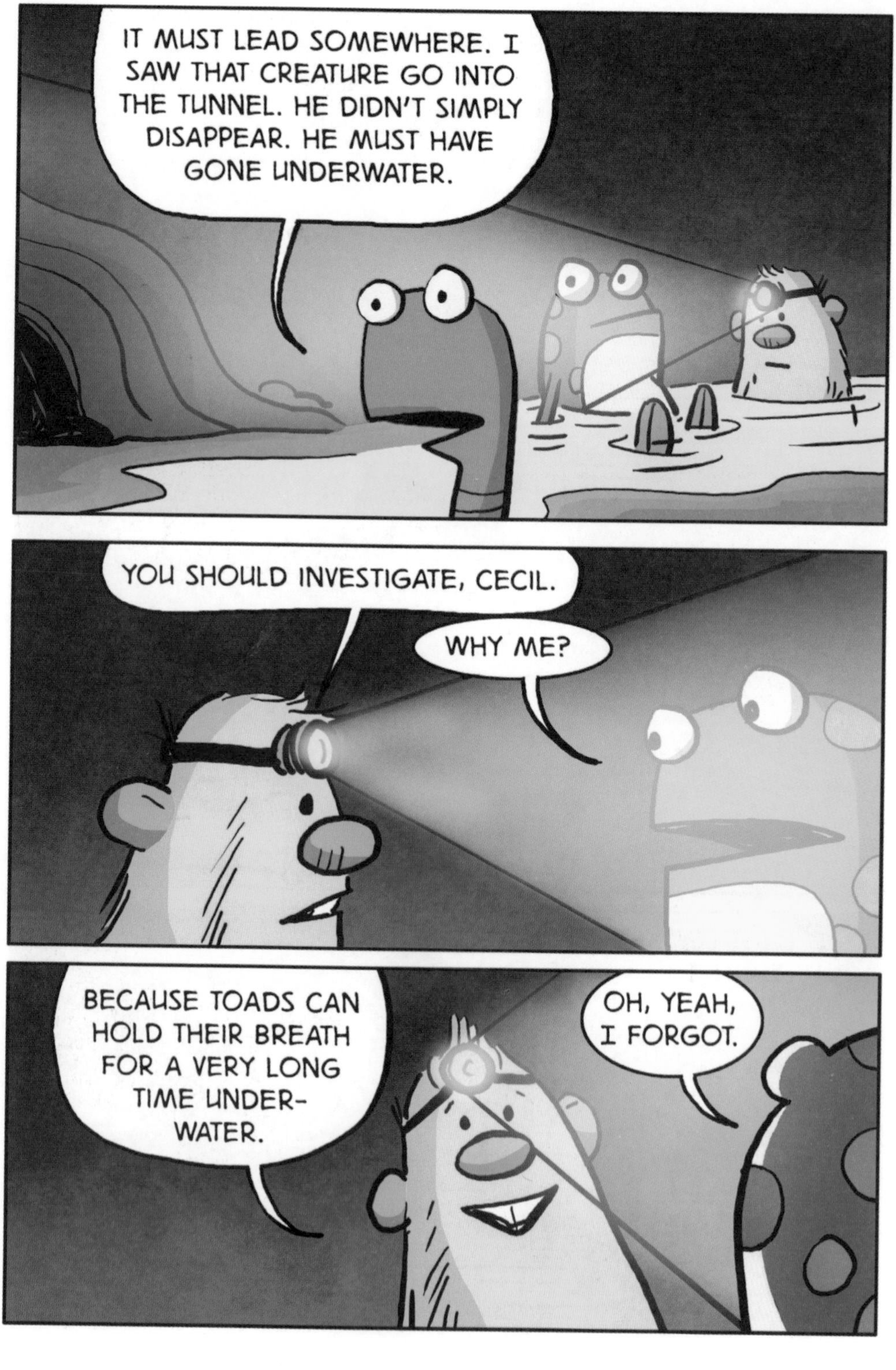
IT MUST LEAD SOMEWHERE. I SAW THAT CREATURE GO INTO THE TUNNEL. HE DIDN'T SIMPLY DISAPPEAR. HE MUST HAVE GONE UNDERWATER.
YOU SHOULD INVESTIGATE, CECIL.
WHY ME?
BECAUSE TOADS CAN HOLD THEIR BREATH FOR A VERY LONG TIME UNDER-WATER.
OH, YEAH, I FORGOT.

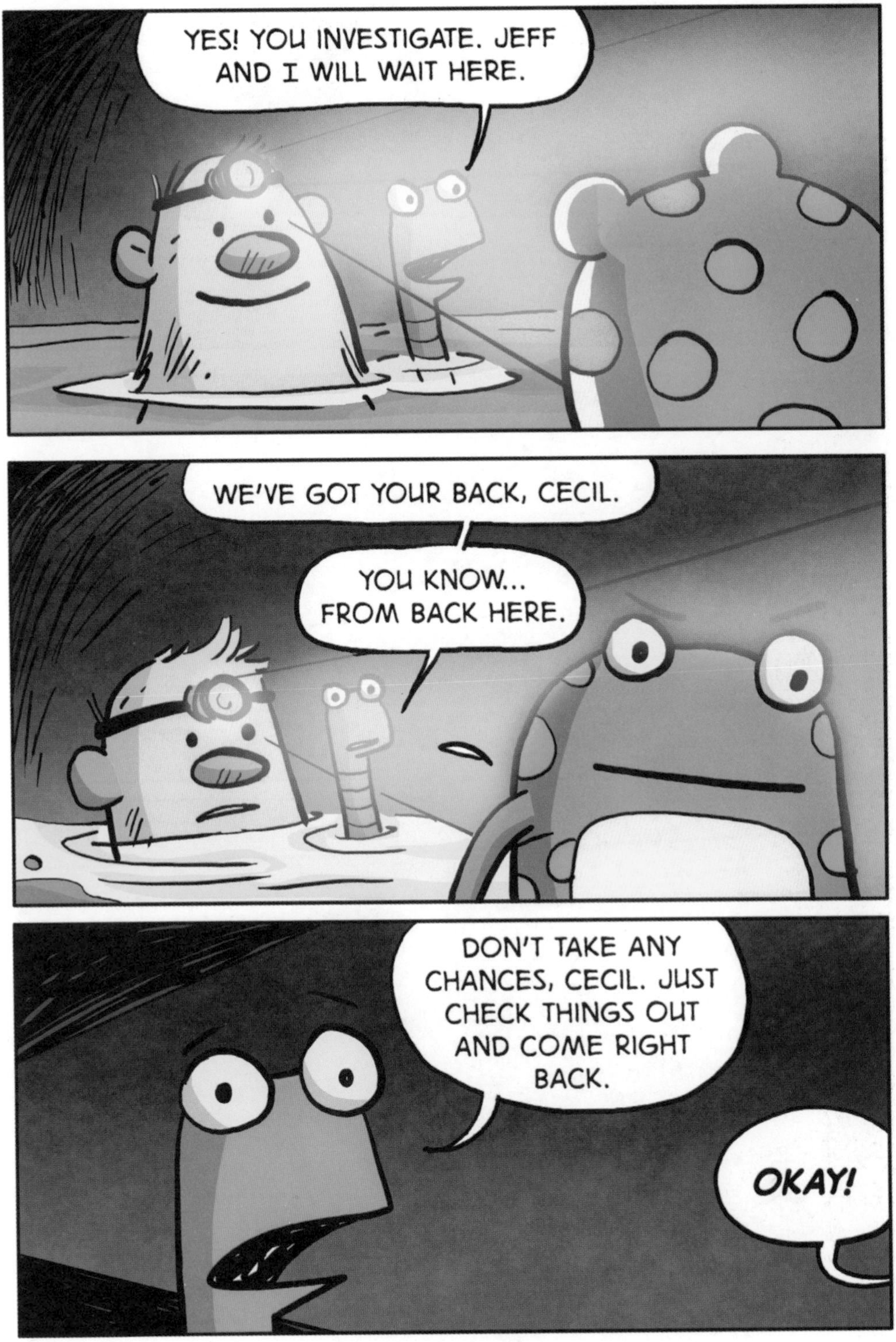
YES! YOU INVESTIGATE. JEFF AND I WILL WAIT HERE.
WE'VE GOT YOUR BACK, CECIL.
YOU KNOW... FROM BACK HERE.
DON'T TAKE ANY CHANCES, CECIL. JUST CHECK THINGS OUT AND COME RIGHT BACK.
OKAY!

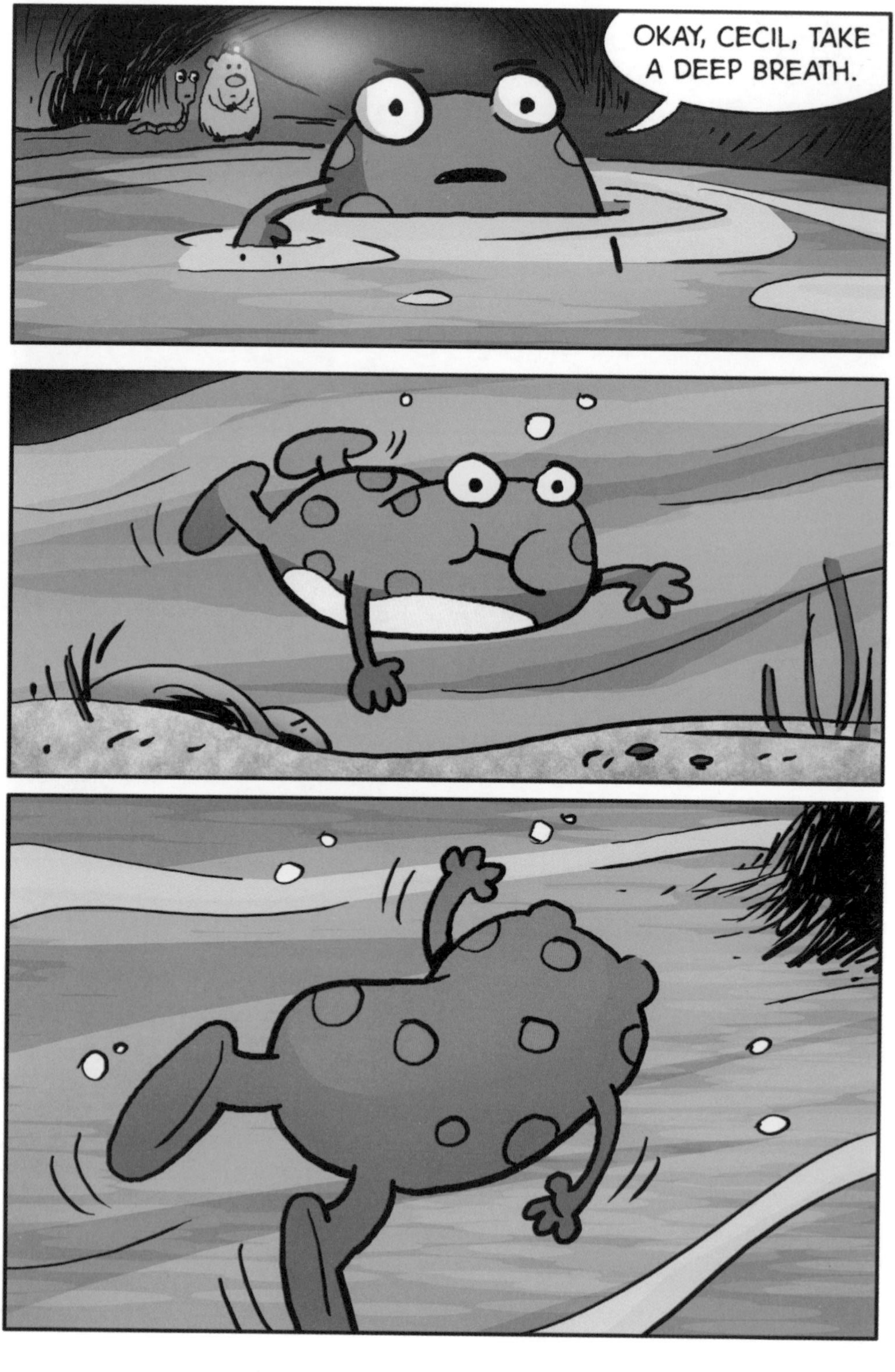
OKAY, CECIL, TAKE A DEEP BREATH.

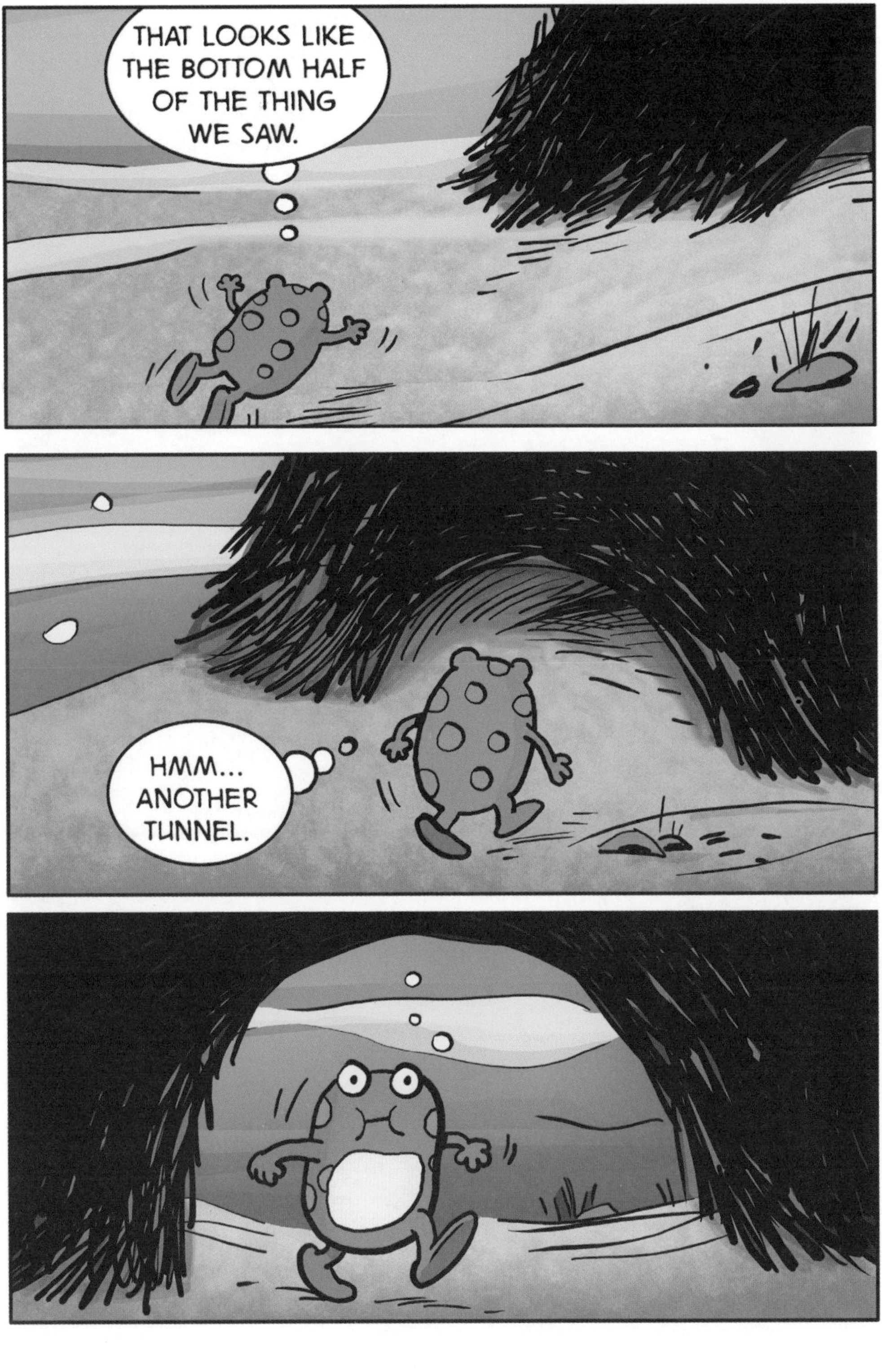
THAT LOOKS LIKE THE BOTTOM HALF OF THE THING WE SAW.
HMM... ANOTHER TUNNEL.

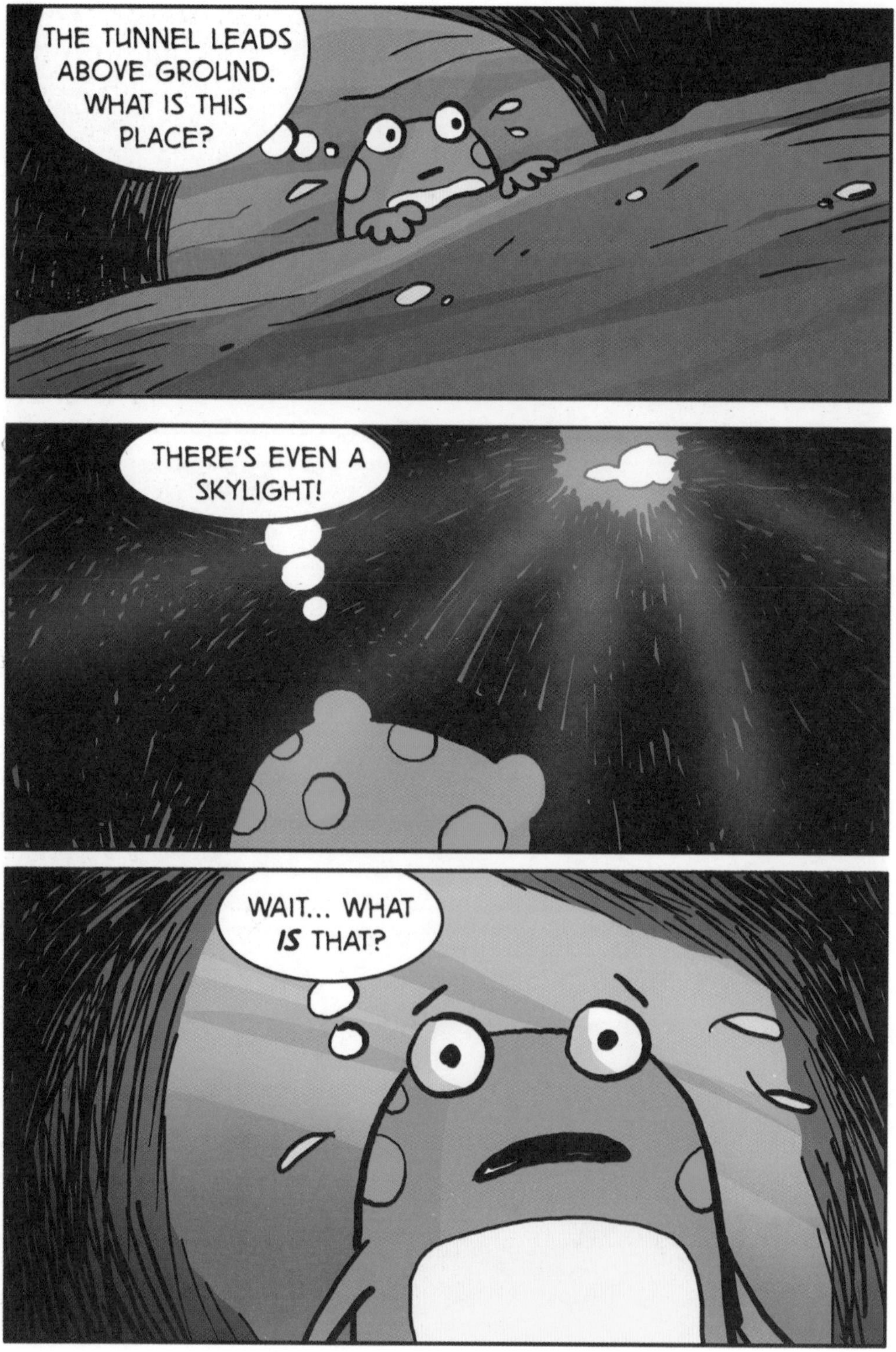
THE TUNNEL LEADS ABOVE GROUND. WHAT IS THIS PLACE?
THERE'S EVEN A SKYLIGHT!
WAIT... WHAT *IS* THAT?

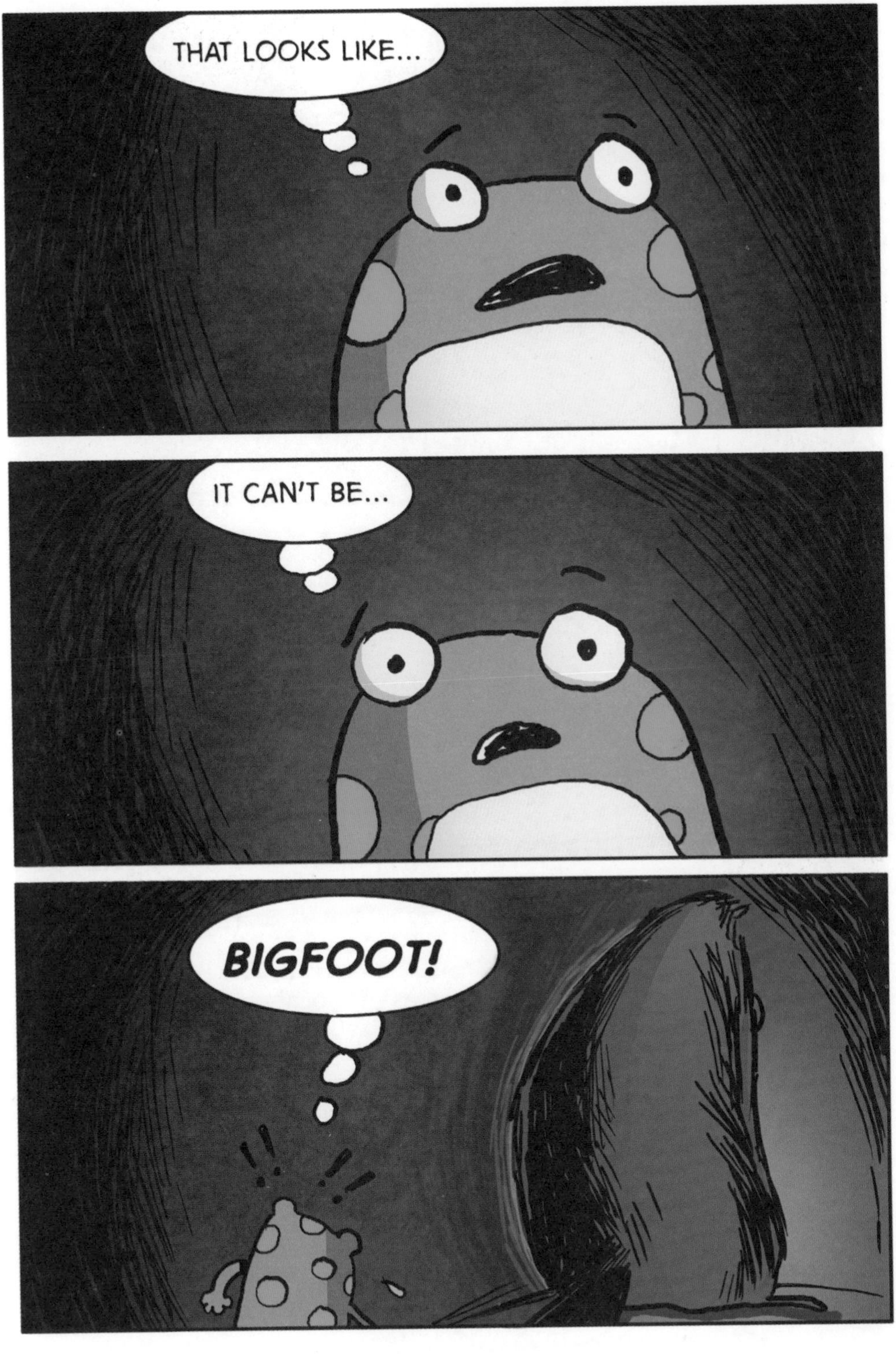
THAT LOOKS LIKE...
IT CAN'T BE...
BIGFOOT!

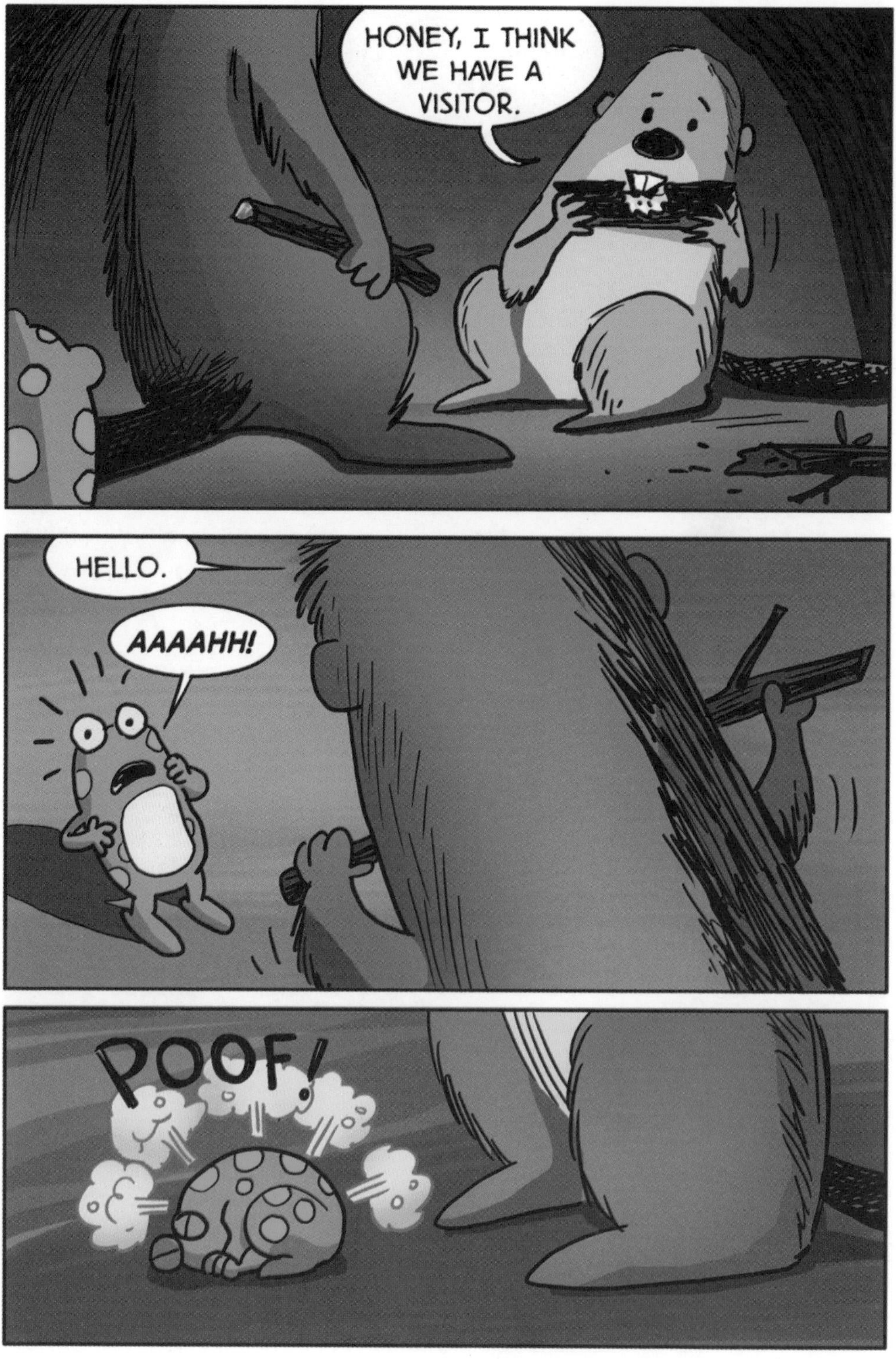
HONEY, I THINK WE HAVE A VISITOR.
HELLO.
AAAAHH!
POOF!

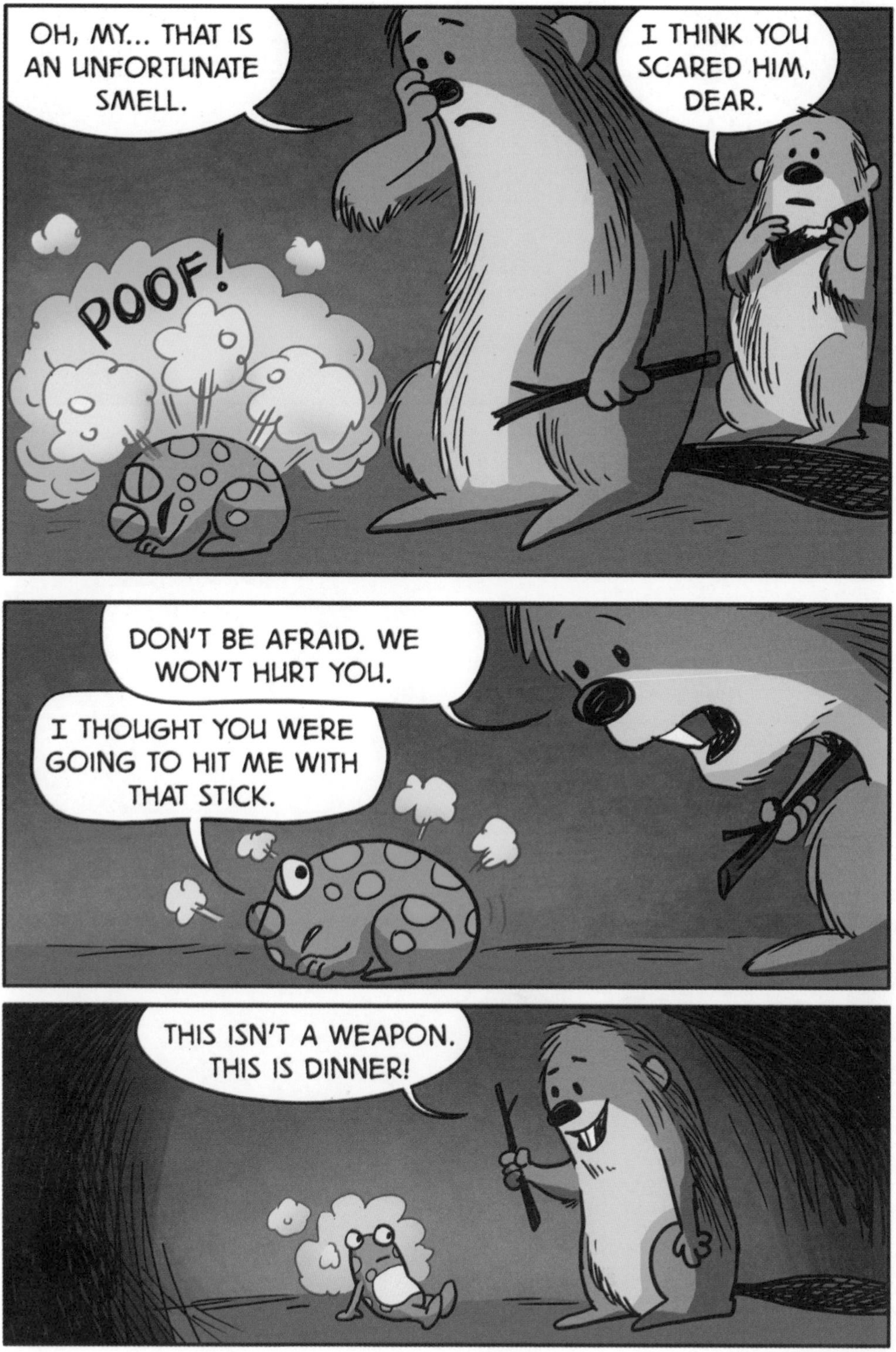
OH, MY... THAT IS AN UNFORTUNATE SMELL.
I THINK YOU SCARED HIM, DEAR.
POOF!
DON'T BE AFRAID. WE WON'T HURT YOU.
I THOUGHT YOU WERE GOING TO HIT ME WITH THAT STICK.
THIS ISN'T A WEAPON. THIS IS DINNER!

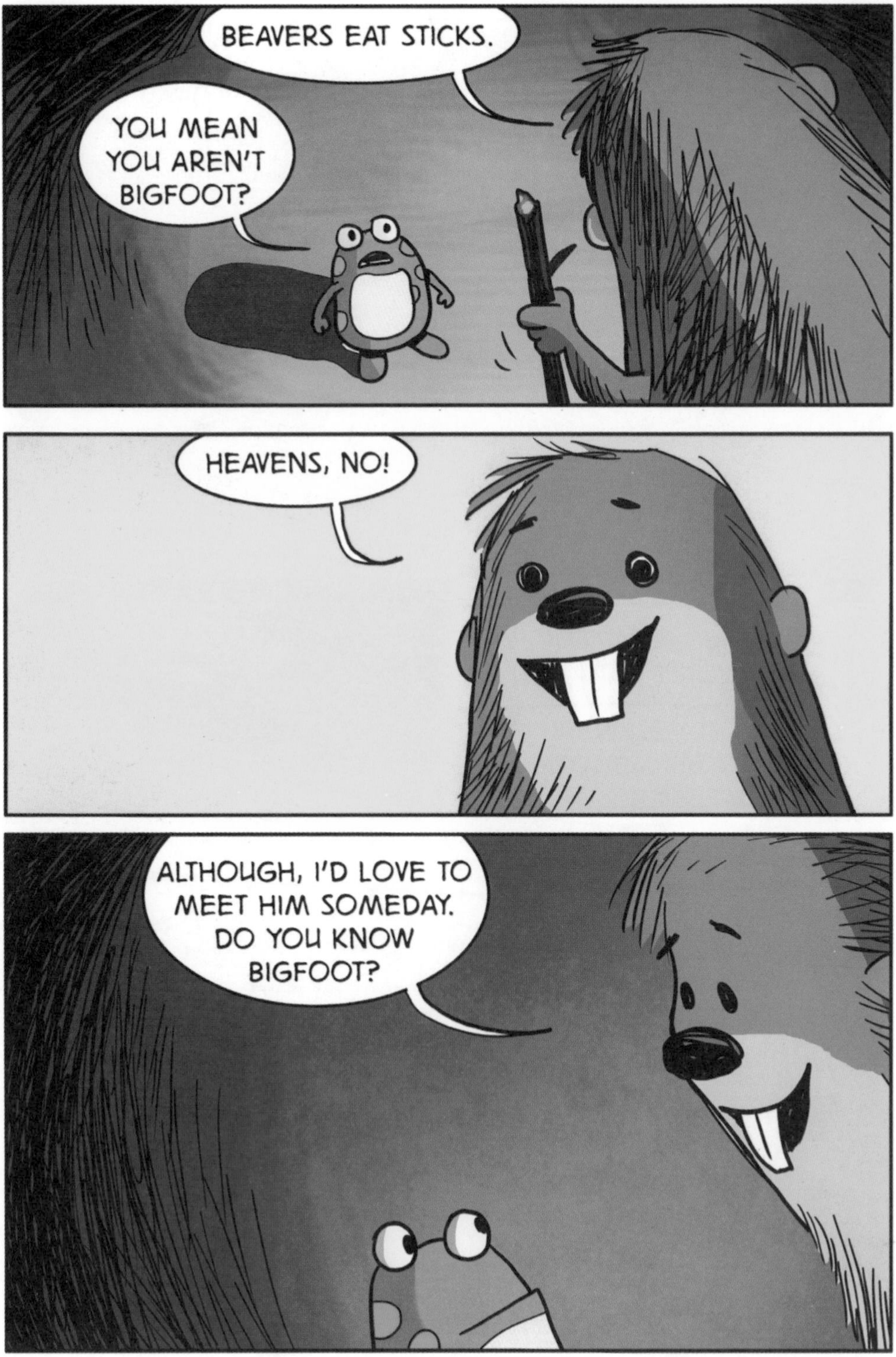
BEAVERS EAT STICKS.
YOU MEAN YOU AREN'T BIGFOOT?
HEAVENS, NO!
ALTHOUGH, I'D LOVE TO MEET HIM SOMEDAY. DO YOU KNOW BIGFOOT?

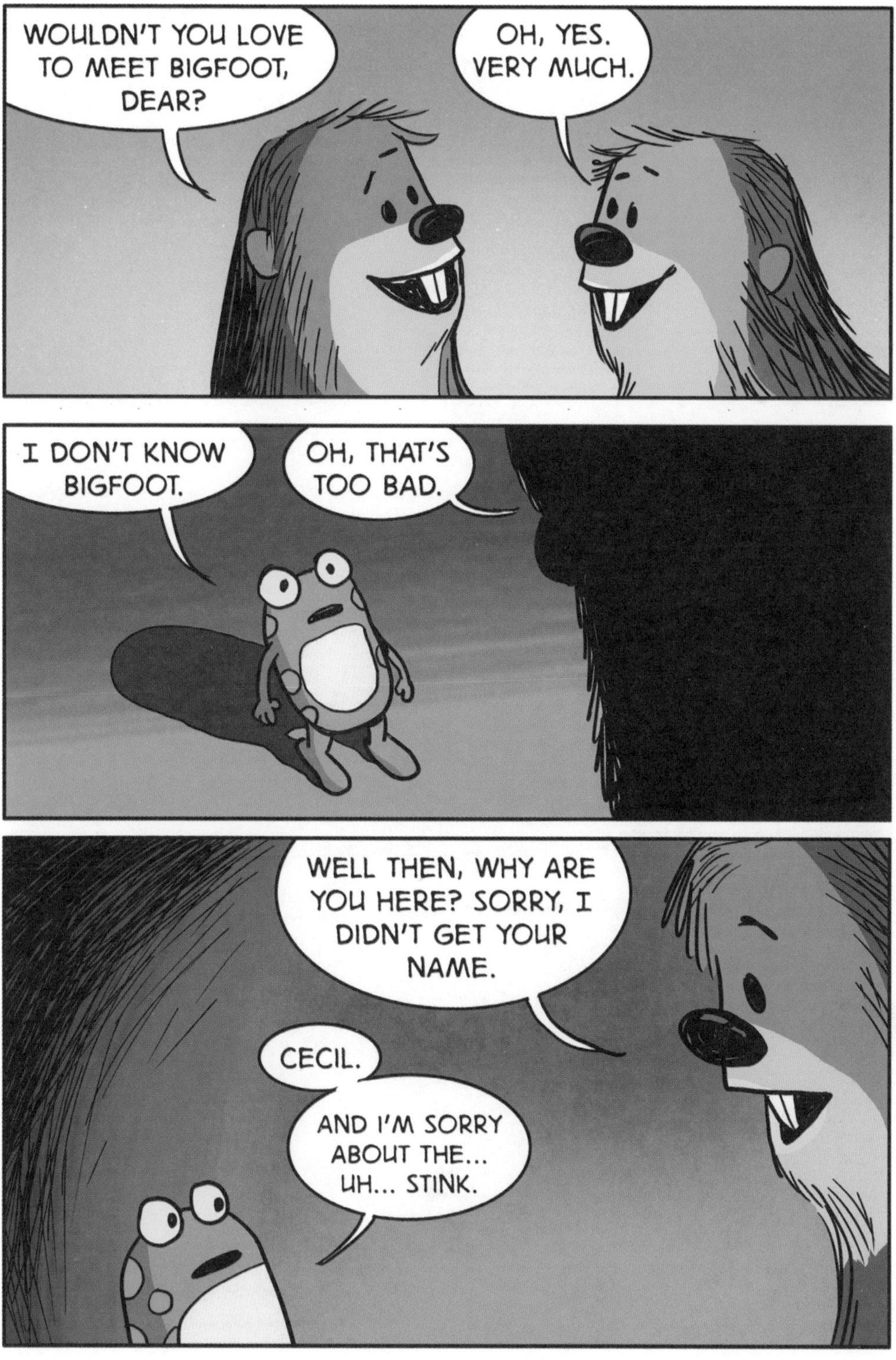
WOULDN'T YOU LOVE TO MEET BIGFOOT, DEAR?
OH, YES. VERY MUCH.
I DON'T KNOW BIGFOOT.
OH, THAT'S TOO BAD.
WELL THEN, WHY ARE YOU HERE? SORRY, I DIDN'T GET YOUR NAME.
CECIL.
AND I'M SORRY ABOUT THE... UH... STINK.

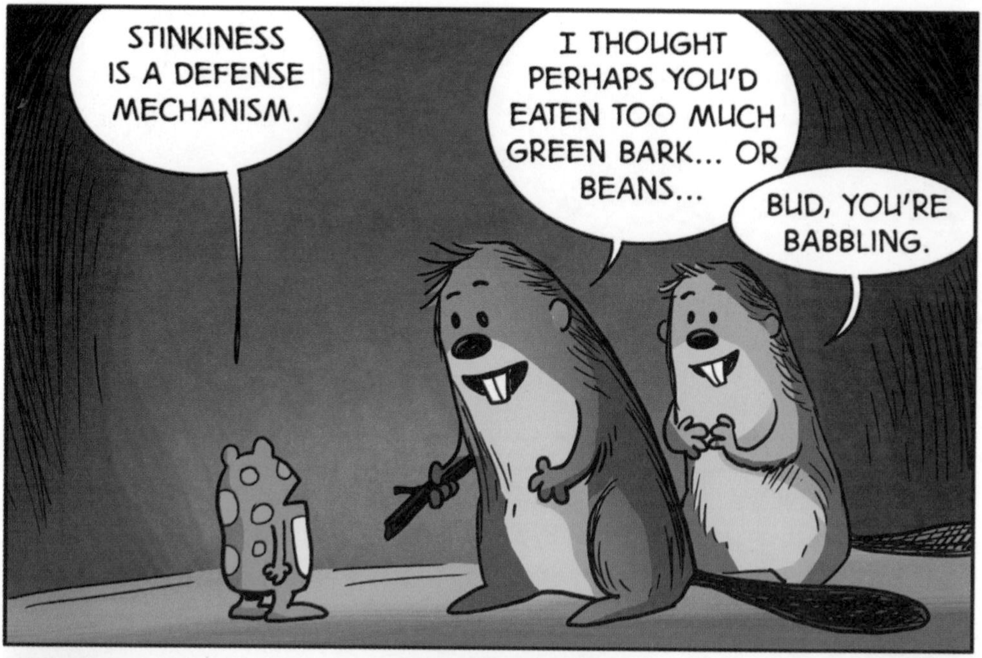
STINKINESS IS A DEFENSE MECHANISM.
I THOUGHT PERHAPS YOU'D EATEN TOO MUCH GREEN BARK... OR BEANS...
BUD, YOU'RE BABBLING.

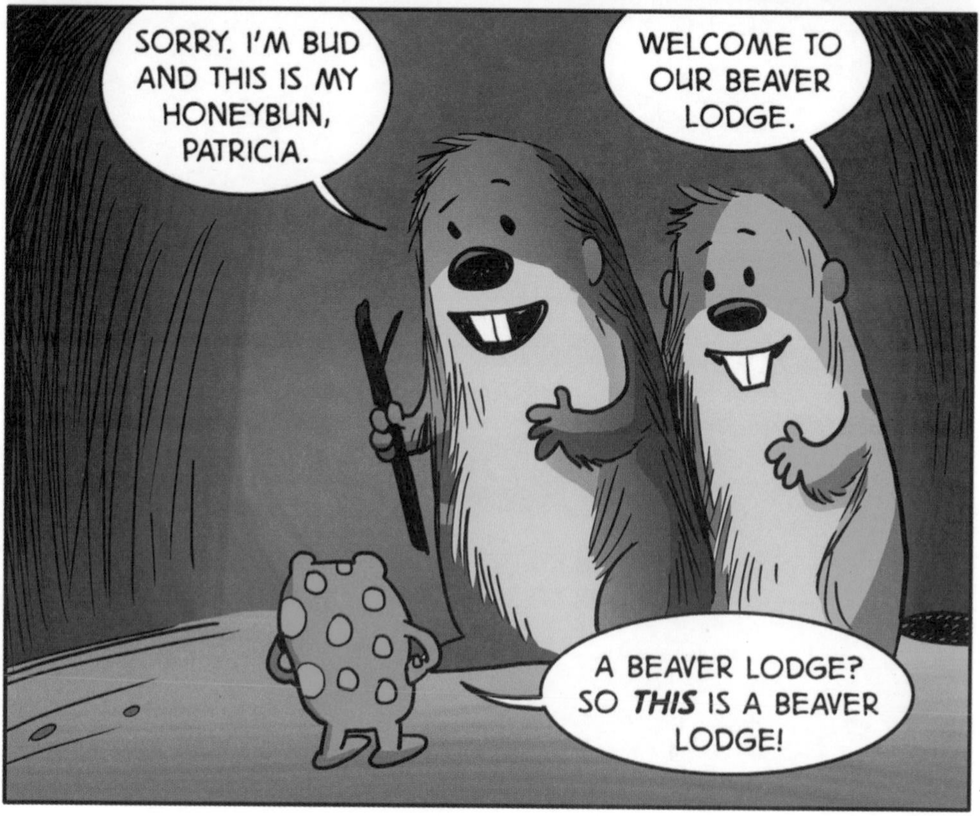
SORRY. I'M BUD AND THIS IS MY HONEYBUN, PATRICIA.
WELCOME TO OUR BEAVER LODGE.
A BEAVER LODGE? SO *THIS* IS A BEAVER LODGE!

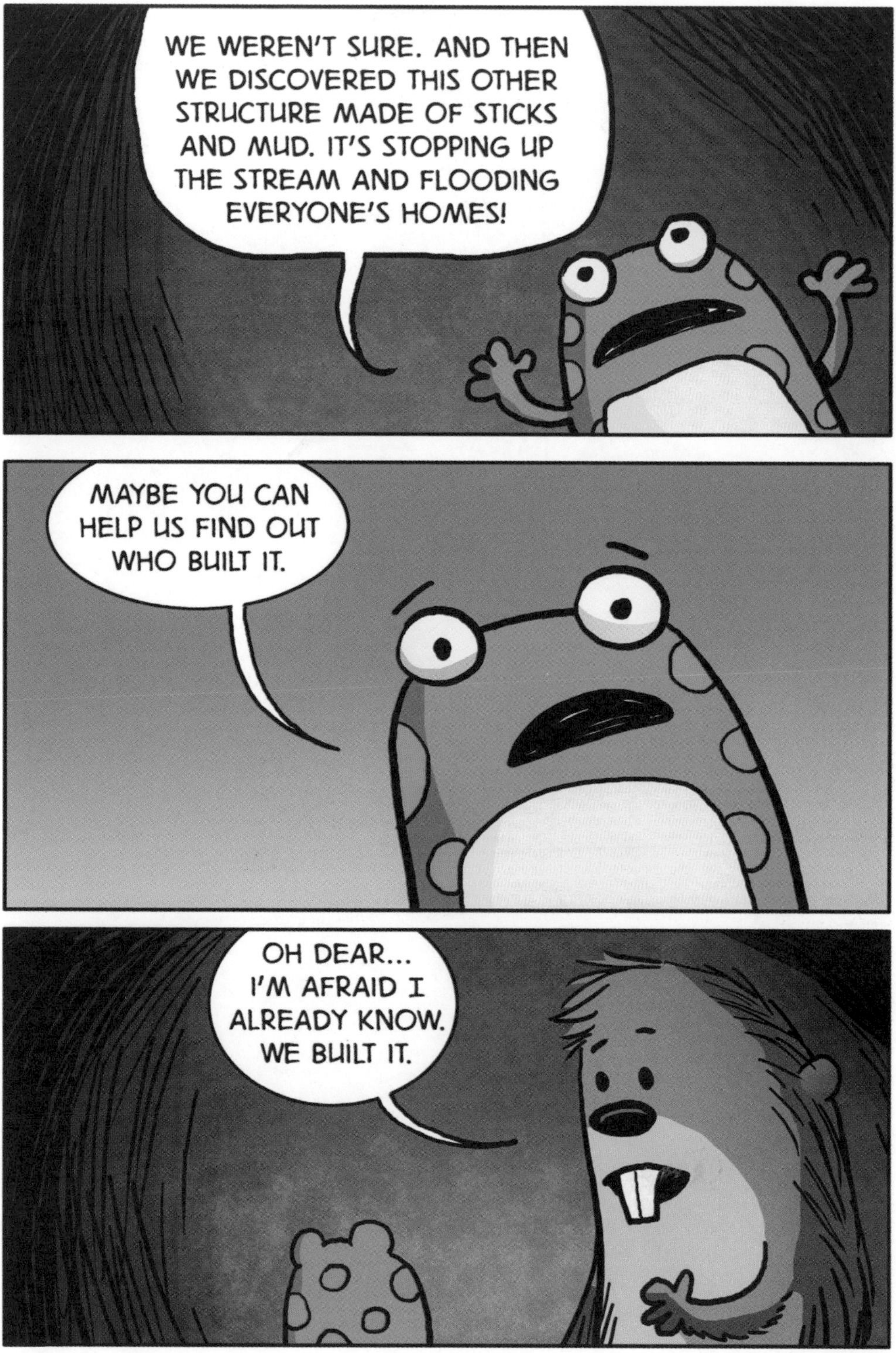
WE WEREN'T SURE. AND THEN WE DISCOVERED THIS OTHER STRUCTURE MADE OF STICKS AND MUD. IT'S STOPPING UP THE STREAM AND FLOODING EVERYONE'S HOMES!
MAYBE YOU CAN HELP US FIND OUT WHO BUILT IT.
OH DEAR... I'M AFRAID I ALREADY KNOW. WE BUILT IT.

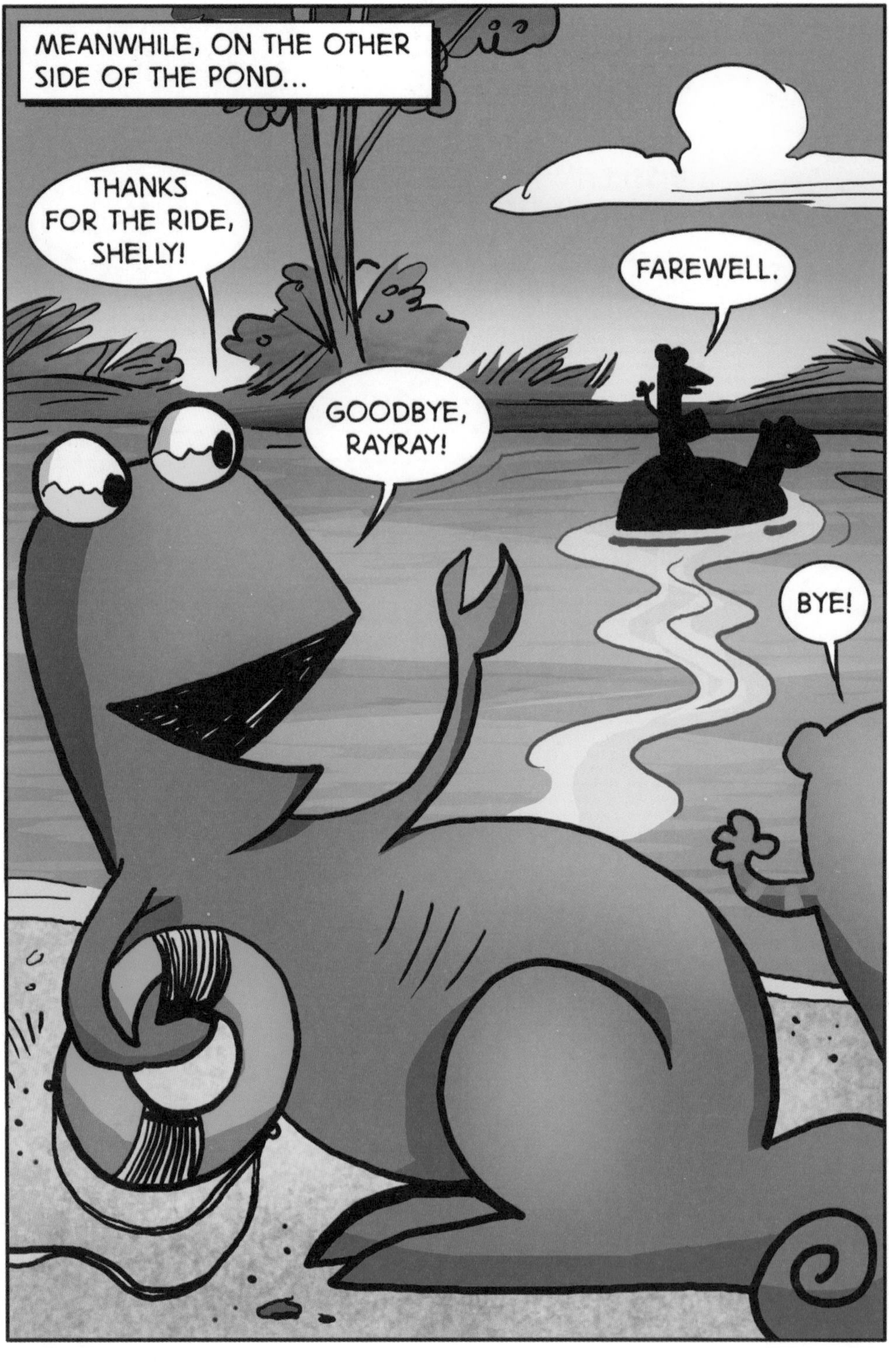

MEANWHILE, ON THE OTHER SIDE OF THE POND...
THANKS FOR THE RIDE, SHELLY!
FAREWELL.
GOODBYE, RAYRAY!
BYE!

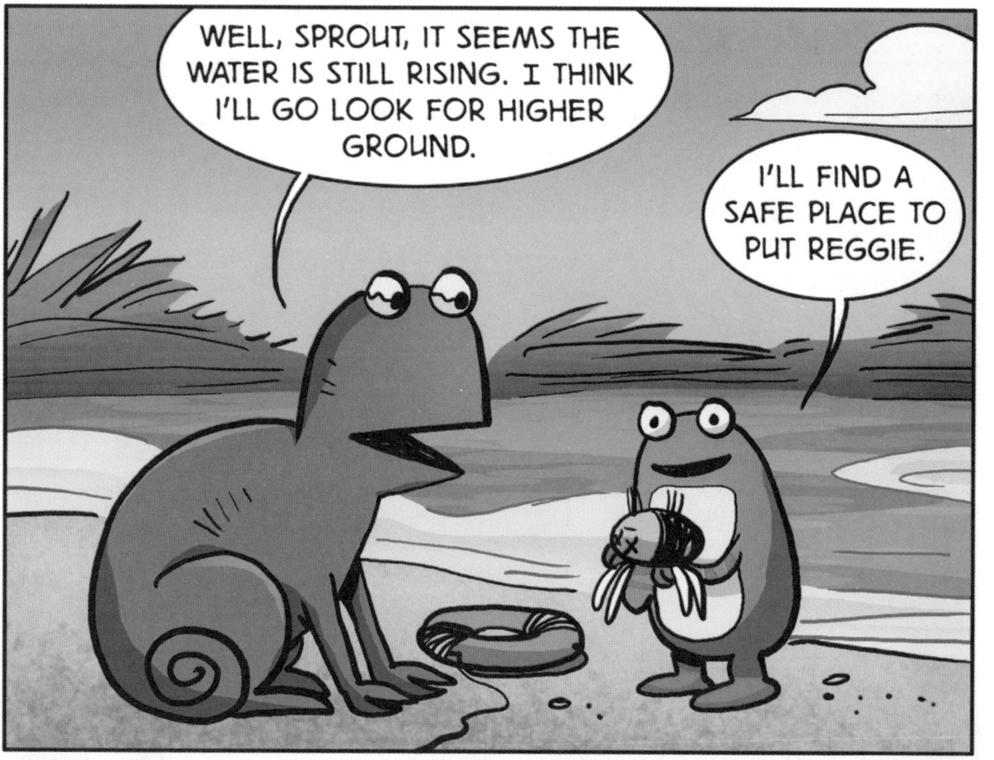
WELL, SPROUT, IT SEEMS THE WATER IS STILL RISING. I THINK I'LL GO LOOK FOR HIGHER GROUND.
I'LL FIND A SAFE PLACE TO PUT REGGIE.

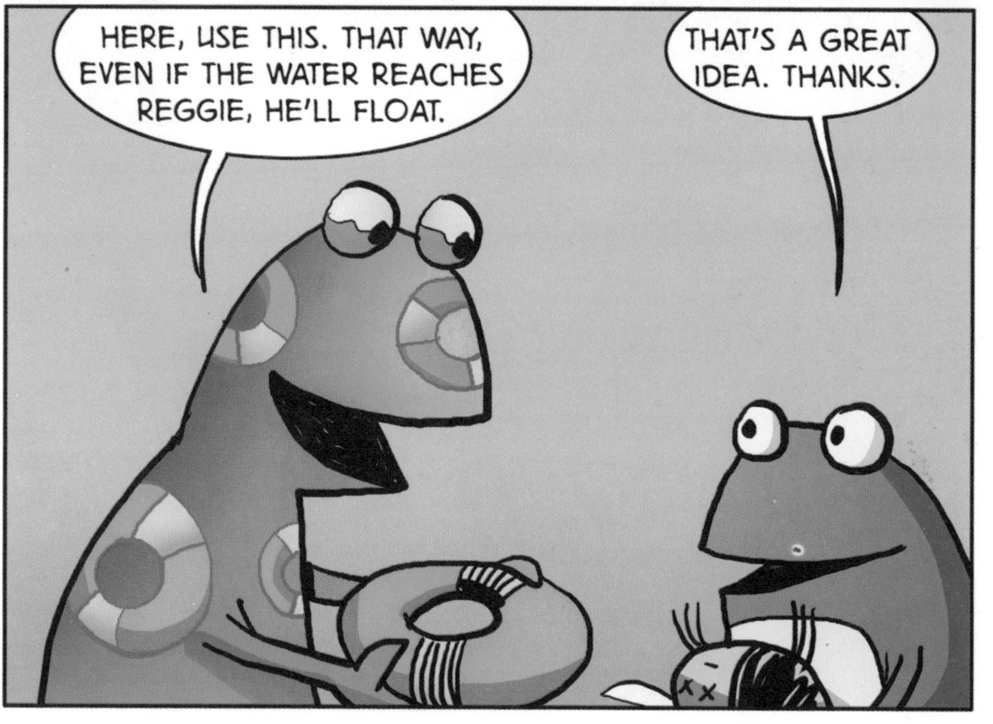
HERE, USE THIS. THAT WAY, EVEN IF THE WATER REACHES REGGIE, HE'LL FLOAT.
THAT'S A GREAT IDEA. THANKS.

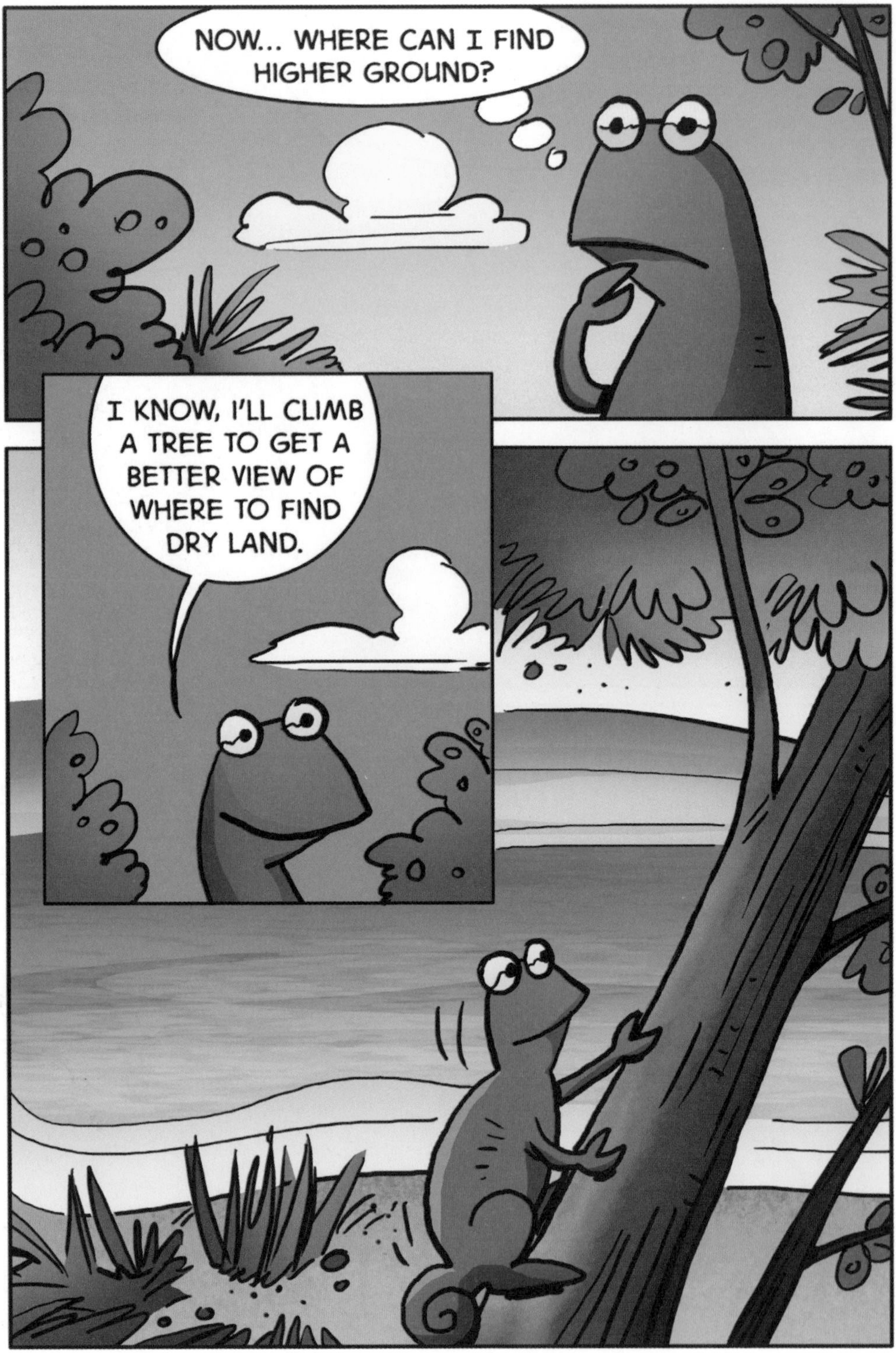
NOW... WHERE CAN I FIND HIGHER GROUND?
I KNOW, I'LL CLIMB A TREE TO GET A BETTER VIEW OF WHERE TO FIND DRY LAND.

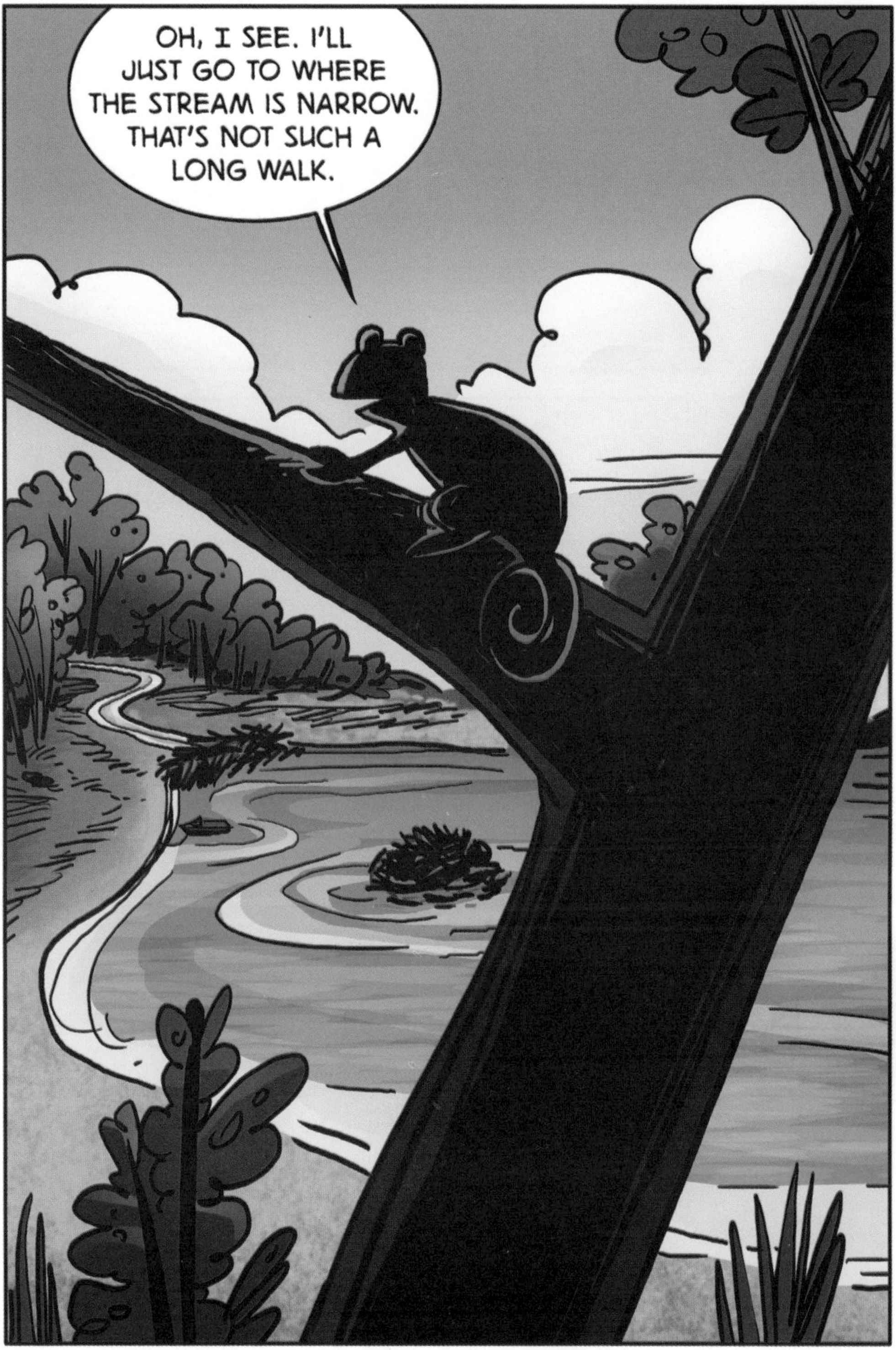
OH, I SEE. I'LL JUST GO TO WHERE THE STREAM IS NARROW. THAT'S NOT SUCH A LONG WALK.

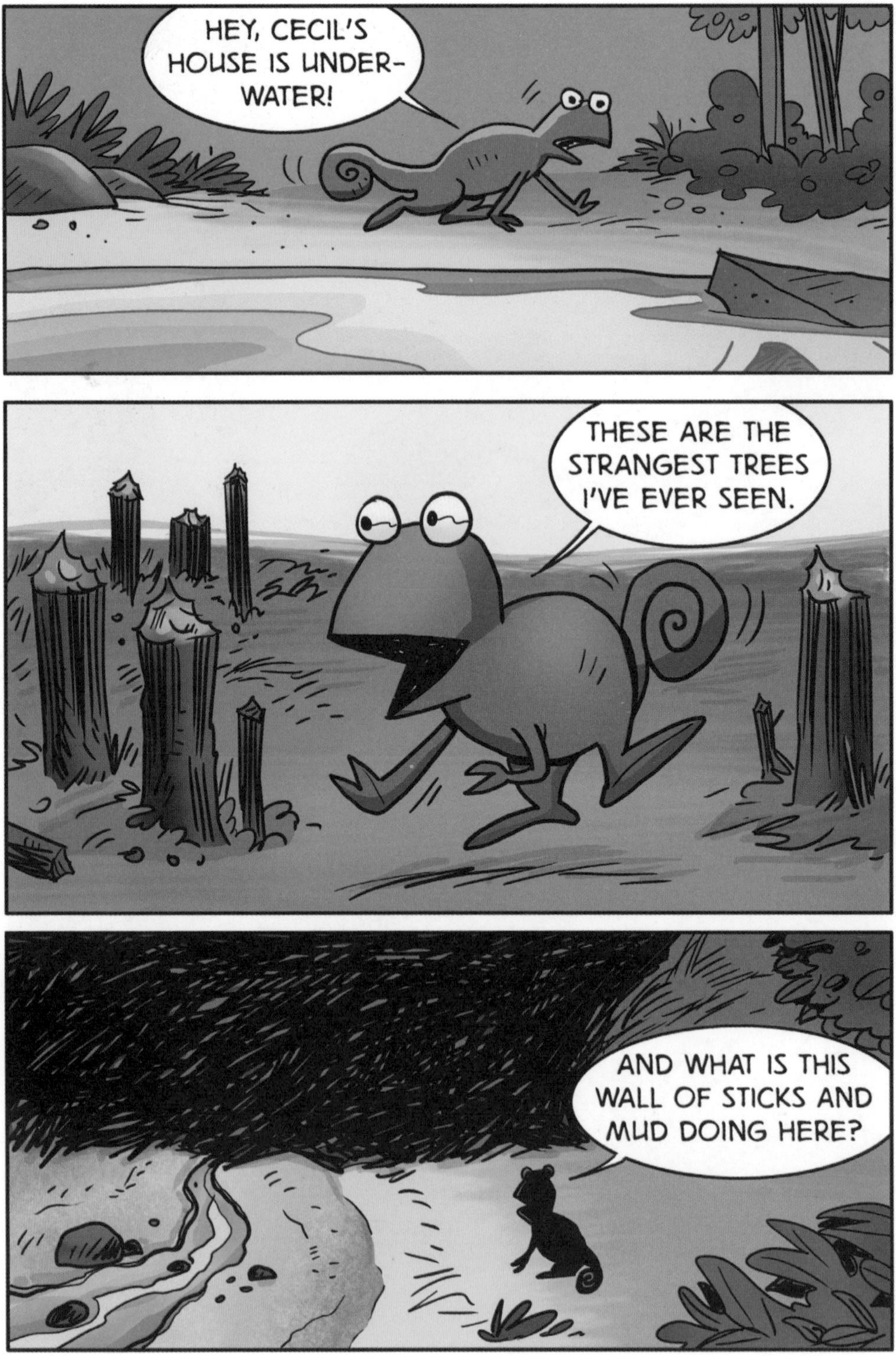
HEY, CECIL'S HOUSE IS UNDER-WATER!
THESE ARE THE STRANGEST TREES I'VE EVER SEEN.
AND WHAT IS THIS WALL OF STICKS AND MUD DOING HERE?

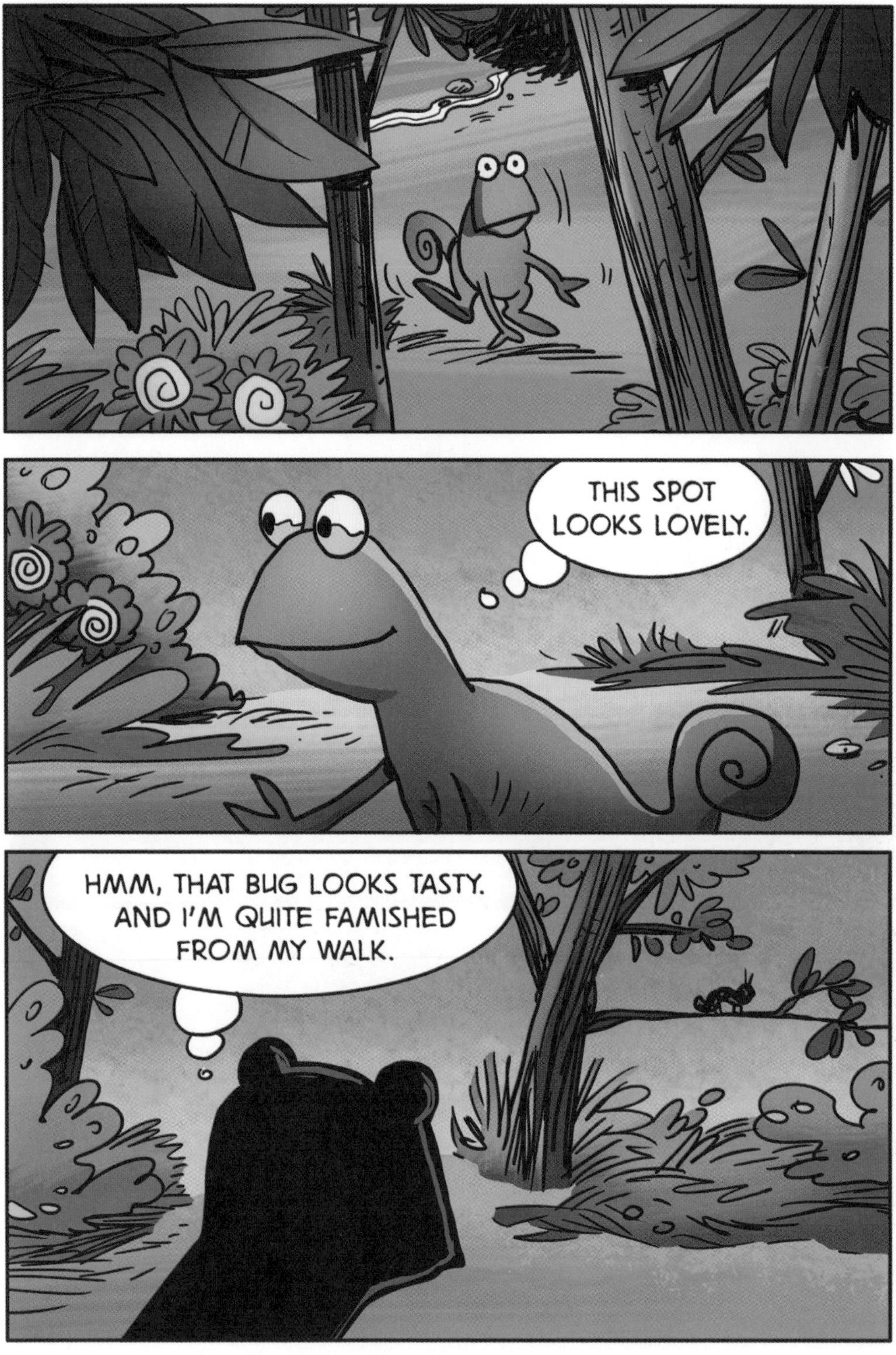
THIS SPOT LOOKS LOVELY.
HMM, THAT BUG LOOKS TASTY. AND I'M QUITE FAMISHED FROM MY WALK.

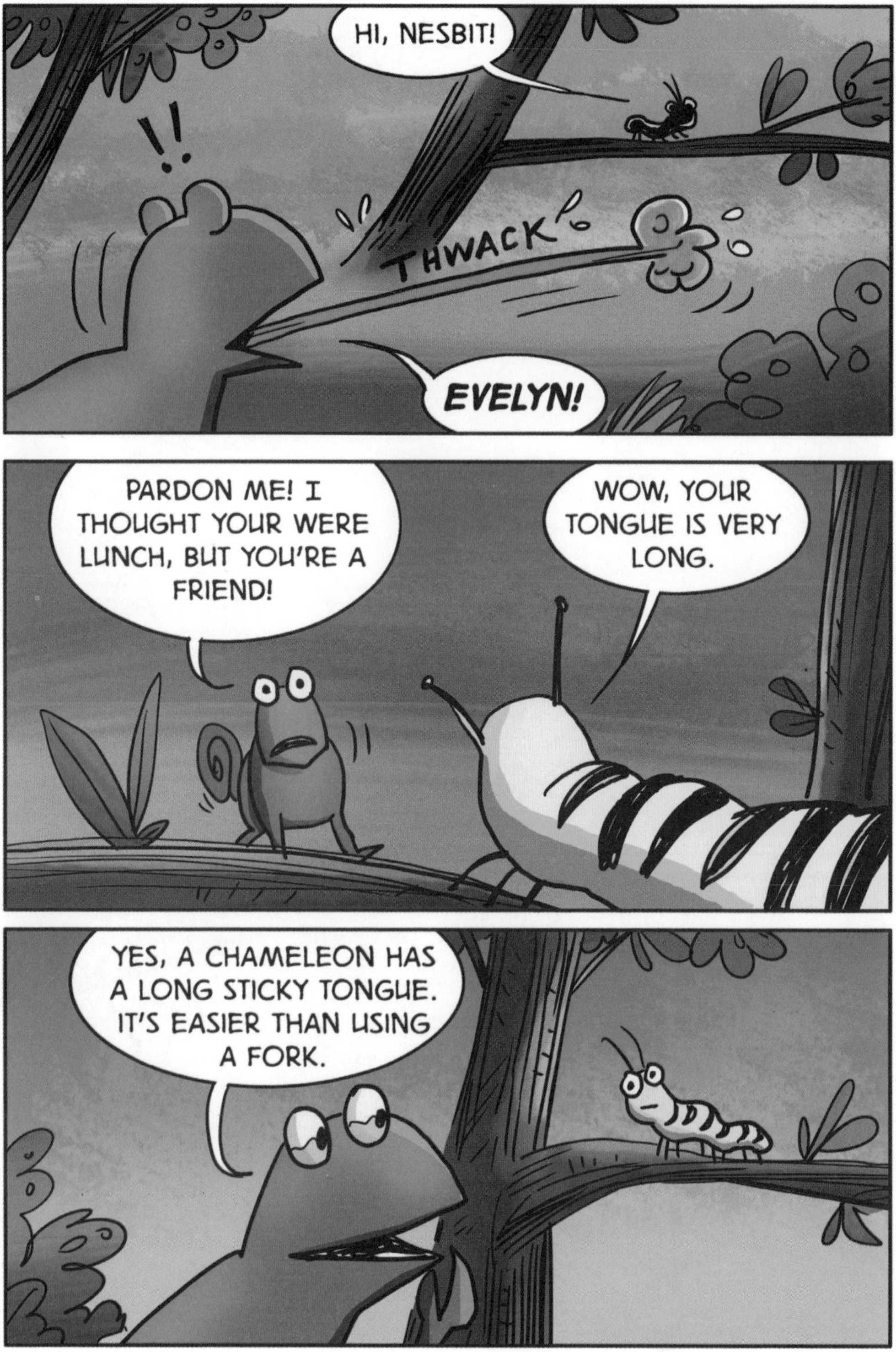
HI, NESBIT!
!!
THWACK
EVELYN!
PARDON ME! I THOUGHT YOUR WERE LUNCH, BUT YOU'RE A FRIEND!
WOW, YOUR TONGUE IS VERY LONG.
YES, A CHAMELEON HAS A LONG STICKY TONGUE. IT'S EASIER THAN USING A FORK.

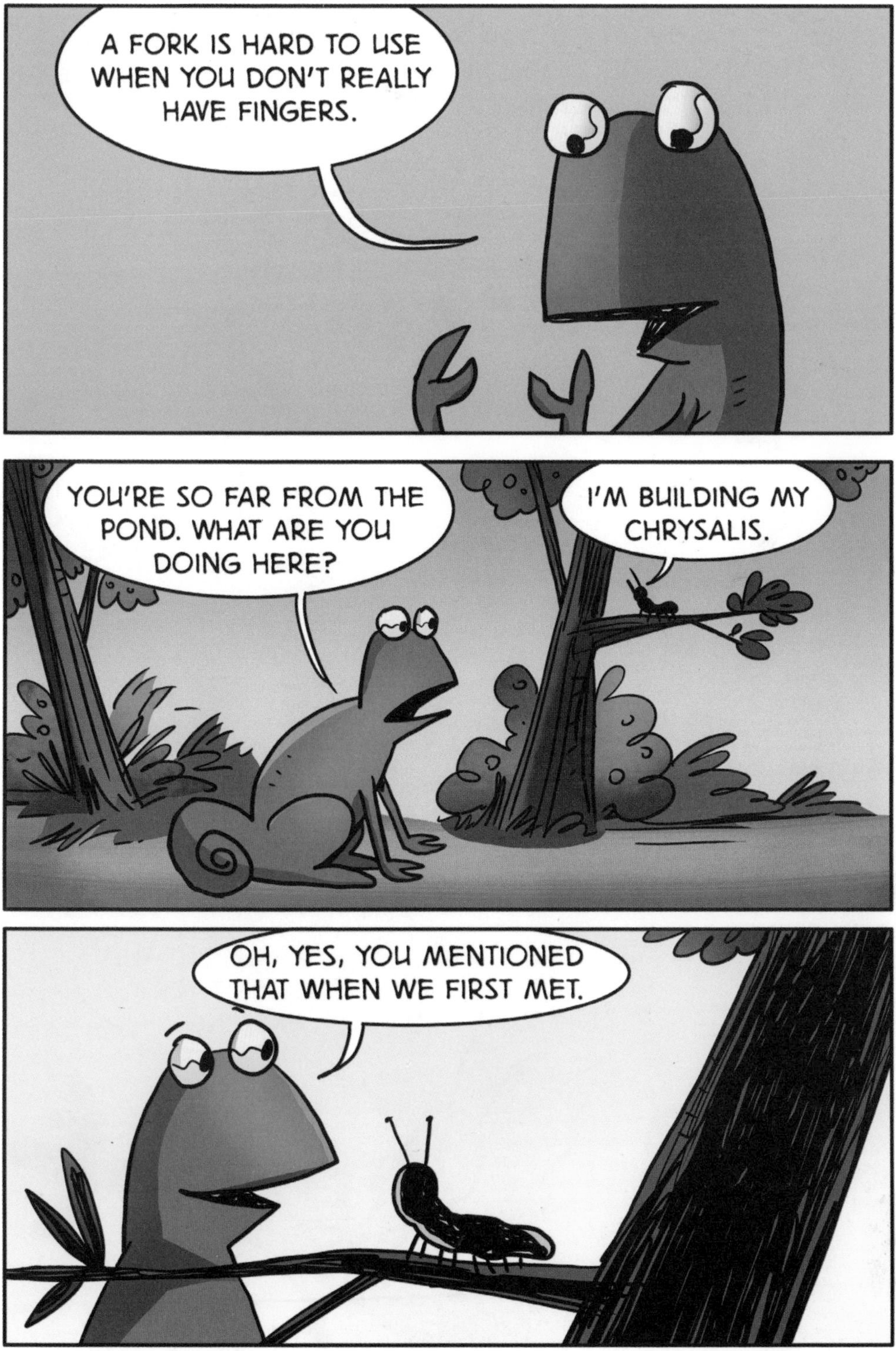
A FORK IS HARD TO USE WHEN YOU DON'T REALLY HAVE FINGERS.
YOU'RE SO FAR FROM THE POND. WHAT ARE YOU DOING HERE?
I'M BUILDING MY CHRYSALIS.
OH, YES, YOU MENTIONED THAT WHEN WE FIRST MET.

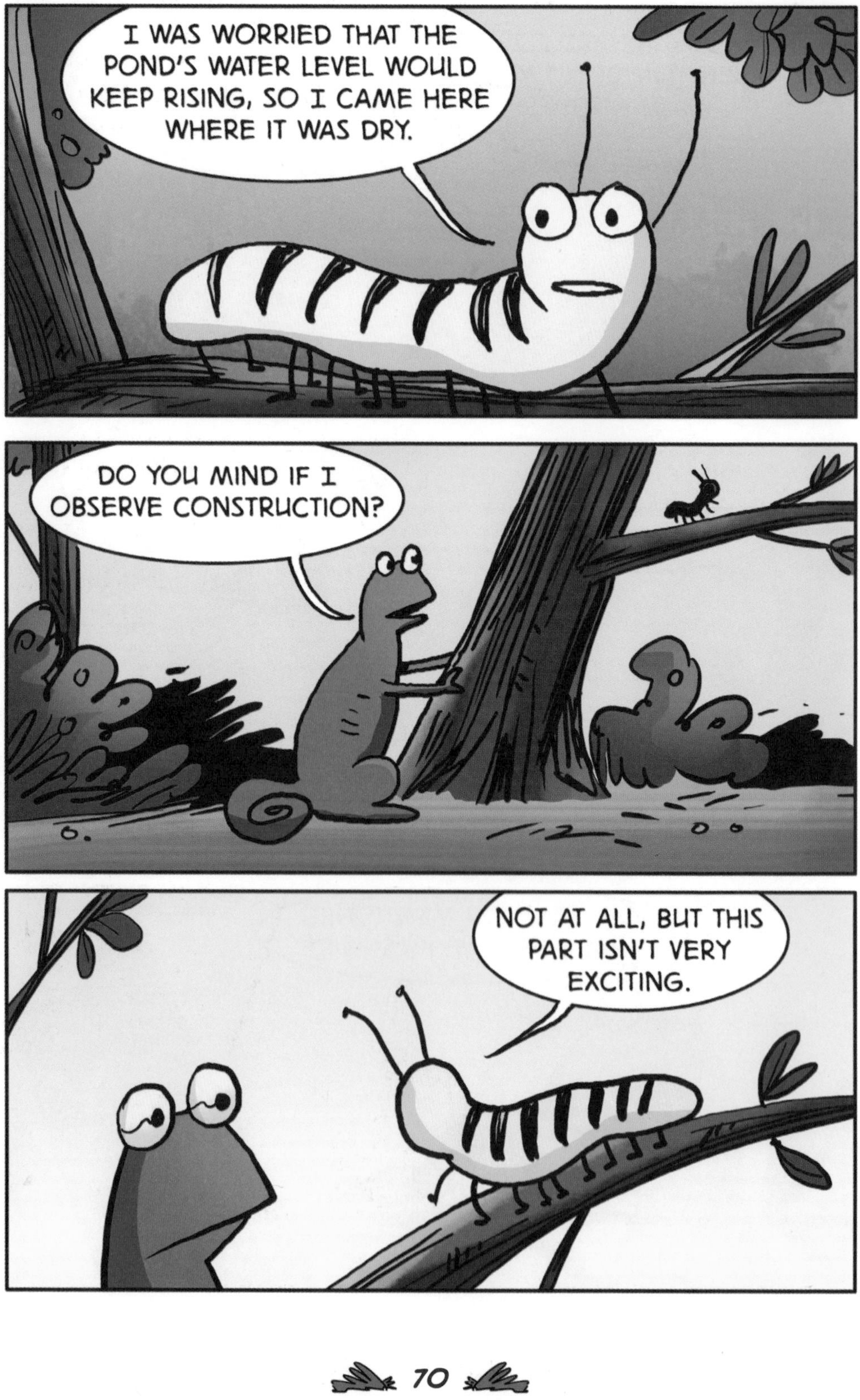
I WAS WORRIED THAT THE POND'S WATER LEVEL WOULD KEEP RISING, SO I CAME HERE WHERE IT WAS DRY.
DO YOU MIND IF I OBSERVE CONSTRUCTION?
NOT AT ALL, BUT THIS PART ISN'T VERY EXCITING.

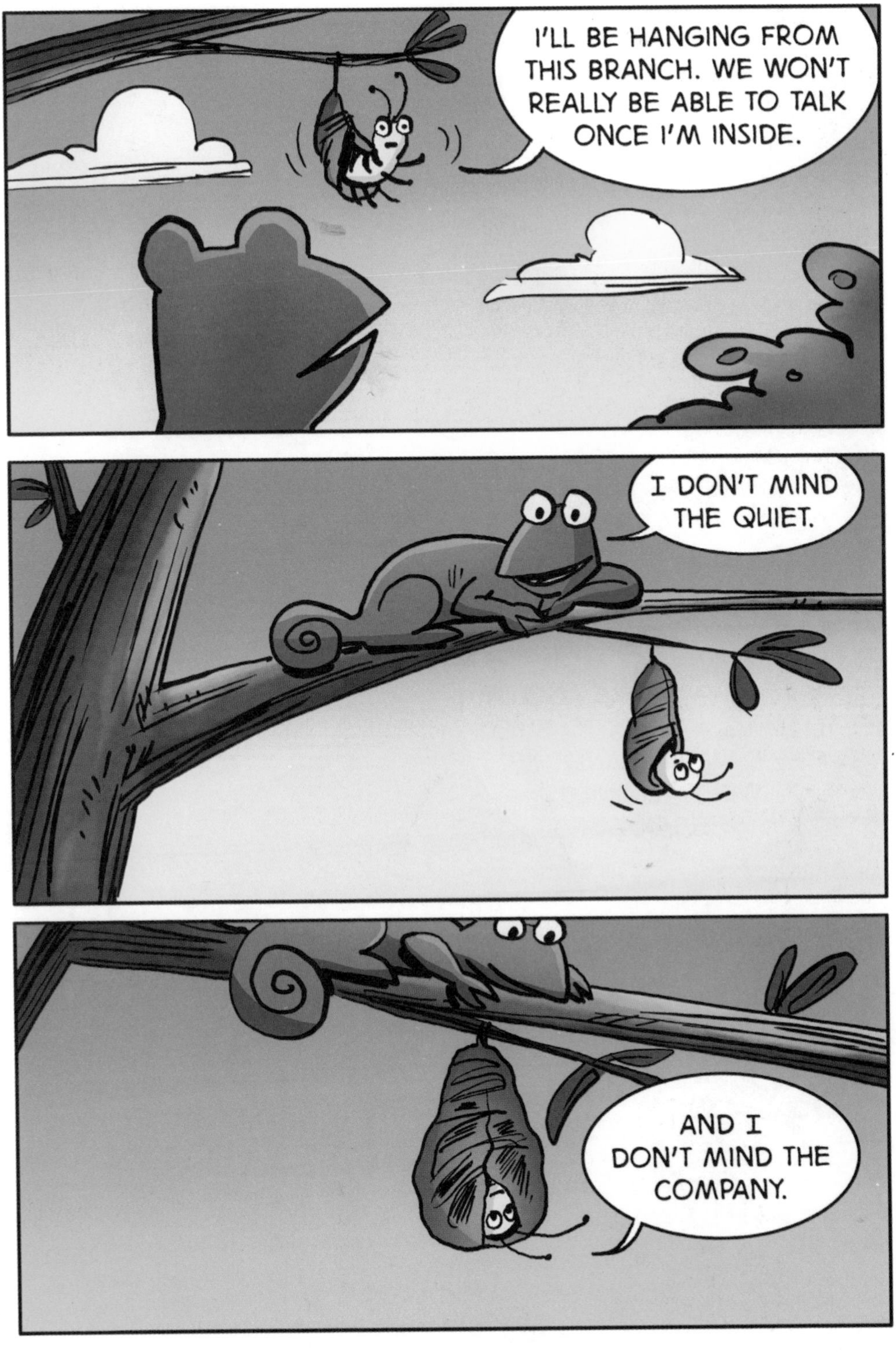
I'LL BE HANGING FROM THIS BRANCH. WE WON'T REALLY BE ABLE TO TALK ONCE I'M INSIDE.
I DON'T MIND THE QUIET.
AND I DON'T MIND THE COMPANY.

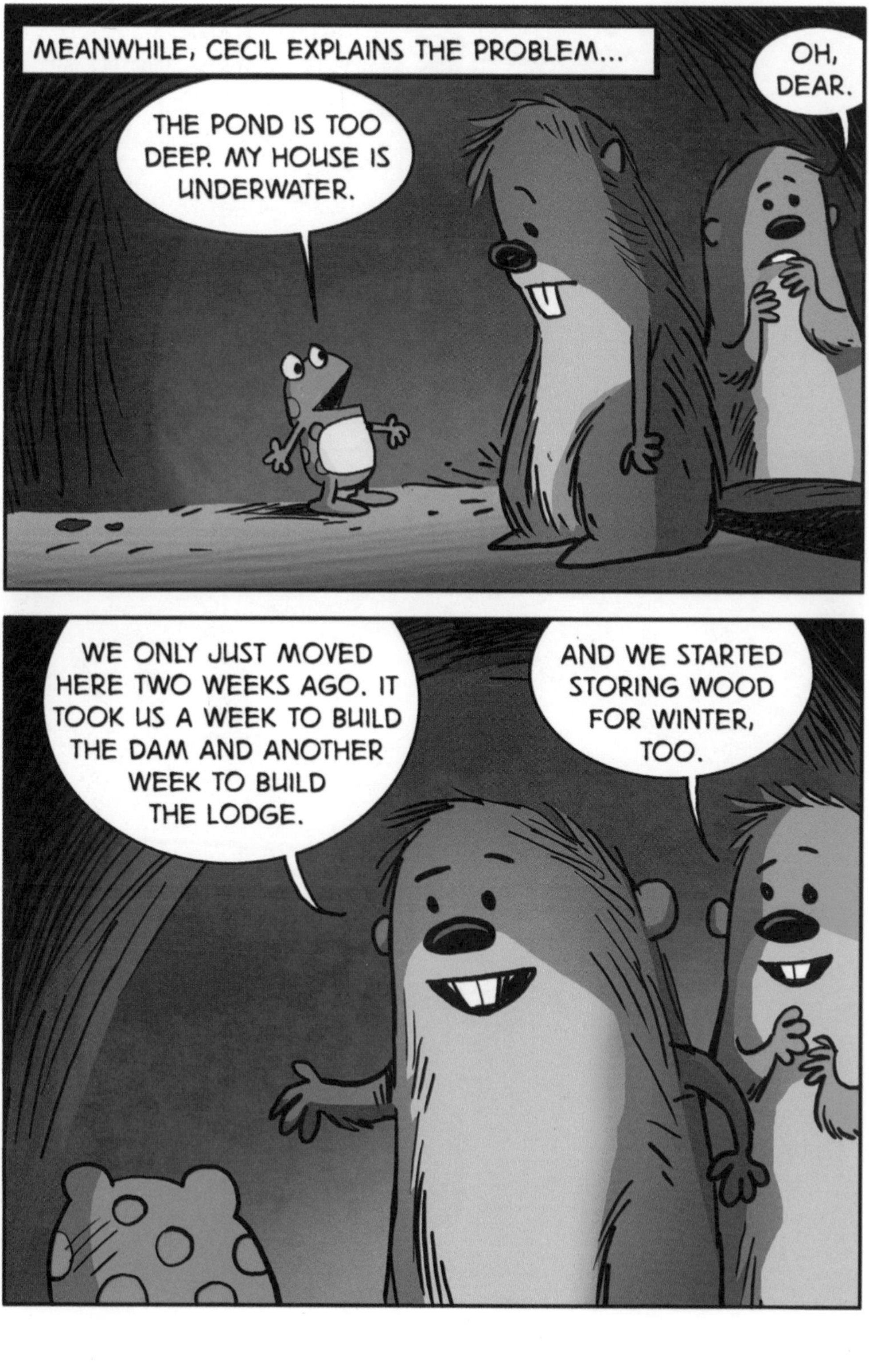
MEANWHILE, CECIL EXPLAINS THE PROBLEM...
THE POND IS TOO DEEP. MY HOUSE IS UNDERWATER.
OH, DEAR.
WE ONLY JUST MOVED HERE TWO WEEKS AGO. IT TOOK US A WEEK TO BUILD THE DAM AND ANOTHER WEEK TO BUILD THE LODGE.
AND WE STARTED STORING WOOD FOR WINTER, TOO.

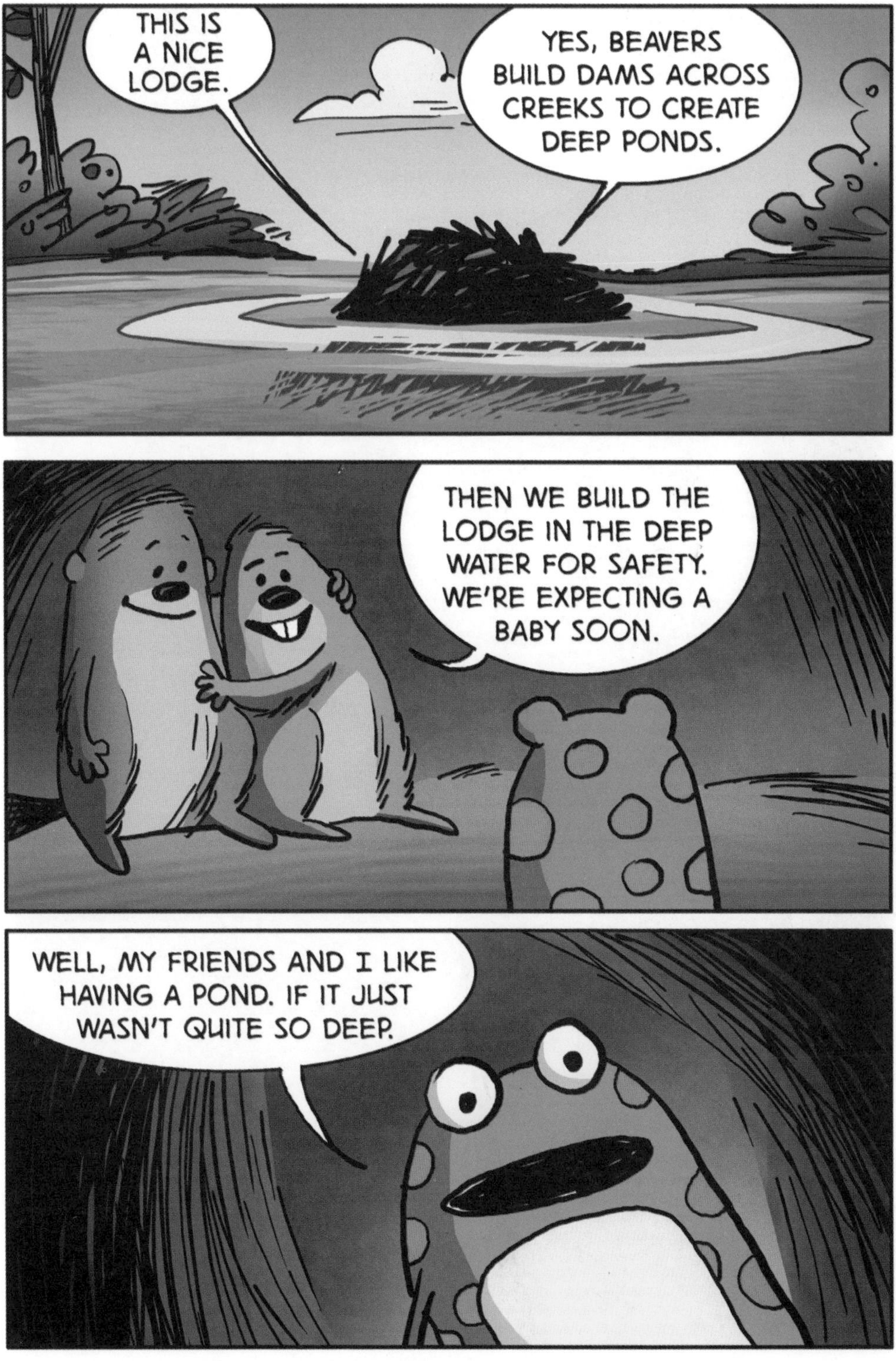
THIS IS A NICE LODGE.
YES, BEAVERS BUILD DAMS ACROSS CREEKS TO CREATE DEEP PONDS.
THEN WE BUILD THE LODGE IN THE DEEP WATER FOR SAFETY. WE'RE EXPECTING A BABY SOON.
WELL, MY FRIENDS AND I LIKE HAVING A POND. IF IT JUST WASN'T QUITE SO DEEP.

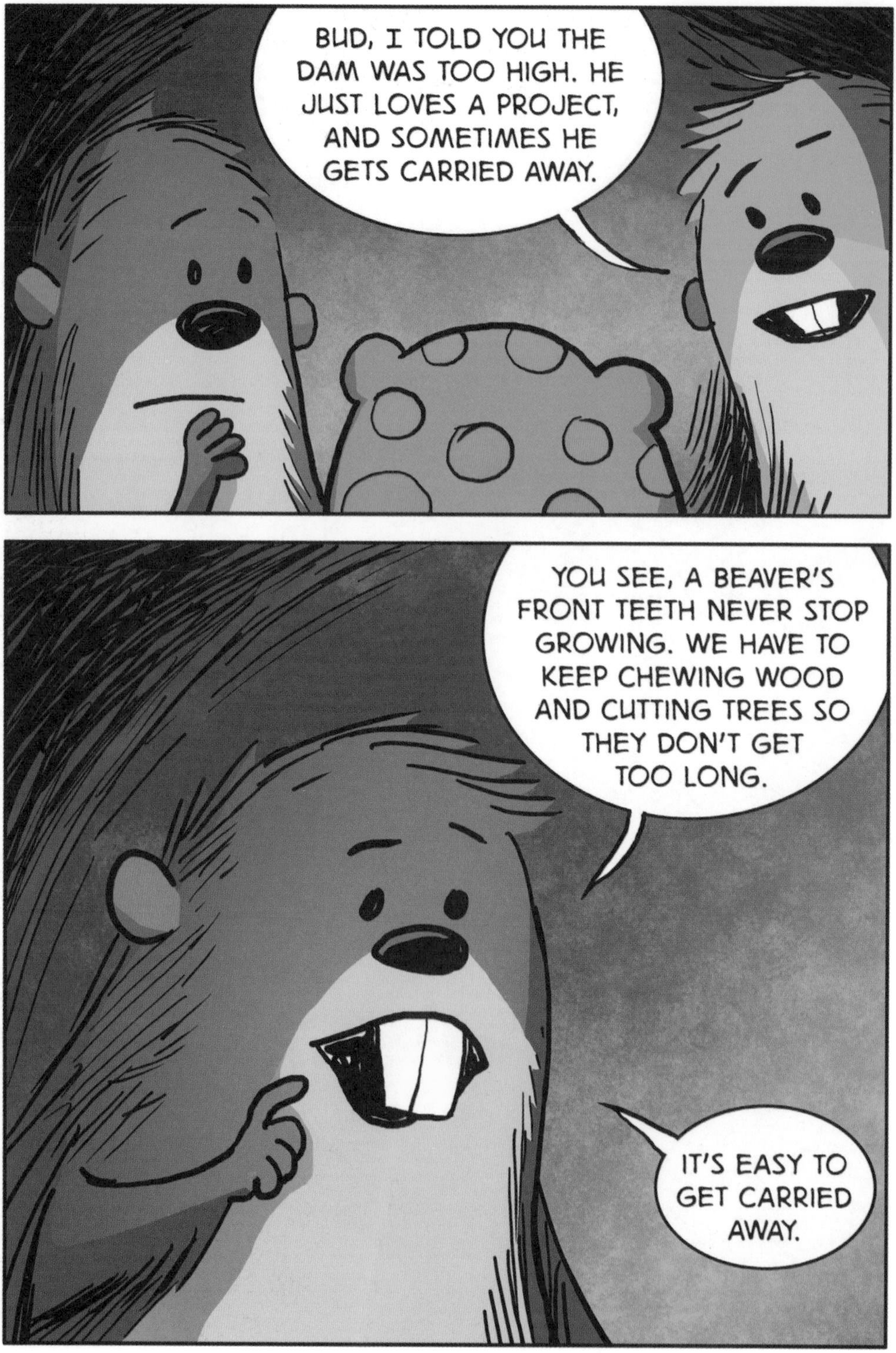
BUD, I TOLD YOU THE DAM WAS TOO HIGH. HE JUST LOVES A PROJECT, AND SOMETIMES HE GETS CARRIED AWAY.
YOU SEE, A BEAVER'S FRONT TEETH NEVER STOP GROWING. WE HAVE TO KEEP CHEWING WOOD AND CUTTING TREES SO THEY DON'T GET TOO LONG.
IT'S EASY TO GET CARRIED AWAY.

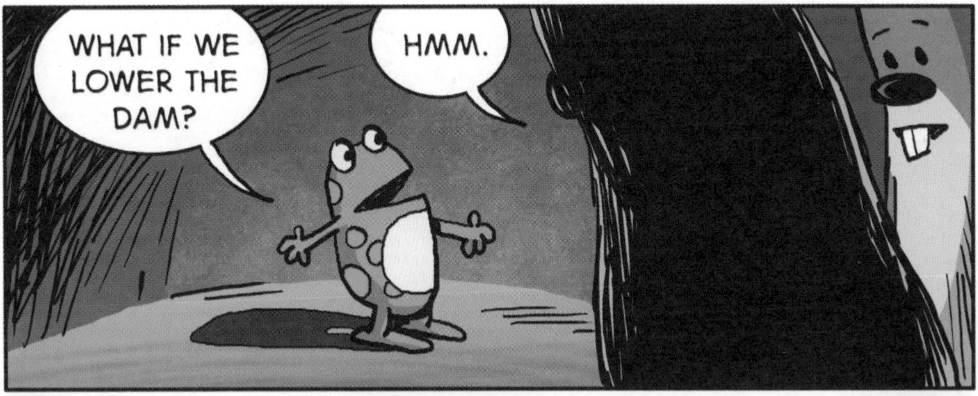
WHAT IF WE LOWER THE DAM?
HMM.

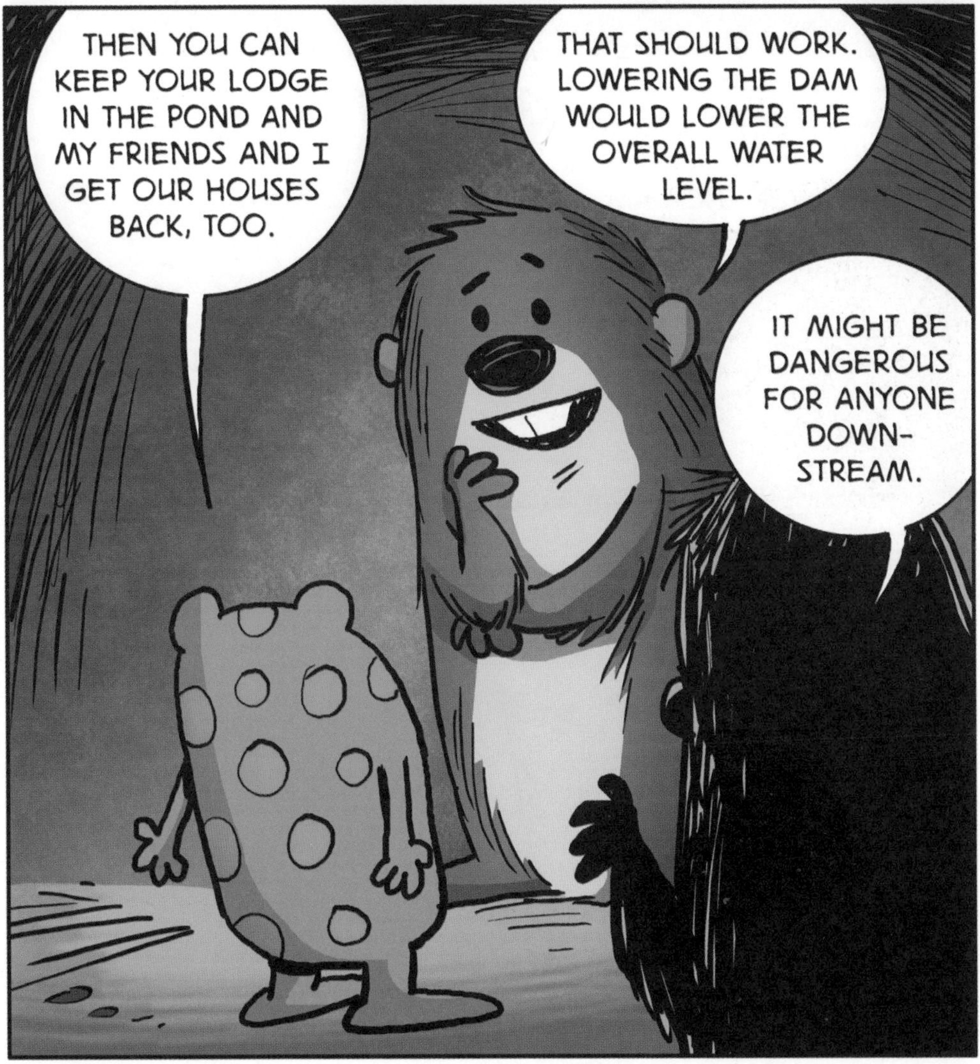
THEN YOU CAN KEEP YOUR LODGE IN THE POND AND MY FRIENDS AND I GET OUR HOUSES BACK, TOO.
THAT SHOULD WORK. LOWERING THE DAM WOULD LOWER THE OVERALL WATER LEVEL.
IT MIGHT BE DANGEROUS FOR ANYONE DOWN-STREAM.

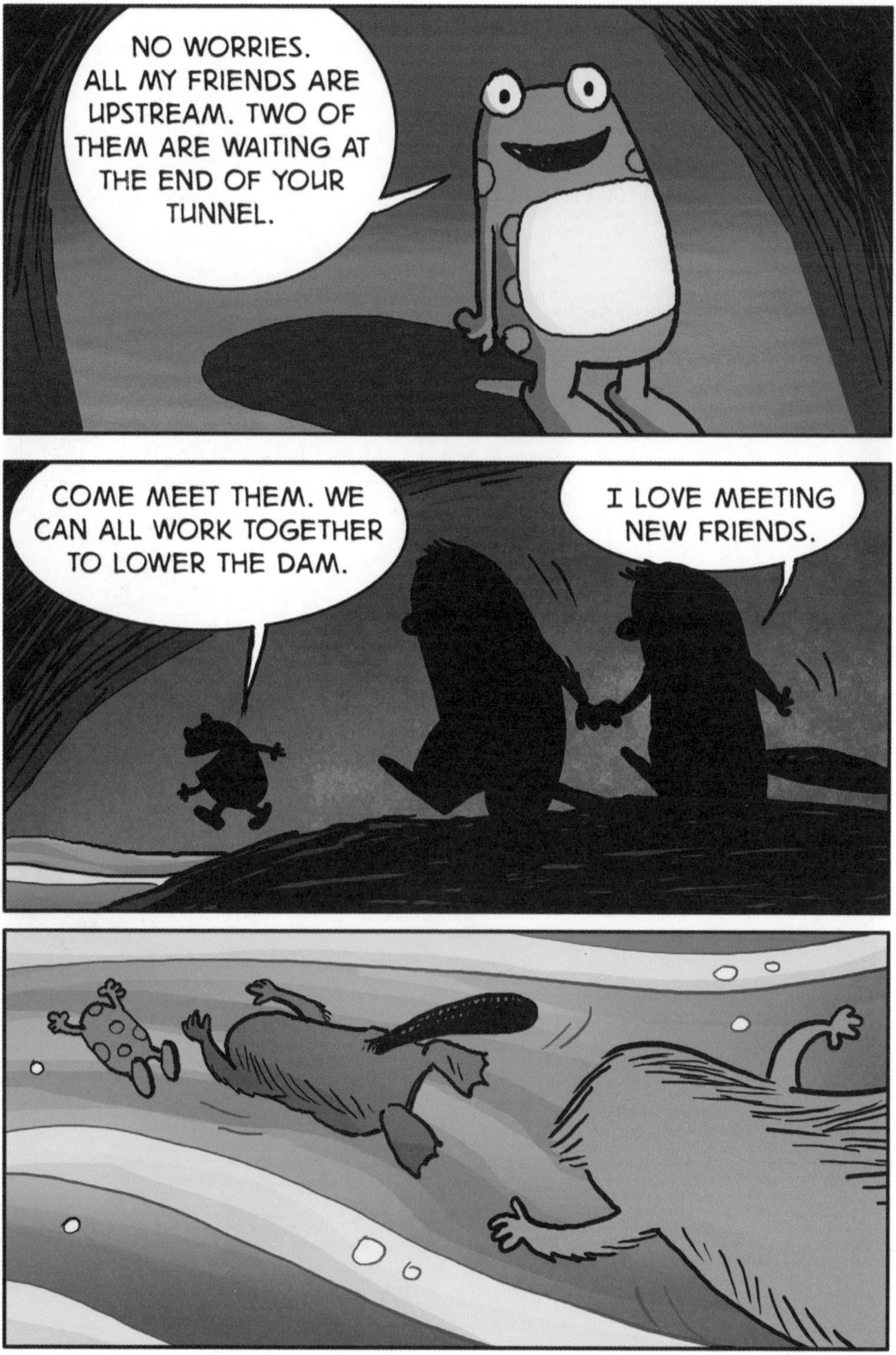
NO WORRIES. ALL MY FRIENDS ARE UPSTREAM. TWO OF THEM ARE WAITING AT THE END OF YOUR TUNNEL.
COME MEET THEM. WE CAN ALL WORK TOGETHER TO LOWER THE DAM.
I LOVE MEETING NEW FRIENDS.

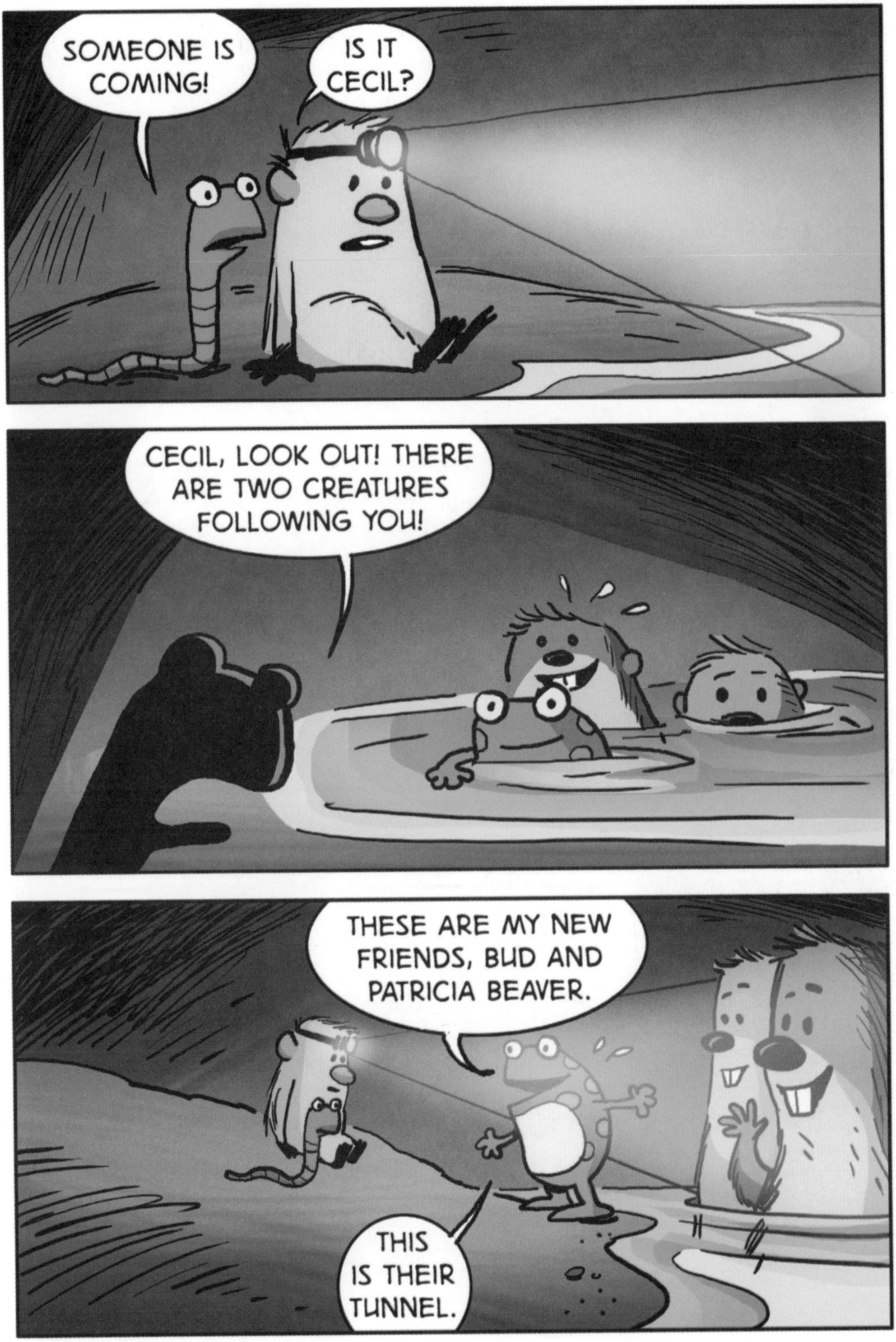
SOMEONE IS COMING!
IS IT CECIL?
CECIL, LOOK OUT! THERE ARE TWO CREATURES FOLLOWING YOU!
THESE ARE MY NEW FRIENDS, BUD AND PATRICIA BEAVER.
THIS IS THEIR TUNNEL.

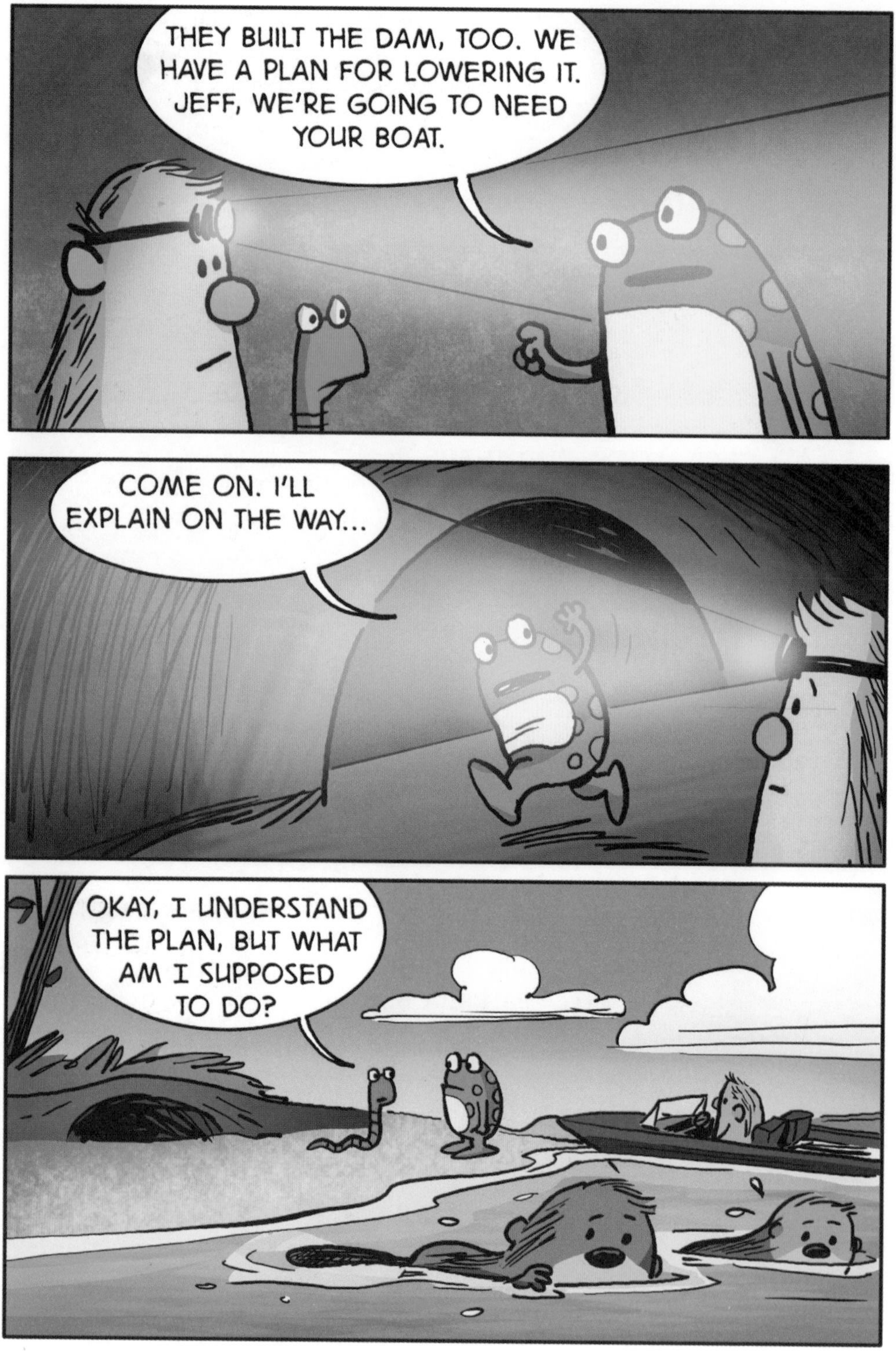
THEY BUILT THE DAM, TOO. WE HAVE A PLAN FOR LOWERING IT. JEFF, WE'RE GOING TO NEED YOUR BOAT.
COME ON. I'LL EXPLAIN ON THE WAY...
OKAY, I UNDERSTAND THE PLAN, BUT WHAT AM I SUPPOSED TO DO?

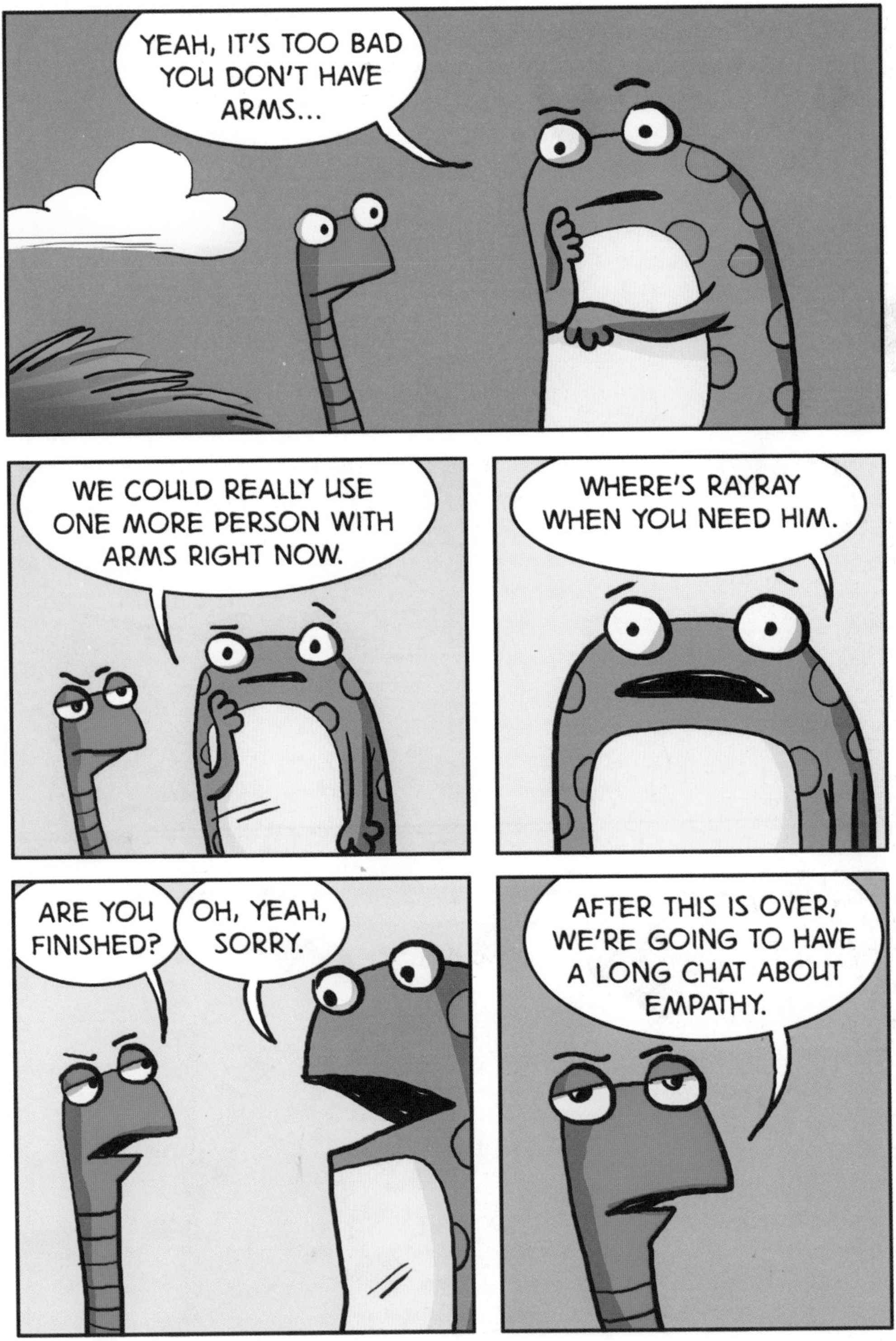
YEAH, IT'S TOO BAD YOU DON'T HAVE ARMS...
WE COULD REALLY USE ONE MORE PERSON WITH ARMS RIGHT NOW.
WHERE'S RAYRAY WHEN YOU NEED HIM.
ARE YOU FINISHED?
OH, YEAH, SORRY.
AFTER THIS IS OVER, WE'RE GOING TO HAVE A LONG CHAT ABOUT EMPATHY.

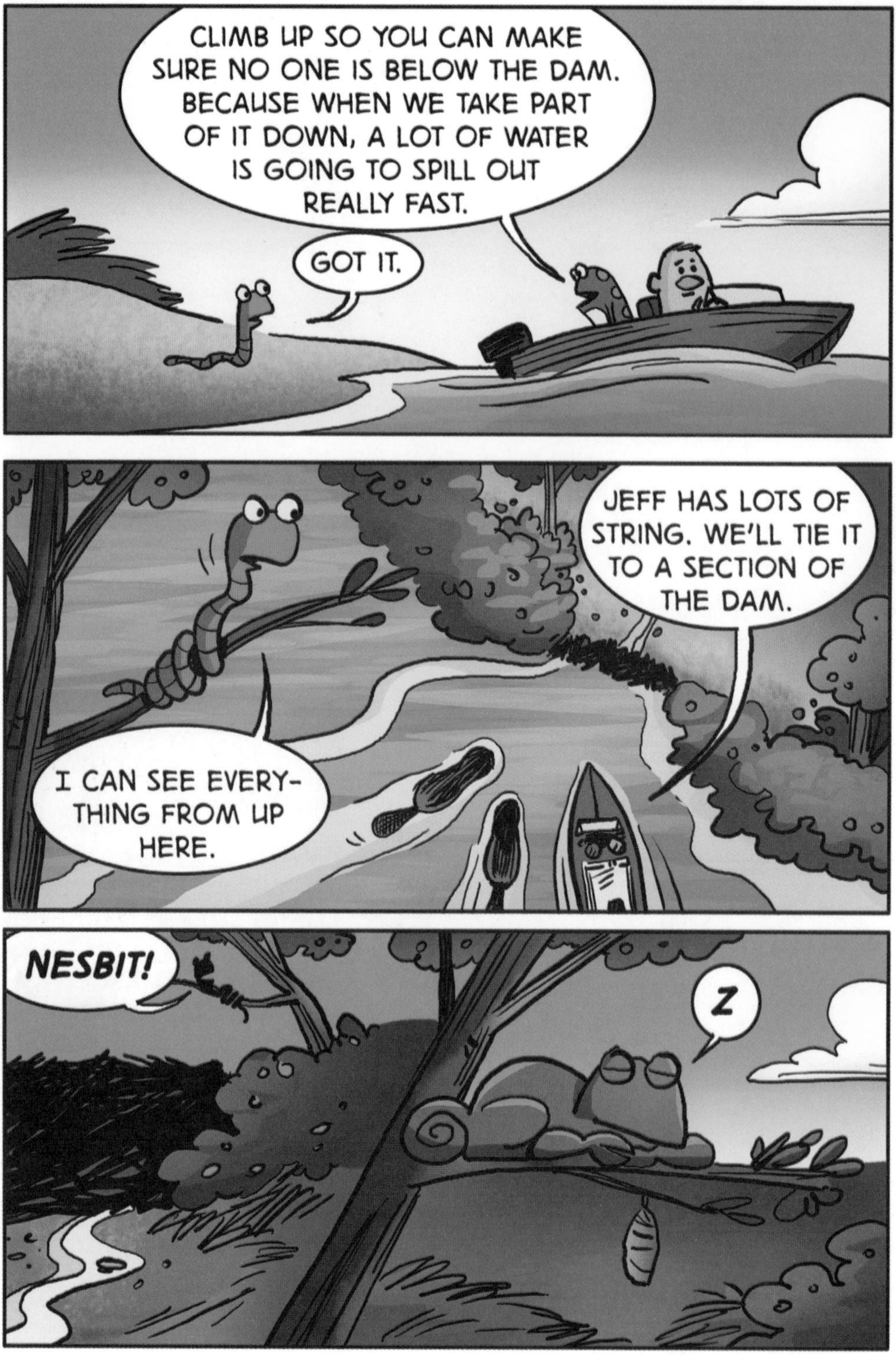
CLIMB UP SO YOU CAN MAKE SURE NO ONE IS BELOW THE DAM. BECAUSE WHEN WE TAKE PART OF IT DOWN, A LOT OF WATER IS GOING TO SPILL OUT REALLY FAST.
GOT IT.
JEFF HAS LOTS OF STRING. WE'LL TIE IT TO A SECTION OF THE DAM.
I CAN SEE EVERY-THING FROM UP HERE.
NESBIT!
Z

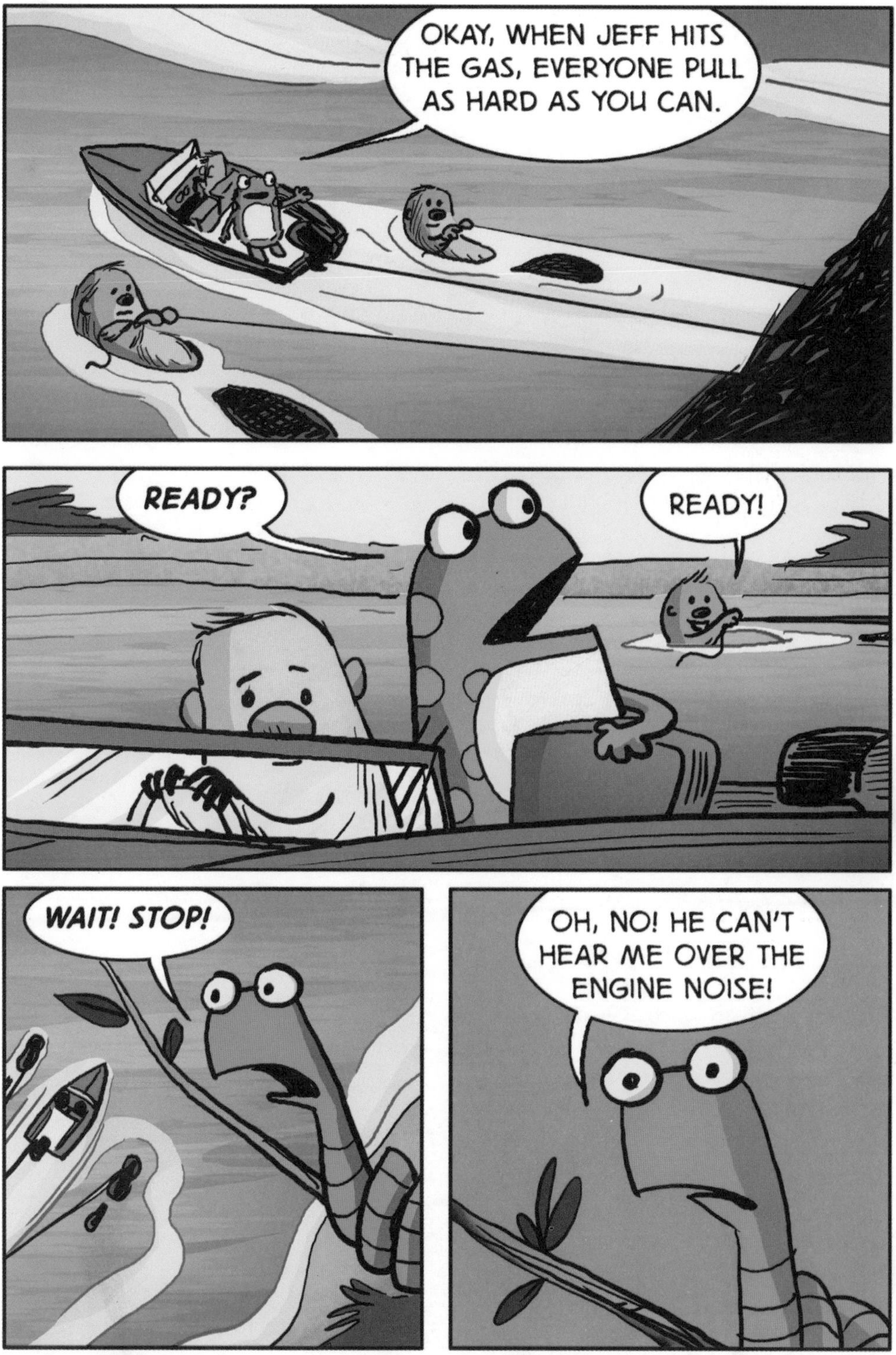
OKAY, WHEN JEFF HITS THE GAS, EVERYONE PULL AS HARD AS YOU CAN.
READY?
READY!
WAIT! STOP!
OH, NO! HE CAN'T HEAR ME OVER THE ENGINE NOISE!

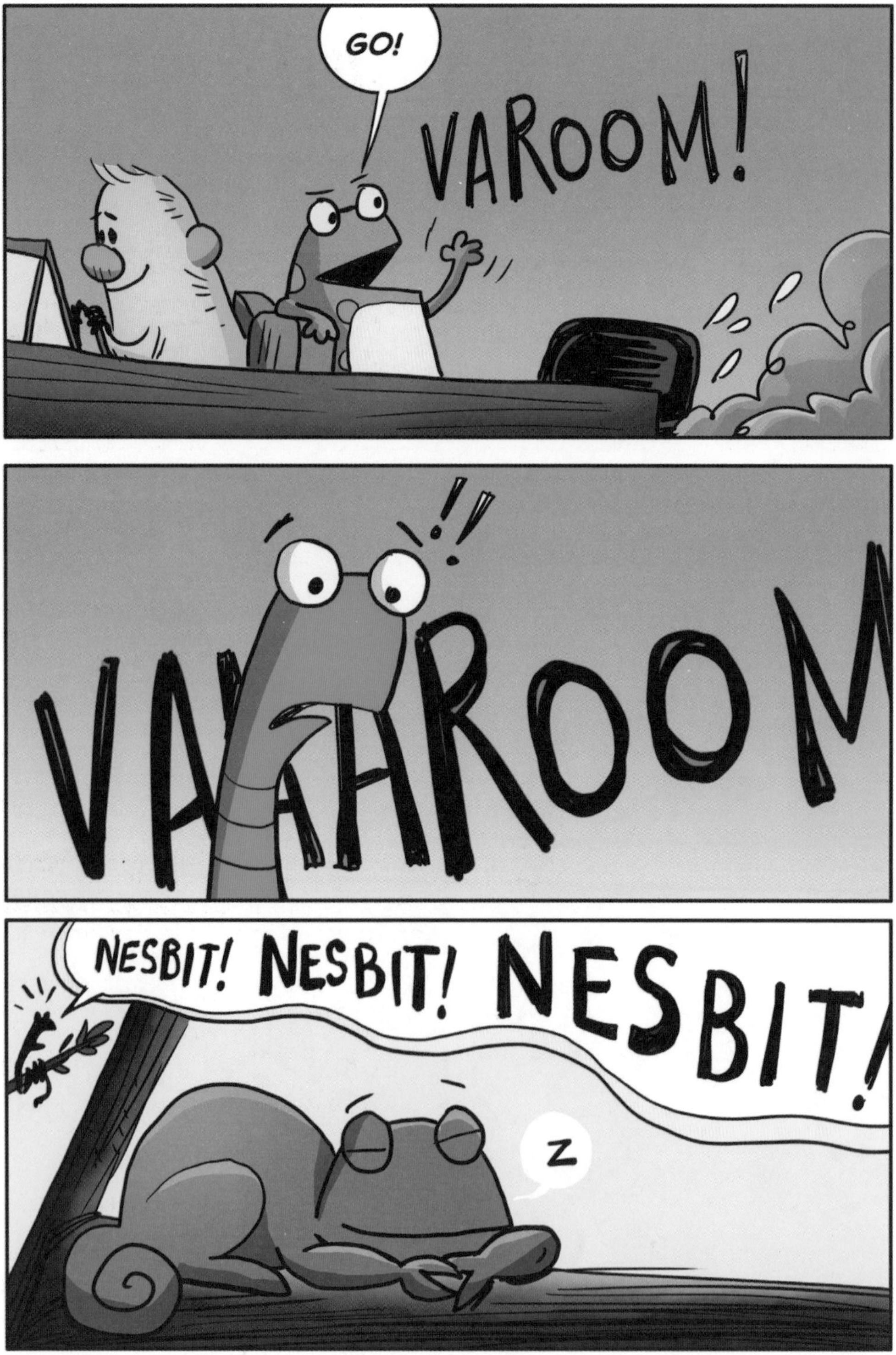
GO!
VAROOM!
!!
VAHROOM
NESBIT! NESBIT! NESBIT!
Z

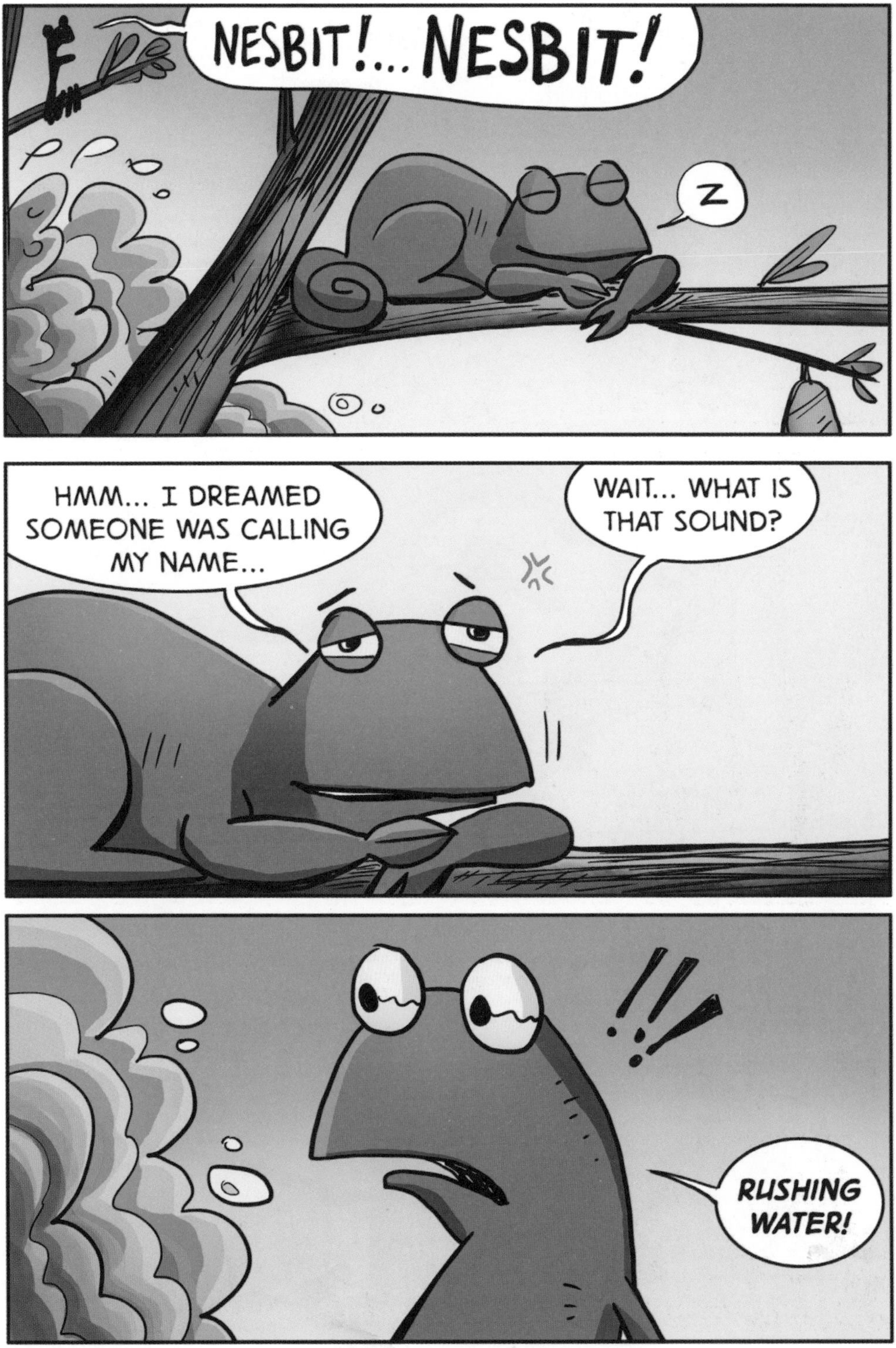
NESBIT!... NESBIT!
Z
HMM... I DREAMED SOMEONE WAS CALLING MY NAME...
WAIT... WHAT IS THAT SOUND?
!!
RUSHING WATER!

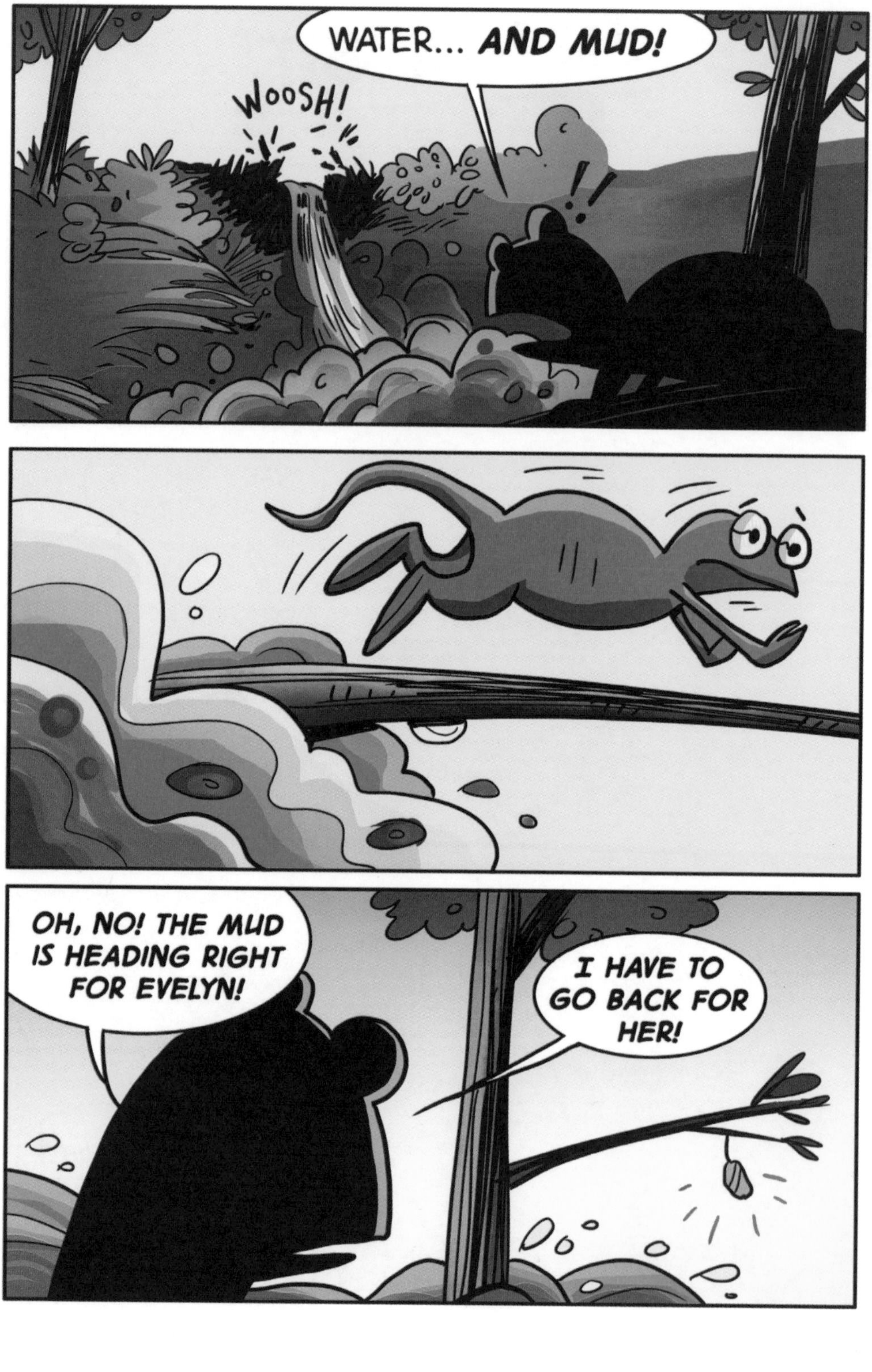
WATER... AND MUD!
WOOSH!
!!
OH, NO! THE MUD IS HEADING RIGHT FOR EVELYN!
I HAVE TO GO BACK FOR HER!

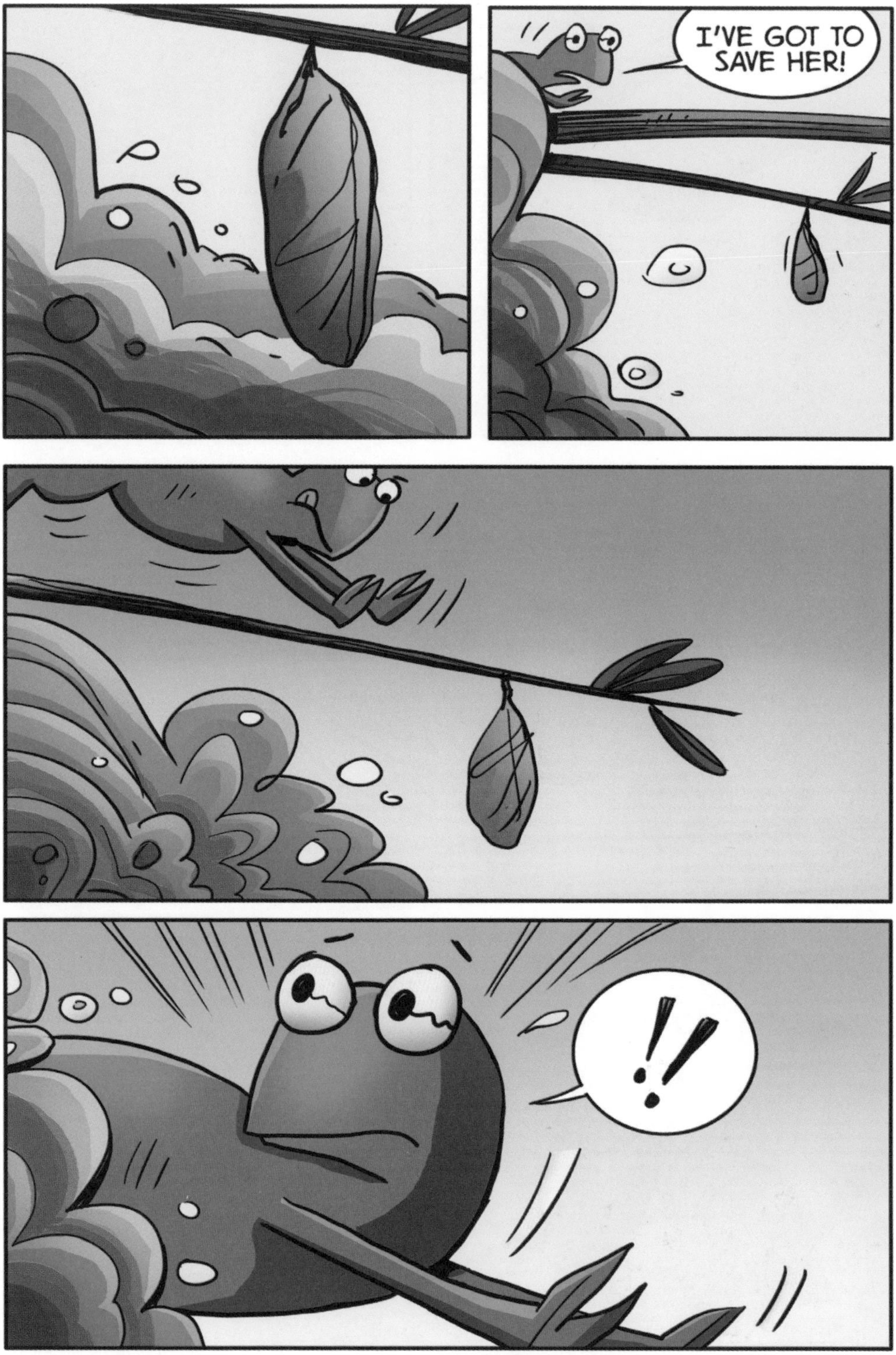
I'VE GOT TO SAVE HER!
!!

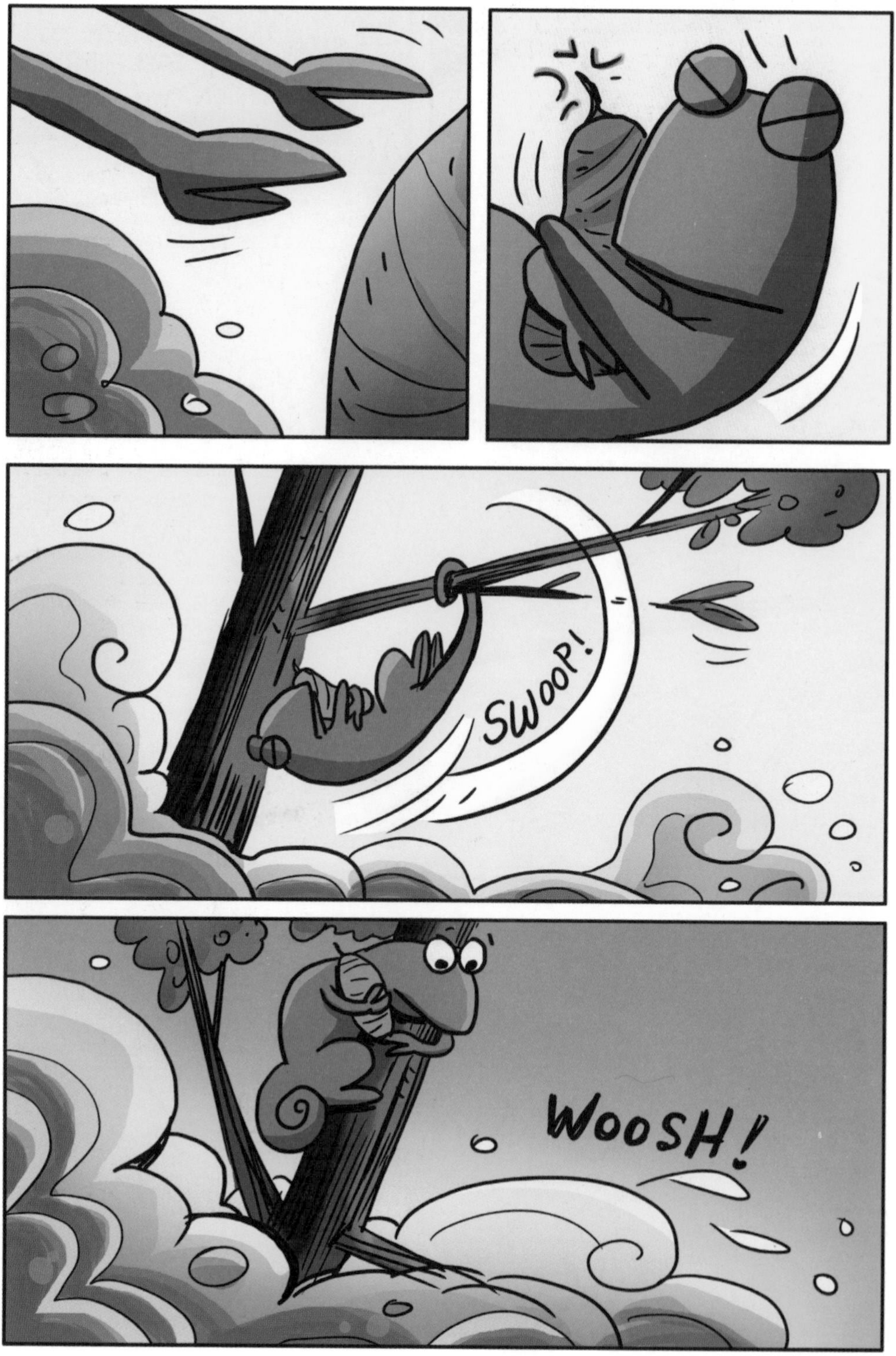
SWOOP!
WOOSH!

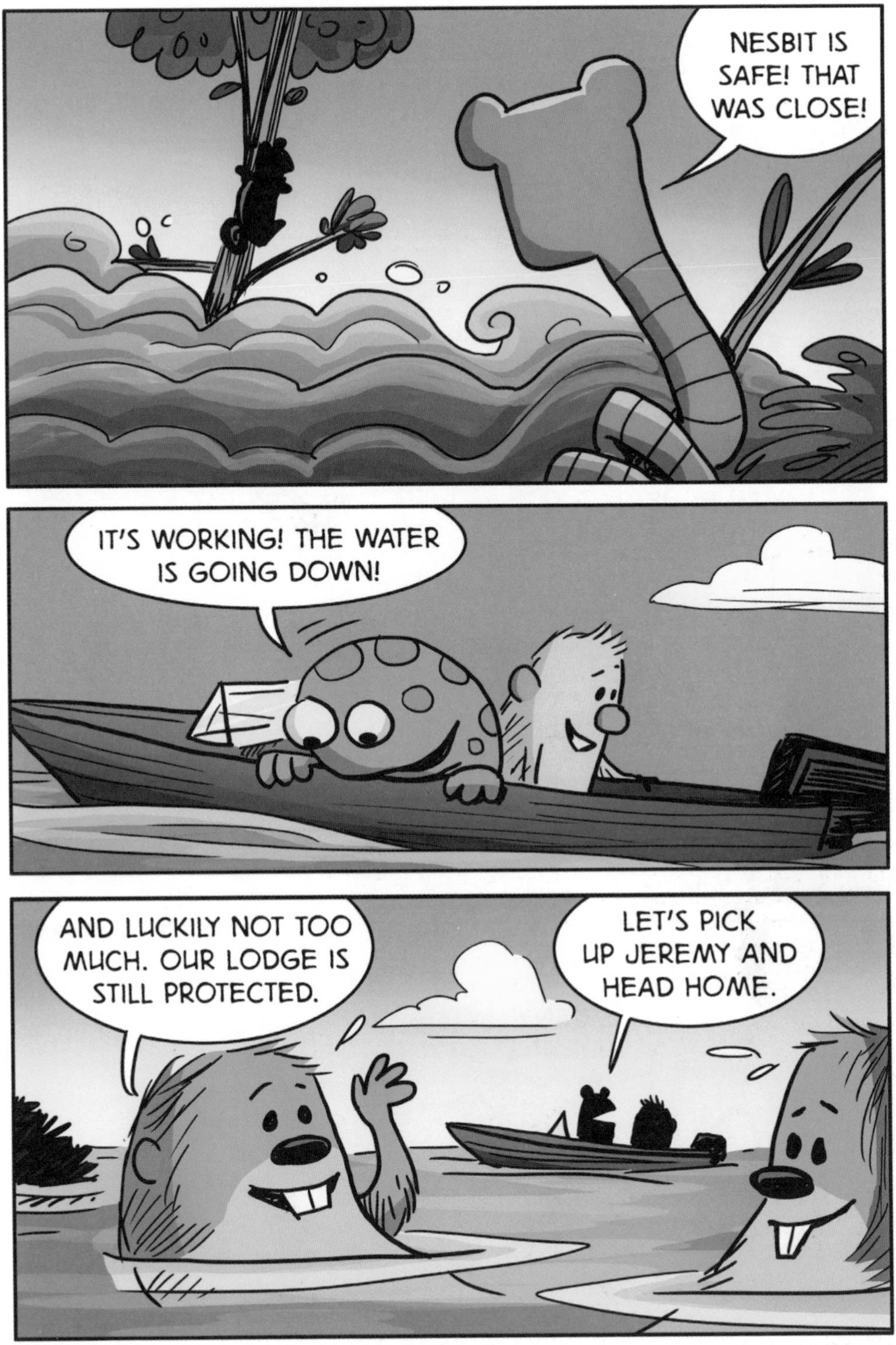
NESBIT IS SAFE! THAT WAS CLOSE!
IT'S WORKING! THE WATER IS GOING DOWN!
AND LUCKILY NOT TOO MUCH. OUR LODGE IS STILL PROTECTED.
LET'S PICK UP JEREMY AND HEAD HOME.

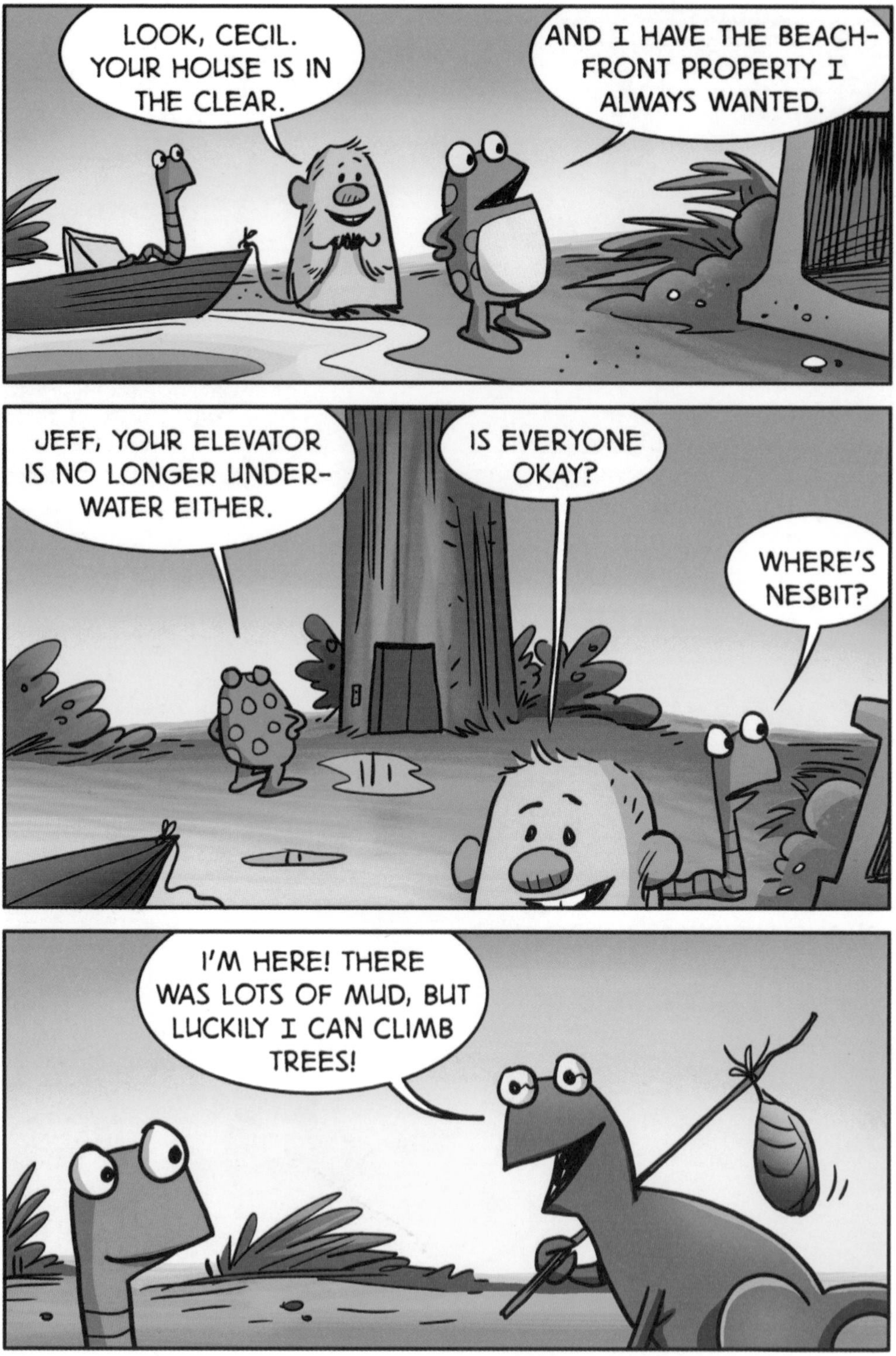
LOOK, CECIL. YOUR HOUSE IS IN THE CLEAR.
AND I HAVE THE BEACH-FRONT PROPERTY I ALWAYS WANTED.
JEFF, YOUR ELEVATOR IS NO LONGER UNDER-WATER EITHER.
IS EVERYONE OKAY?
WHERE'S NESBIT?
I'M HERE! THERE WAS LOTS OF MUD, BUT LUCKILY I CAN CLIMB TREES!

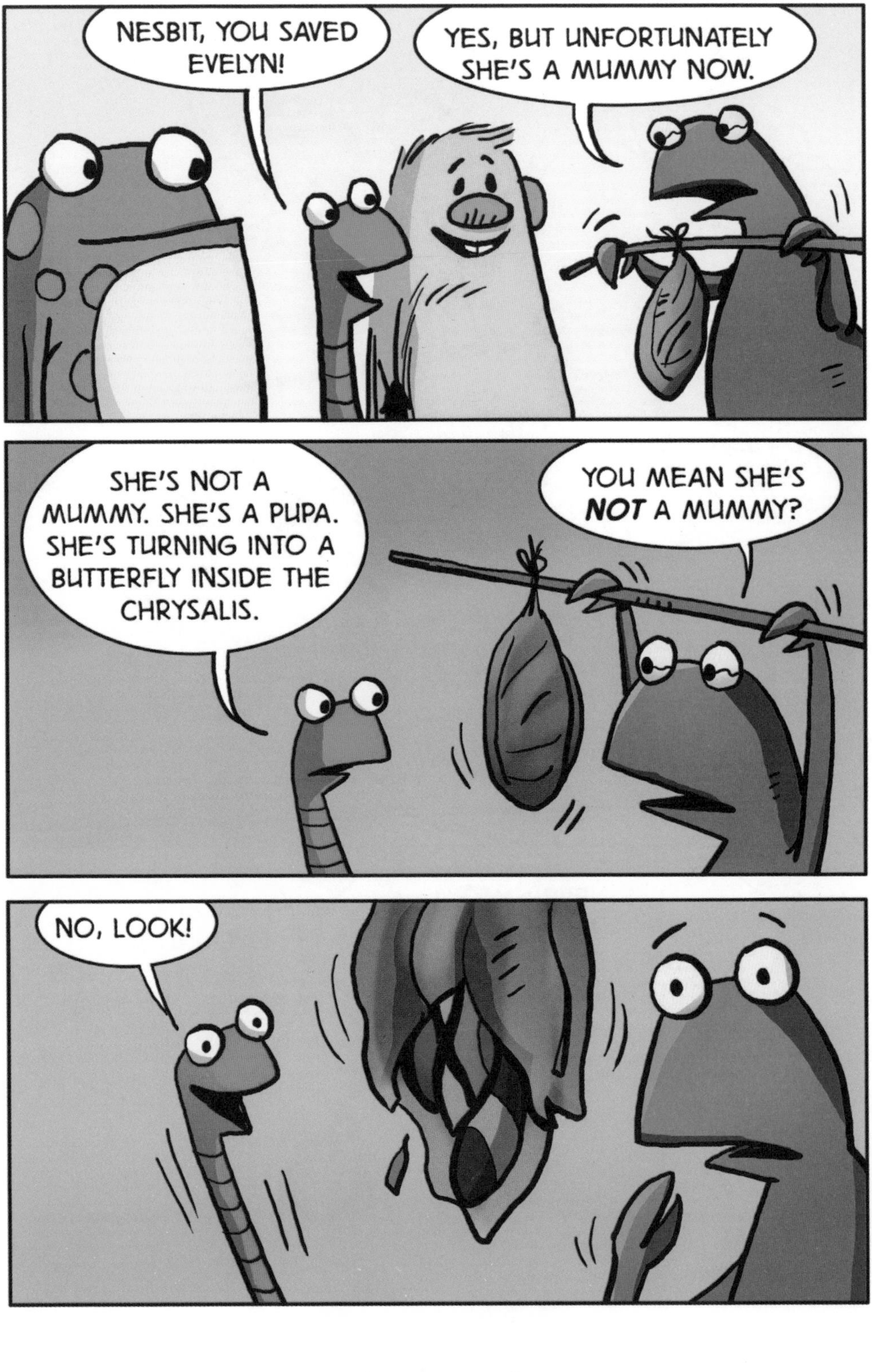
NESBIT, YOU SAVED EVELYN!
YES, BUT UNFORTUNATELY SHE'S A MUMMY NOW.
SHE'S NOT A MUMMY. SHE'S A PUPA. SHE'S TURNING INTO A BUTTERFLY INSIDE THE CHRYSALIS.
YOU MEAN SHE'S **NOT** A MUMMY?
NO, LOOK!

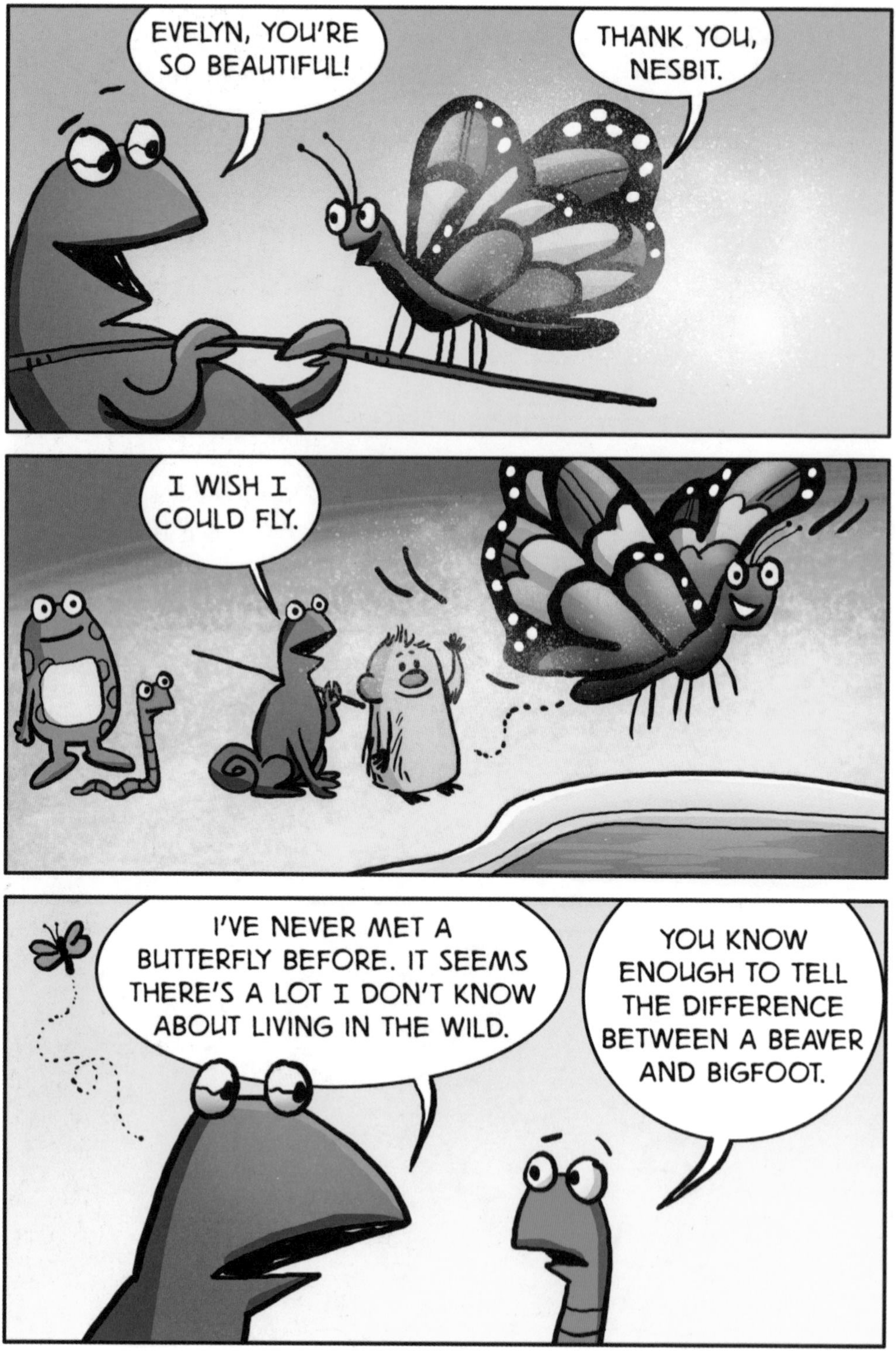
EVELYN, YOU'RE SO BEAUTIFUL!
THANK YOU, NESBIT.
I WISH I COULD FLY.
I'VE NEVER MET A BUTTERFLY BEFORE. IT SEEMS THERE'S A LOT I DON'T KNOW ABOUT LIVING IN THE WILD.
YOU KNOW ENOUGH TO TELL THE DIFFERENCE BETWEEN A BEAVER AND BIGFOOT.

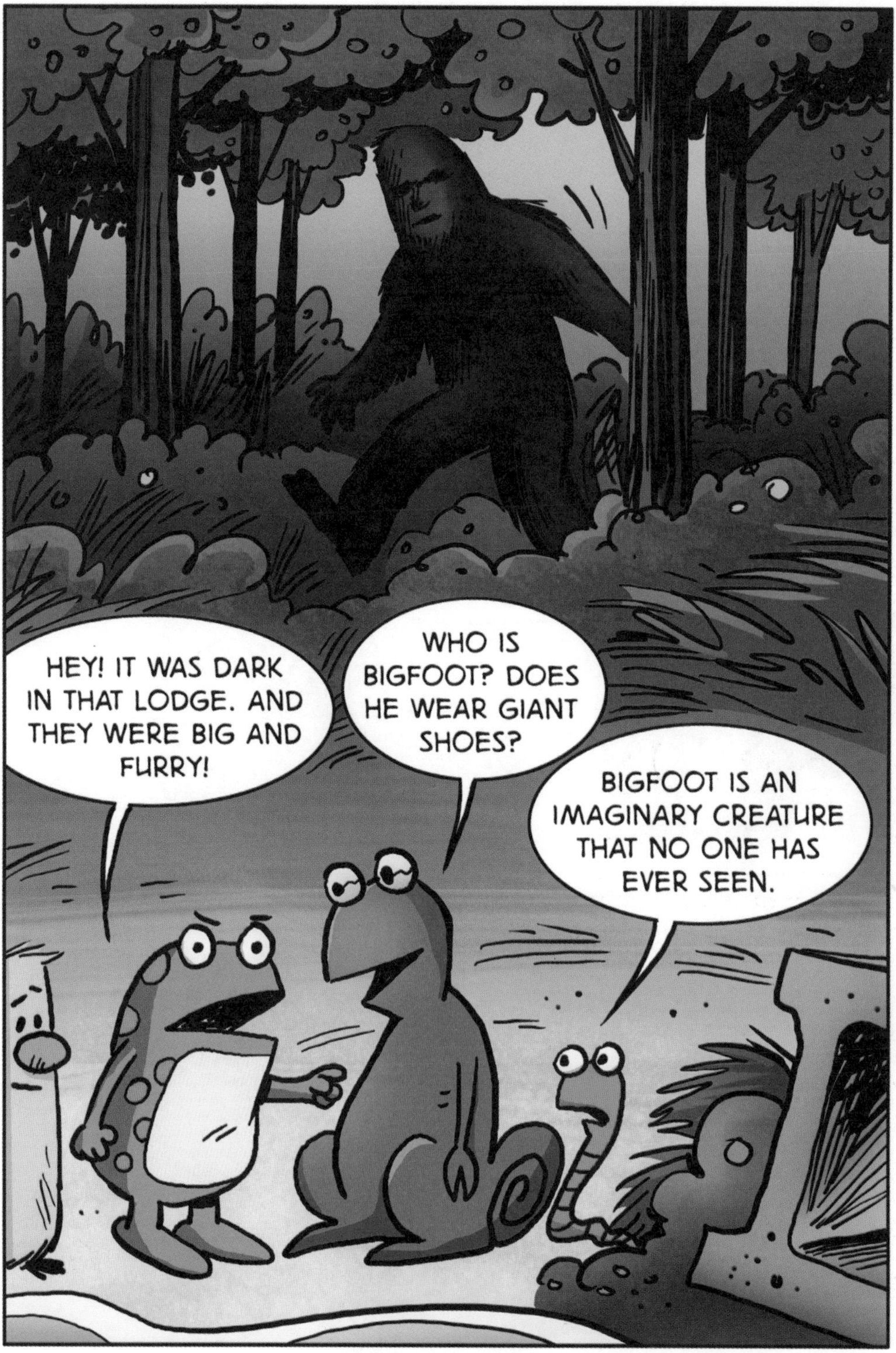
HEY! IT WAS DARK IN THAT LODGE. AND THEY WERE BIG AND FURRY!
WHO IS BIGFOOT? DOES HE WEAR GIANT SHOES?
BIGFOOT IS AN IMAGINARY CREATURE THAT NO ONE HAS EVER SEEN.

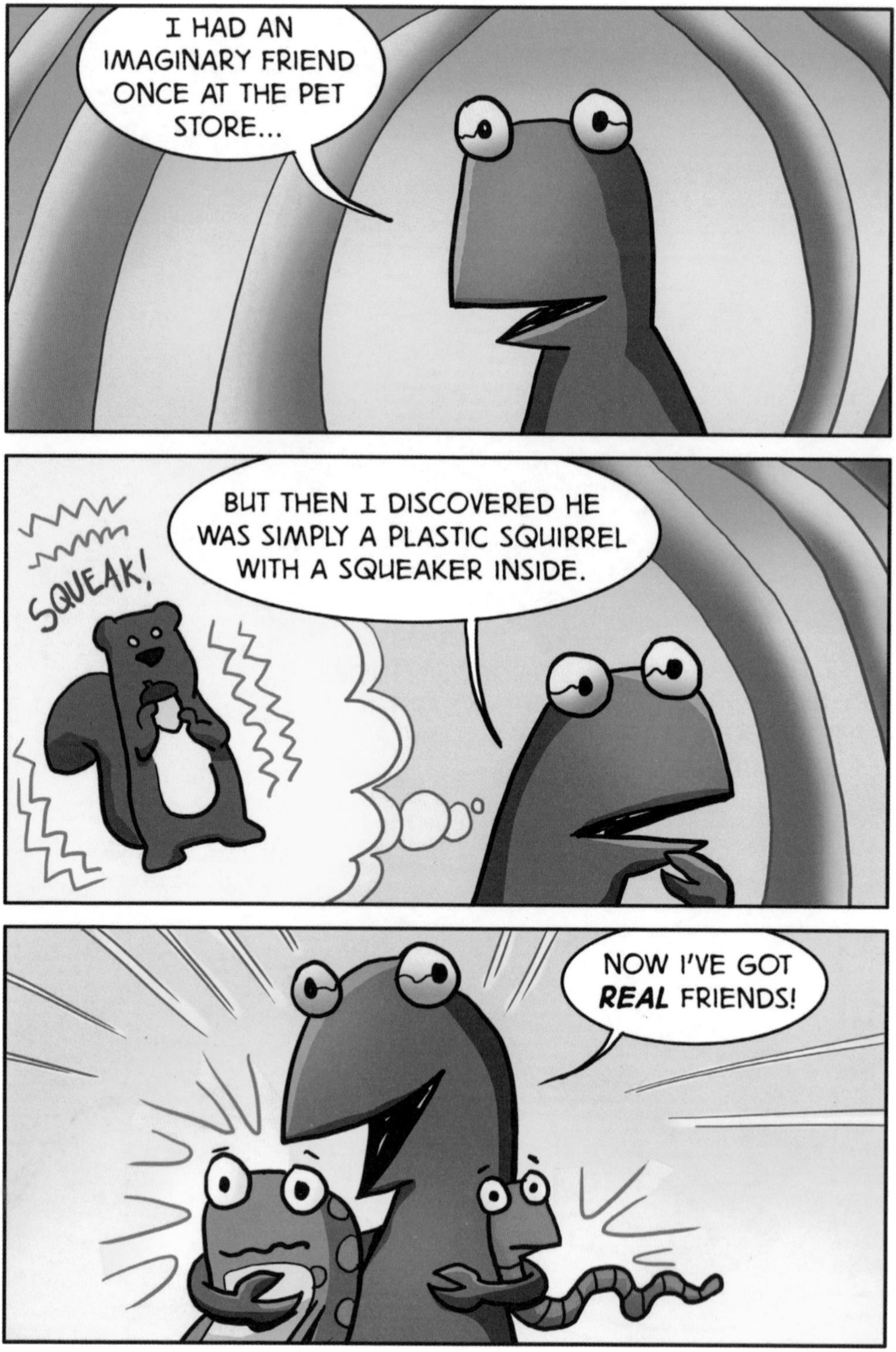
I HAD AN IMAGINARY FRIEND ONCE AT THE PET STORE...
BUT THEN I DISCOVERED HE WAS SIMPLY A PLASTIC SQUIRREL WITH A SQUEAKER INSIDE.
SQUEAK!
NOW I'VE GOT **REAL** FRIENDS!

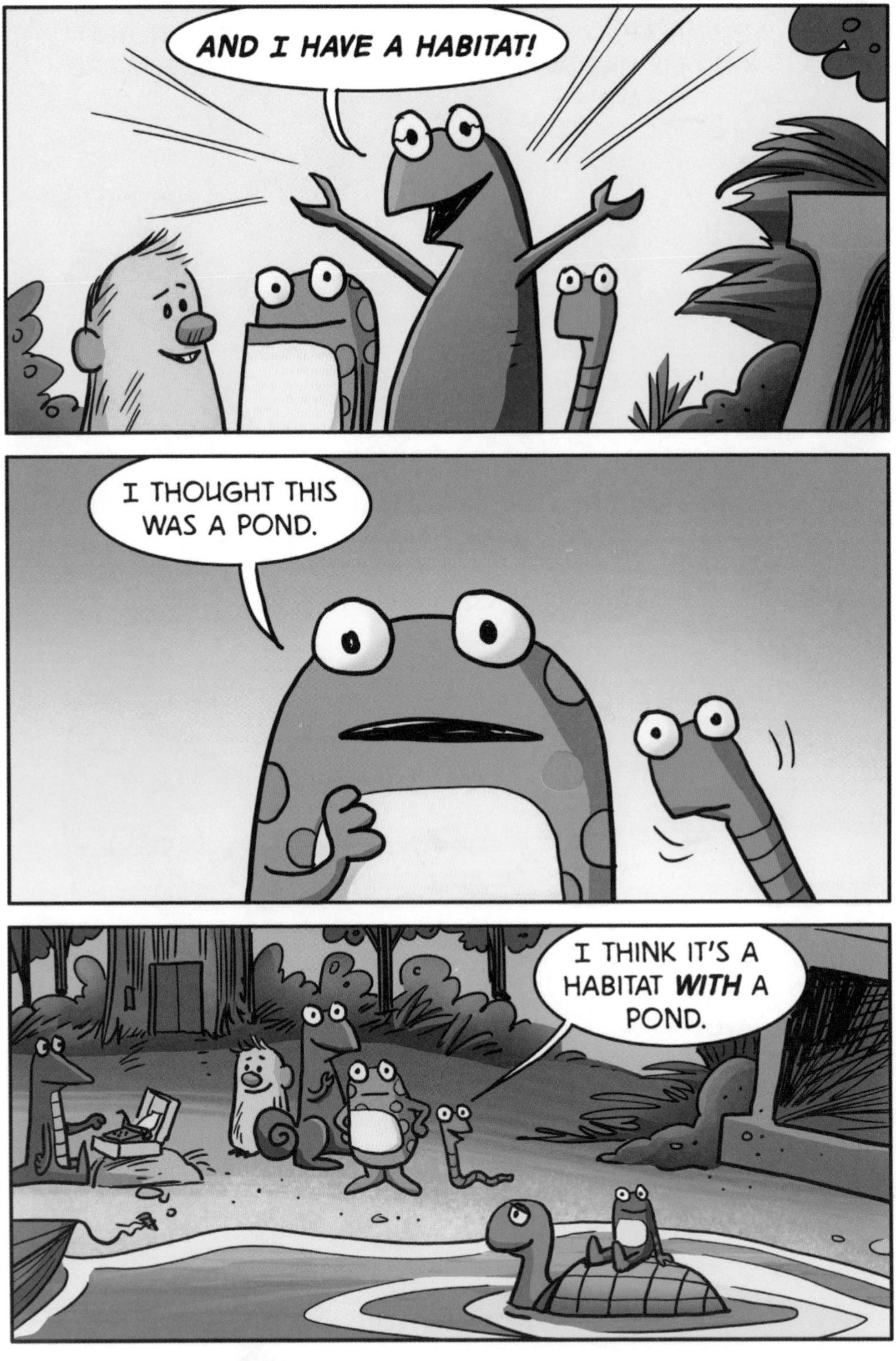
AND I HAVE A HABITAT!
I THOUGHT THIS WAS A POND.
I THINK IT'S A HABITAT **WITH** A POND.

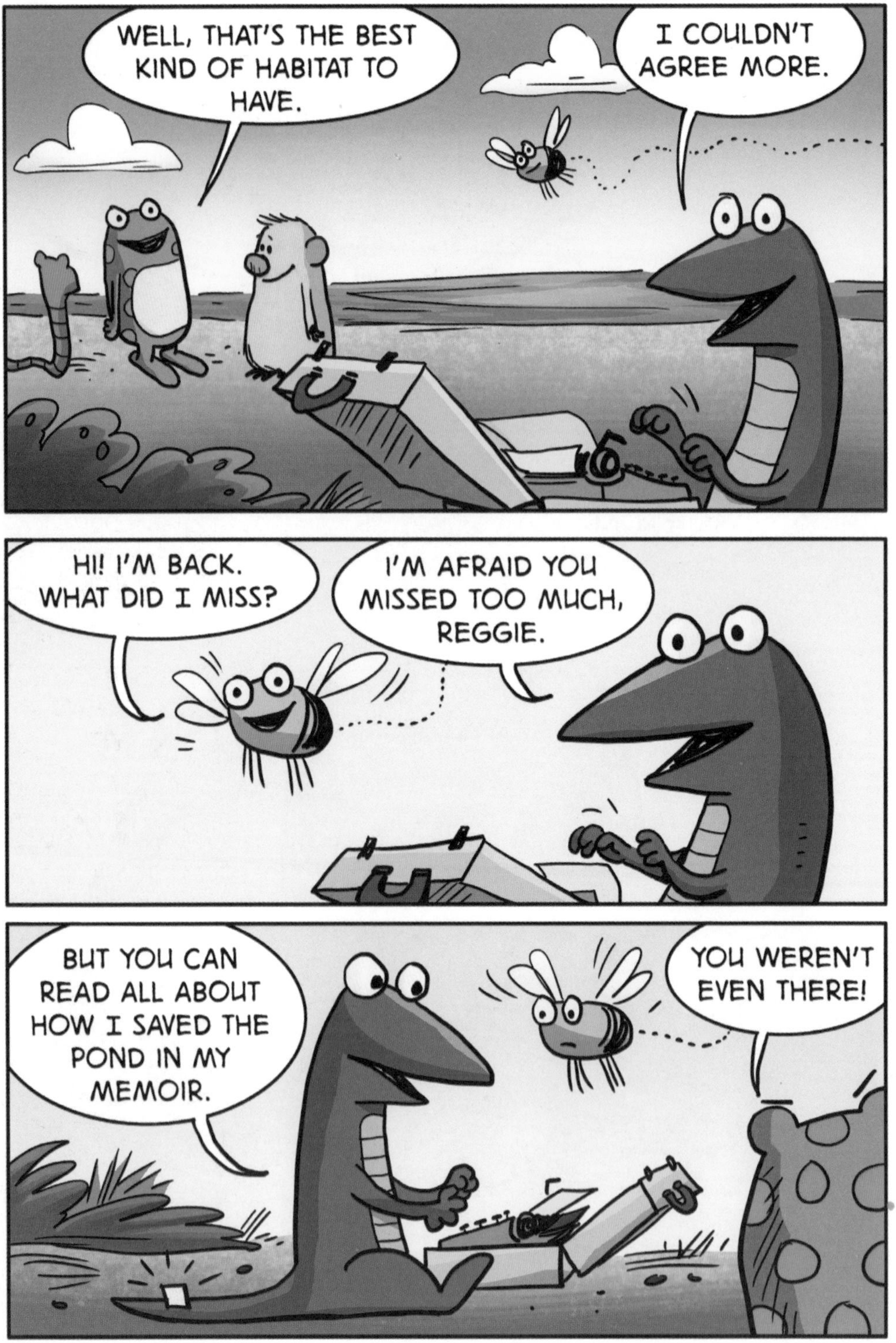
WELL, THAT'S THE BEST KIND OF HABITAT TO HAVE.
I COULDN'T AGREE MORE.
HI! I'M BACK. WHAT DID I MISS?
I'M AFRAID YOU MISSED TOO MUCH, REGGIE.
BUT YOU CAN READ ALL ABOUT HOW I SAVED THE POND IN MY MEMOIR.
YOU WEREN'T EVEN THERE!

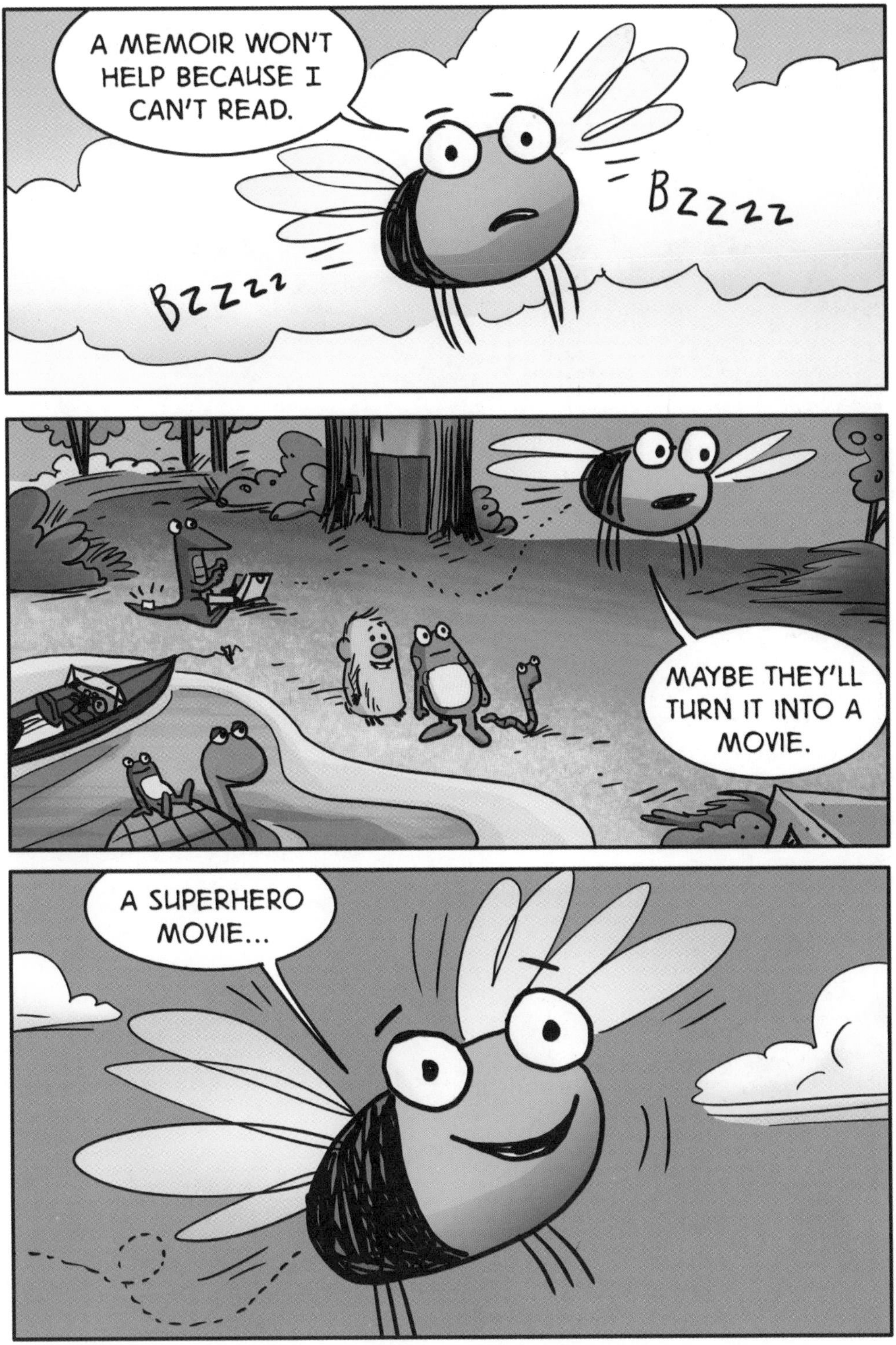
A MEMOIR WON'T HELP BECAUSE I CAN'T READ.
Bzzzz
Bzzzz
MAYBE THEY'LL TURN IT INTO A MOVIE.
A SUPERHERO MOVIE...

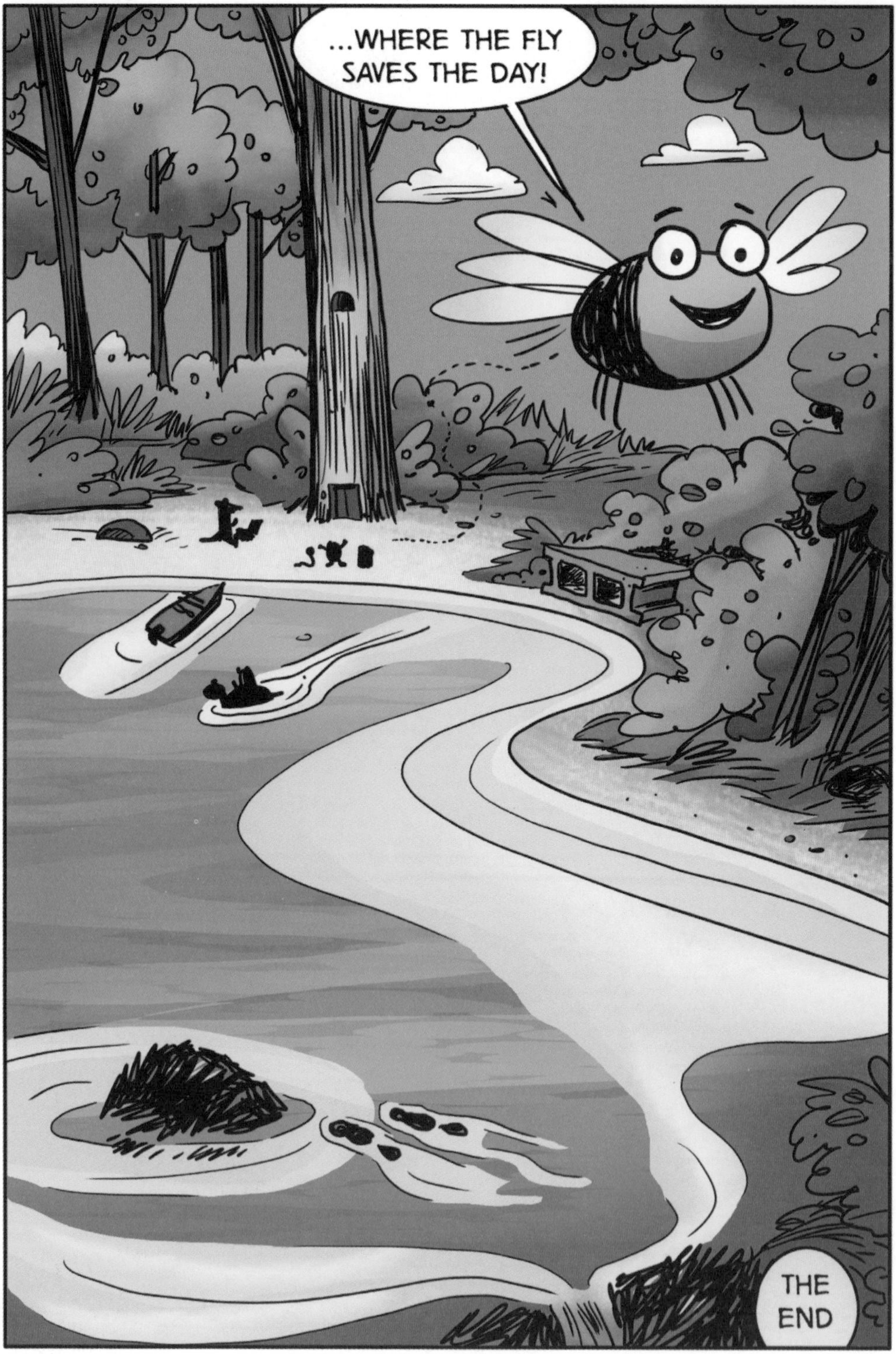
...WHERE THE FLY SAVES THE DAY!
THE END

MORE
TO EXPLORE!
FEATURING FUN FACTS!

ABOUT THE BEAVER

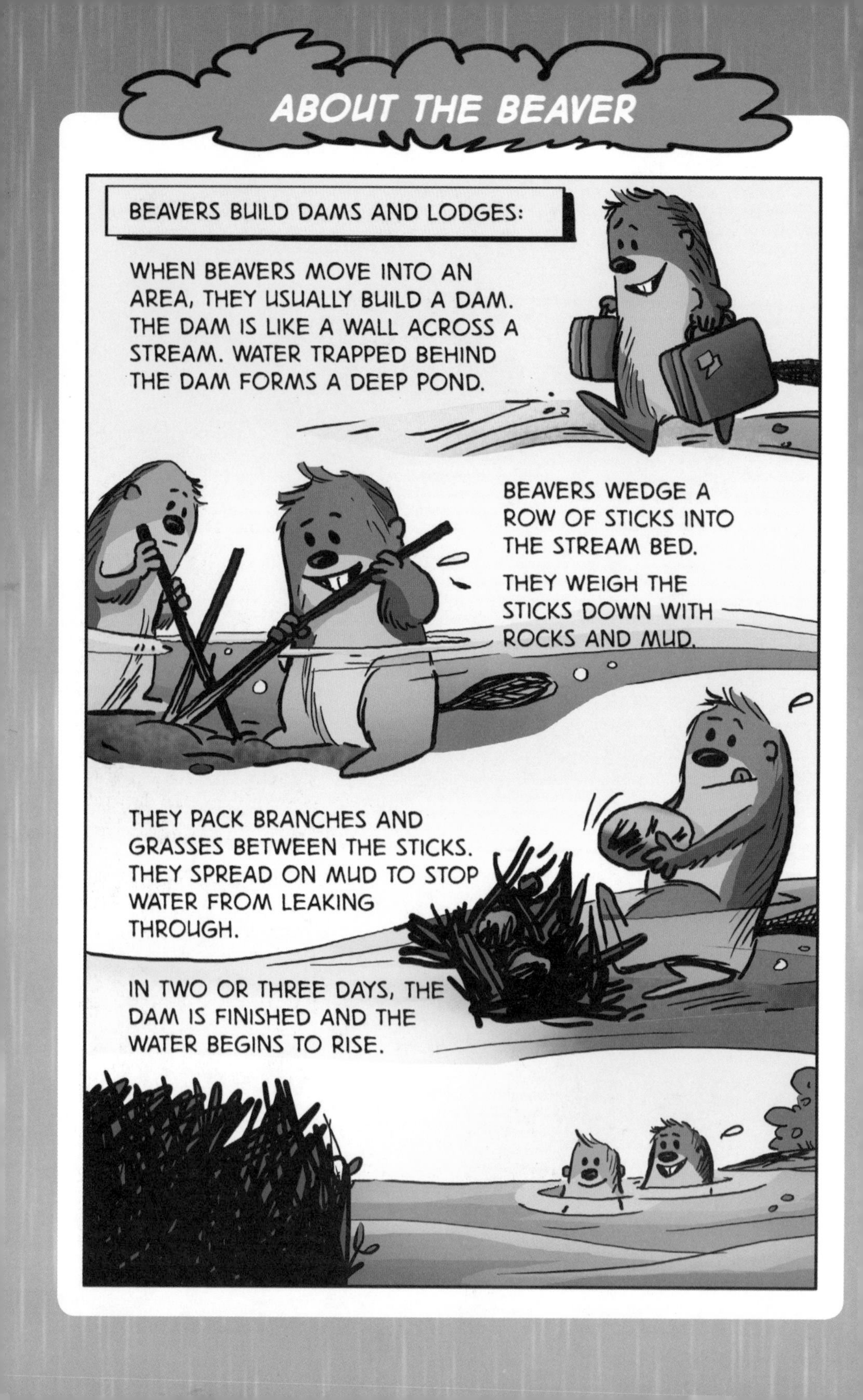

BEAVERS BUILD DAMS AND LODGES:
WHEN BEAVERS MOVE INTO AN AREA, THEY USUALLY BUILD A DAM. THE DAM IS LIKE A WALL ACROSS A STREAM. WATER TRAPPED BEHIND THE DAM FORMS A DEEP POND.
BEAVERS WEDGE A ROW OF STICKS INTO THE STREAM BED.
THEY WEIGH THE STICKS DOWN WITH ROCKS AND MUD.
THEY PACK BRANCHES AND GRASSES BETWEEN THE STICKS. THEY SPREAD ON MUD TO STOP WATER FROM LEAKING THROUGH.
IN TWO OR THREE DAYS, THE DAM IS FINISHED AND THE WATER BEGINS TO RISE.

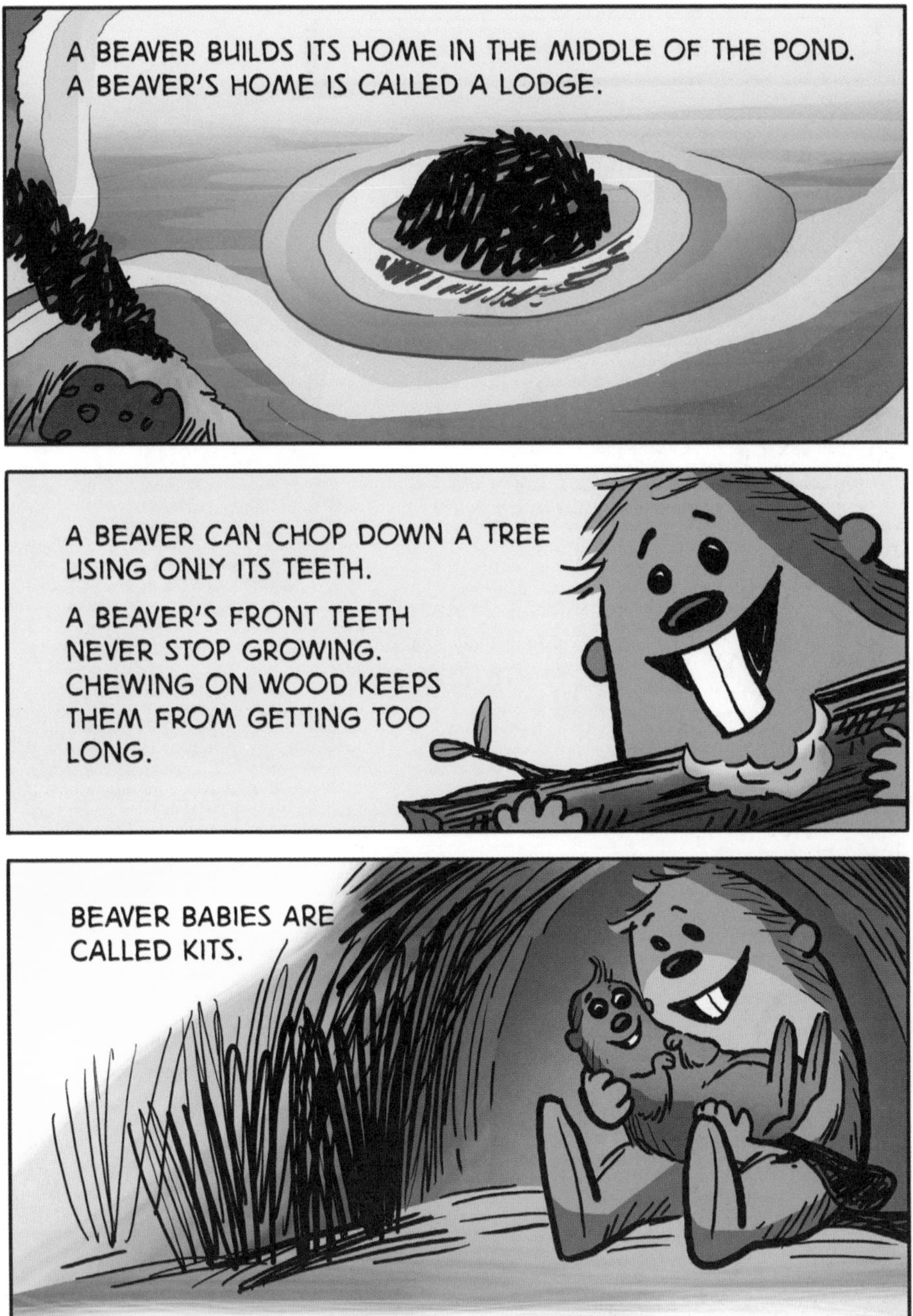
A BEAVER BUILDS ITS HOME IN THE MIDDLE OF THE POND.
A BEAVER'S HOME IS CALLED A LODGE.
A BEAVER CAN CHOP DOWN A TREE USING ONLY ITS TEETH.
A BEAVER'S FRONT TEETH NEVER STOP GROWING. CHEWING ON WOOD KEEPS THEM FROM GETTING TOO LONG.
BEAVER BABIES ARE CALLED KITS.

Source: *Beavers* by Deborah Hodge, Kids Can Press Wildlife Series

ABOUT THE MONARCH BUTTERFLY

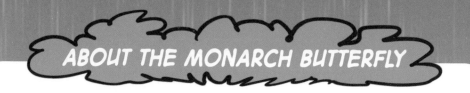

LIFE CYCLE OF A MONARCH BUTTERFLY:

BUTTERFLIES HAVE FOUR SEPARATE STAGES. EACH STAGE LOOKS COMPLETELY DIFFERENT AND SERVES A DIFFERENT PURPOSE IN THE LIFE OF THE INSECT.

MONARCH BUTTERFLIES LIVE IN DIFFERENT PLACES DURING COLD AND HOT MONTHS. THEY CAN'T LIVE IN ICY TEMPERATURES. FROM SPRING AND SUMMER UNTIL EARLY FALL, YOU CAN SEE THEM ANYWHERE YOU FIND LOTS OF MILKWEED SINCE THEY LAY THEIR EGGS ON TOP OF MILKWEED.

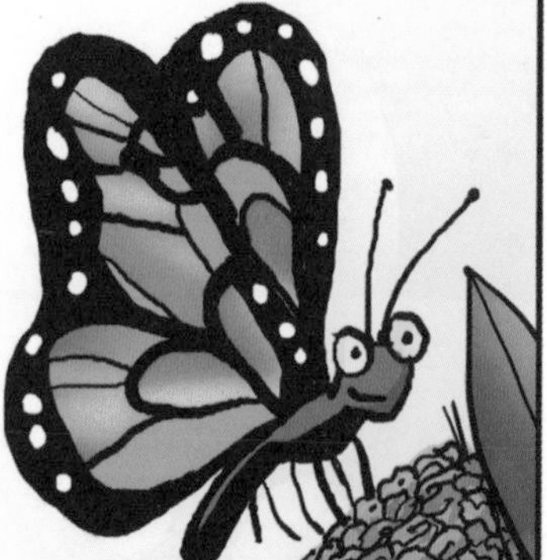

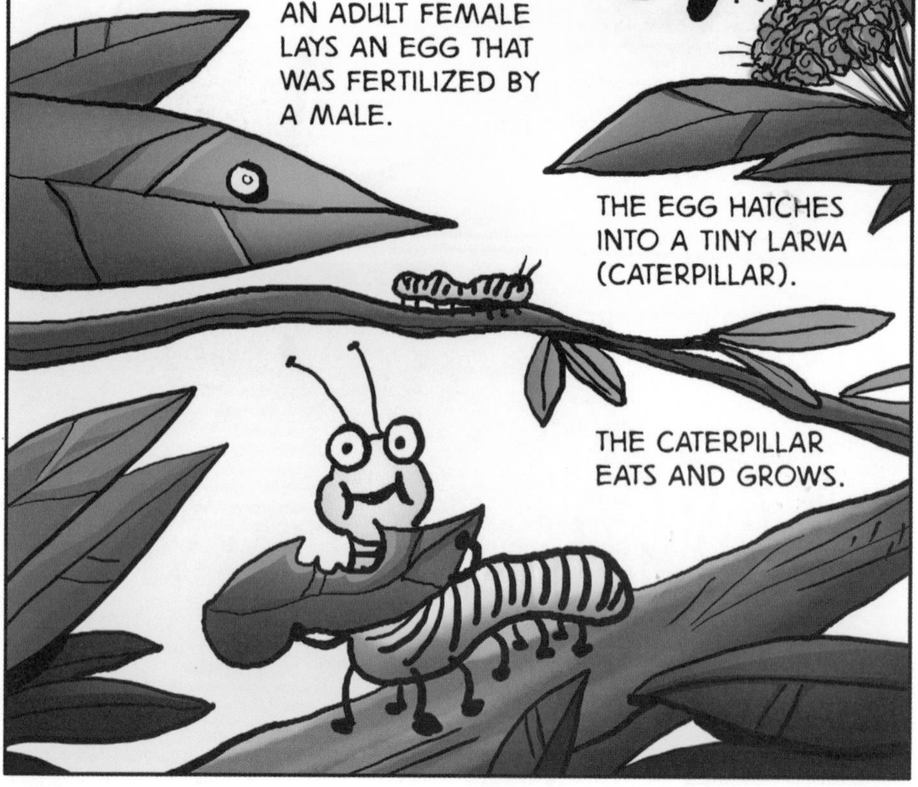

AN ADULT FEMALE LAYS AN EGG THAT WAS FERTILIZED BY A MALE.
THE EGG HATCHES INTO A TINY LARVA (CATERPILLAR).
THE CATERPILLAR EATS AND GROWS.

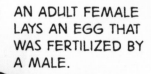

THEN THE CATERPILLAR ATTACHES ITSELF TO A TWIG AND FORMS A CHRYSALIS (PUPA).

INSIDE THE PUPA, A CATERPILLAR CHANGES INTO A BUTTERFLY. A FULLY GROWN BUTTERFLY EMERGES FROM THE CHRYSALIS.

THE NEW BUTTERFLY BREAKS OUT OF THE CHRYSALIS AND STRETCHES ITS WINGS UNTIL THEY ARE FLAT.

THE MONARCH BUTTERFLY MIGRATES, LEAVING THE UNITED STATES DURING LATE SUMMER, OR AUTUMN IN SOUTHERN CANADA, FOR COASTAL CALIFORNIA AND MEXICO AND COMES BACK TO THE NORTHERN REGION DURING SPRING. THIS HAPPENS DURING THE LIFE SPAN OF 3-4 GENERATIONS OF THIS BUTTERFLY.

Source: Lotts, Kelly C., Thomas Naberhaus, and Paul A. Opler. 2017. The Children's Butterfly Site. Butterfly and Moth Information Network. http://www.kidsbutterfly.org/; http://www.monarch-butterfly.com

ACKNOWLEDGMENTS

It was really fun to collaborate with colorist Jose Flores on this book. I'd also like to say thanks to my editor, Dorothy. Thank you to my parents, Bud and Pat, for all of their support over the years of my life in comics. Special thanks to my very detailed beta reader, my wife, Evelyn. And last, but certainly not least, a note of appreciation to my always encouraging, always supportive comics pals, Lex Fajardo and Art Roche. Oh, and to Donna for introducing me to some new digital brushes!

Andrews McMeel Publishing
a division of Andrews McMeel Universal
1130 Walnut Street, Kansas City, Missouri 64106

www.andrewsmcmeel.com

18 19 20 21 22 SDB 10 9 8 7 6 5 4 3 2 1

ISBN: 978-1-4494-8937-3

Library of Congress Control Number: 2017940296

Color by Jose Mari Flores
Font created by Nate Piekos (Blambot.com)

Made by:
Shenzhen Donnelley Printing Company Ltd.
Address and location of manufacturer:
No. 47, Wuhe Nan Road, Bantian Ind. Zone,
Shenzhen China, 518129
1st Printing—12/4/17

Look for these books!

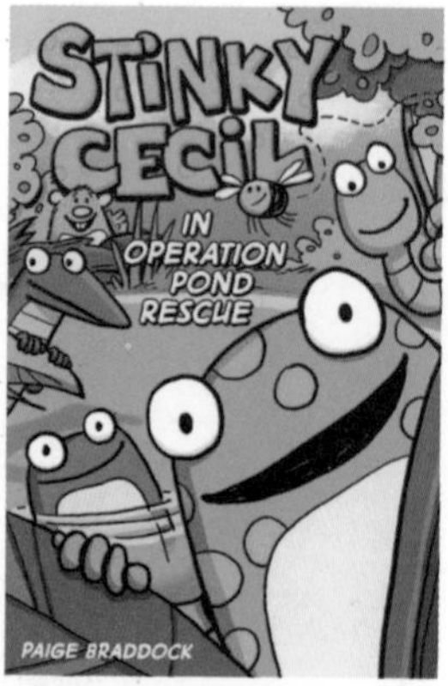
STINKY CECIL
IN OPERATION POND RESCUE
PAIGE BRADDOCK

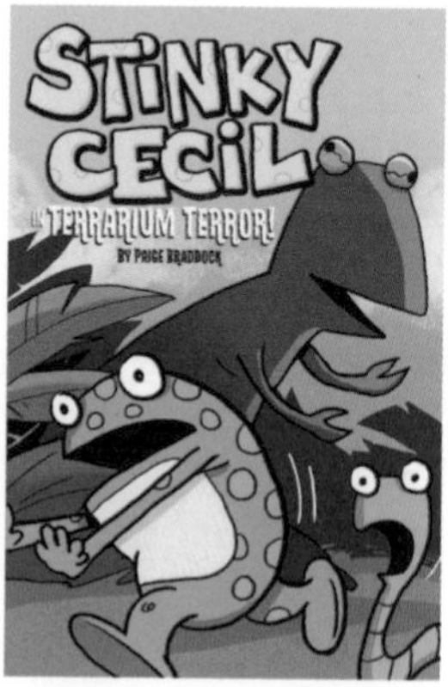
STINKY CECIL
TERRARIUM TERROR!
BY PAIGE BRADDOCK

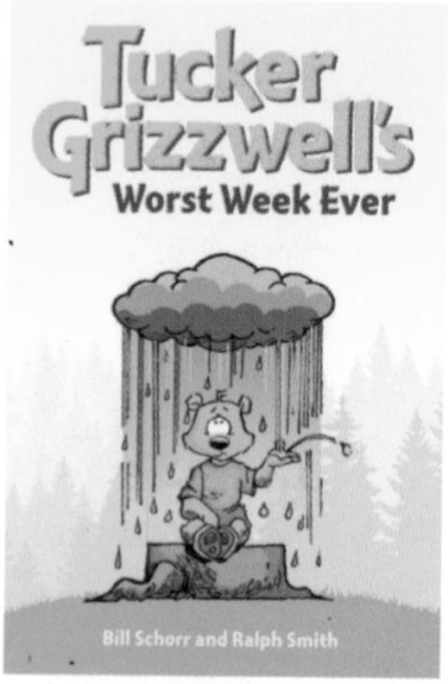
Tucker Grizzwell's
Worst Week Ever
Bill Schorr and Ralph Smith

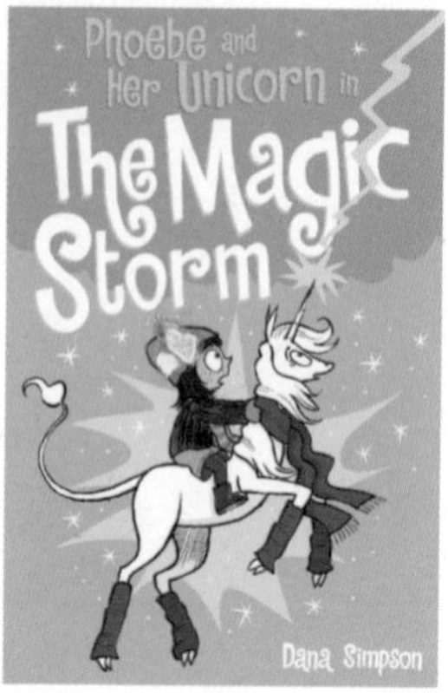
Phoebe and Her Unicorn in
The Magic Storm
Dana Simpson

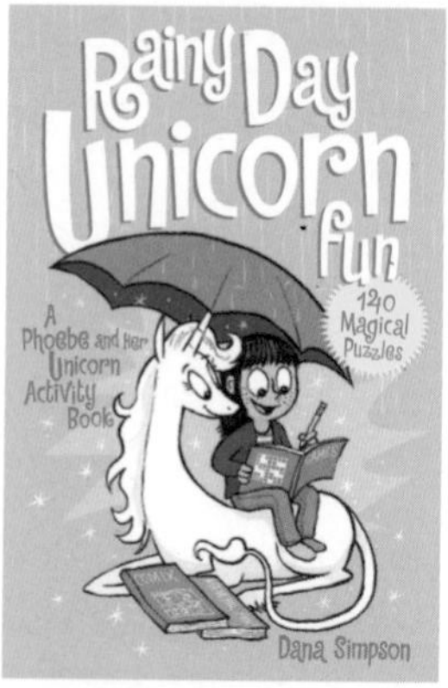
Rainy Day Unicorn Fun
A Phoebe and Her Unicorn Activity Book
140 Magical Puzzles
Dana Simpson

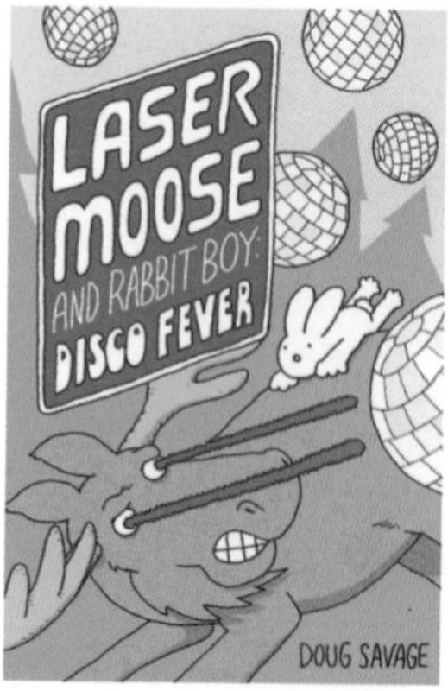
LASER MOOSE AND RABBIT BOY
DISCO FEVER
DOUG SAVAGE

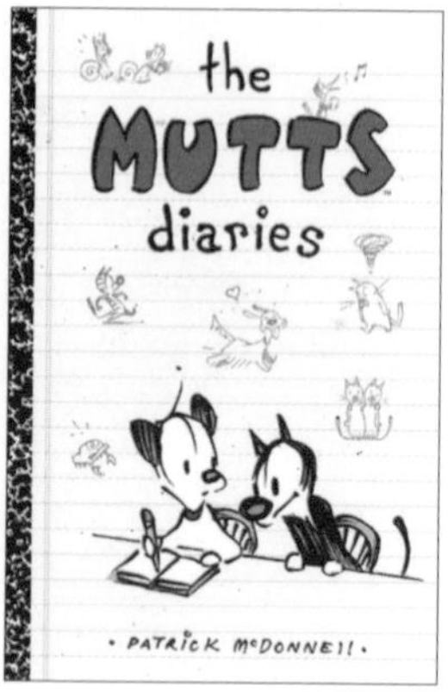
the MUTTS diaries
PATRICK McDONNELL

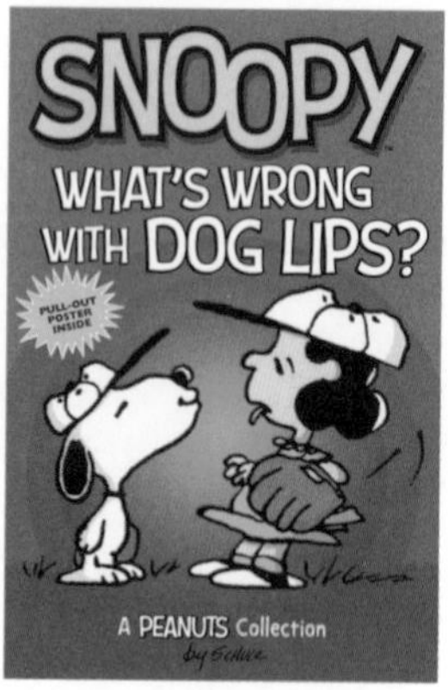
SNOOPY
WHAT'S WRONG WITH DOG LIPS?
PULL-OUT POSTER INSIDE
A PEANUTS Collection
by Schulz

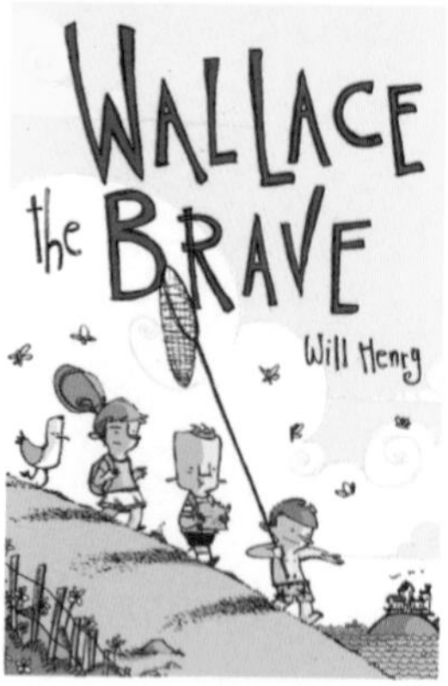
WALLACE the BRAVE
Will Henry